DEATH
TAKES A BOW

Praise for David S. Pederson

Death Checks In

"David Pederson does a great job with this classic murder mystery set in 1947 and the attention to its details…"—*The Novel Approach*

"This noir whodunit is a worthwhile getaway with that old-black-and-white-movie feel that you know you love, and it's sweetly chaste, in a late-1940s way…"—*Outsmart Magazine*

"This is a classic murder mystery; an old-fashioned style mystery à la Agatha Christie…"—*Reviews by Amos Lassen*

Death Comes Darkly

"Agatha Christie…if Miss Marple were a gay police detective in post–WWII Milwaukee."—*PrideSource: Between the Lines*

"The mystery is one that isn't easily solved. It's a cozy mystery unraveled in the drawing room type of story, but well worked out."—*Bookwinked*

"If you LOVE Agatha Christie, you shouldn't miss this one. The writing is very pleasant, the mystery is old-fashioned, but in a good meaning, intriguing plot, well developed characters. I'd like to read more of Heath Barrington and Alan Keyes in the future. This couple has a big potential."—*Gay Book Reviews*

"[A] thoroughly entertaining read from beginning to end. A detective story in the best Agatha Christie tradition with all the trimmings."—*Sinfully Gay Romance Book Review*

Death Goes Overboard

"[A]uthor David S. Pederson has packed a lot in this novel. You don't normally find a soft-sided, poetry-writing mobster in a noir mystery, for instance, but he's here…this novel is both predictable and not, making it a nice diversion for a weekend or vacation."—*Washington Blade*

"Pederson takes a lot of the tropes of mysteries and utilizes them to the fullest, giving the story a knowable form. However, the unique characters and accurate portrayal of the struggles of gay relationships in 1940s America make this an enjoyable, thought-provoking read."—*Gay, Lesbian, Bisexual, and Transgender Round Table of the American Library Association*

By the Author

Death Comes Darkly

Death Goes Overboard

Death Checks In

Death Takes a Bow

Visit us at www.boldstrokesbooks.com

Death Goes Overboard

"[A]uthor David S. Pederson has packed a lot in this novel. You don't normally find a soft-sided, poetry-writing mobster in a noir mystery, for instance, but he's here…this novel is both predictable and not, making it a nice diversion for a weekend or vacation."—*Washington Blade*

"Pederson takes a lot of the tropes of mysteries and utilizes them to the fullest, giving the story a knowable form. However, the unique characters and accurate portrayal of the struggles of gay relationships in 1940s America make this an enjoyable, thought-provoking read."—*Gay, Lesbian, Bisexual, and Transgender Round Table of the American Library Association*

By the Author

Death Comes Darkly

Death Goes Overboard

Death Checks In

Death Takes a Bow

Visit us at www.boldstrokesbooks.com

DEATH
TAKES A BOW

by

David S. Pederson

2019

DEATH TAKES A BOW

ISBN 13: 978-1-63555-472-4

This Trade Paperback Original Is Published By
Bold Strokes Books, Inc.
P.O. Box 249
Valley Falls, NY 12185

First Edition: July 2019

Credits
Editors: Jerry L. Wheeler and Stacia Seaman
Production Design: Stacia Seaman
Cover Design by Sheri (hindsightgraphics@gmail.com)

Acknowledgments

I must start by thanking my husband, Alan Karbel. Thank you, Pookie, I love you.

And to all my chosen family, Jacques and Glenn, Mike and Margot, Jeannie and Clif, Dave and Kathy, Justin and Freddy, Liz and Mike, D.C. and Fern, Rick and B.J., Mike P., Randy and Michael, Mary F., Jen and Steve, Derin and David, Ron and Nina, Matthew and Bill, Beth and Bill, and all the rest, including Kim and Pat, Brenda, Deb D., Beth H., Vicki S., Kathi B., and Jeff M., thank you!

Also, thanks to my biological family, whom I would have chosen if I could have, especially my dad, Manford, and my mom, Vondell. My sisters and their husbands, Debbie and John, Julie and Frank; my brother, Brian; and my nephews, Zach and Kevin.

Finally, thanks also to Jerry Wheeler, my editor with the mostest, and everyone at Bold Strokes Books who has helped me so much, especially Sandy, Cindy, and Ruth, and to all my readers. If it weren't for you these books wouldn't exist!

They say friends are the family we choose, and Steve Wingert
was one of my chosen family who left us all too soon.
This book is dedicated to him,
and to his wonderful husband, Mark Bridgeman,
who is also a part of my chosen family. I love you both.

CHAPTER ONE

Thursday, July 10, 1947

I was late for a murder. Frustratingly late, in fact. I sat in the early afternoon traffic on State Street, heading west toward Third Street. A light fog drifted aimlessly about, making it hard to see what the holdup was. I checked my pocket watch for the fourth time in the last twenty minutes and realized I'd missed the whole first act. Of course, I knew *who* was going to be murdered and when and how, as I had read the script. But I wanted to see what the infamous Henry Hawthorne looked like in person, and why Alan couldn't seem to stop talking about him. I'm not the jealous type, but how does one compete with someone whom Alan considers a devilishly handsome actor?

Slowly my '38 Buick Century crawled to the corner of Edison and State, and I realized the State Street Bridge was stuck in the up position. Following the lead of many of my fellow travelers, I turned south on Edison and detoured over the river at Kilbourn. Successful at last at crossing the river, I turned south on Third Street, only to be confounded by multiple red lights that seemed to last an eternity. After at least half of that eternity, I reached the Davidson Theater and found a place to park about a block away. I checked my watch once more. Hopefully I'd see Mr. Hawthorne in the second act, though I couldn't stay long. I had a counterfeiting case that needed my attention, and the day was slipping away.

I hurried through the front doors, across the lobby, and into the auditorium, pausing only long enough to remove my hat and allow my eyes to adjust to the darkness. I quietly found my way down the aisle to a seat front and center. An easy choice, since I was the only one in the audience. It was just a dress rehearsal, after all. On the stage were two women, one older and one younger. The scene was late night, and a thunderstorm was building outside the windows. They were in the main hall of Lochwood, the old, crumbling Clarington family manor, an estate just outside of war-torn London.

"Don't be angry with me anymore, Claire, please," the younger woman said in an accent that sounded like a mix between English and Scottish.

Claire sighed and put her hands in the pockets of her dress, fidgeting with something. "I'm not angry, Charlotte. Not at you, anyway. I know how persuasive Roger can be."

"Yes, that's right. He's an evil man, I see that now. But he's gone. Let's forget him. Let's go back to how it was."

Claire shook her head. "It's too late to ever go back to how it was, I'm sorry. And yes, he's gone, but I fear he'll come back. Maybe even tonight."

"You're waiting for him, aren't you?"

"Yes. I waited for him last night, too, and the night before that. I can't explain it to you, Charlotte. Not now anyway. You wouldn't understand. Go to bed, please."

Charlotte stepped closer yet and put her hand on Claire's shoulder. Claire didn't flinch, but she also didn't turn.

"Go to bed, Charlotte," she said again, more sternly.

Charlotte took her hand away and glanced at Claire just a moment more before turning toward the stairs, her head low. She stopped on the first landing and looked back. I could see the utter sadness in her eyes. Then she turned again and climbed slowly up and away to her room as lightning flashed through the large windows and the thunder boomed.

As soon as she'd gone, Beresford entered from the doorway on the left, dressed in his black butler's livery. He was balancing a china tea service on a silver tray and maneuvered the two steps down into the hall somewhat unsteadily.

"Your tea, madam."

Claire looked at him. "Put it on the table," she said in that powerful, commanding voice.

"Yes, madam."

He moved slowly, the tea service rattling a bit as his hands shook. He put it on the table and stood as erect as he could. He must have been nearly eighty.

"Shall I pour, madam?"

"No." Never "No, thank you" to a servant. It wouldn't be proper, and Claire was clearly an exceptionally proper English woman. Good research from the playwright, I thought.

"Anything else, madam?"

"Not tonight. You may go to bed. Leave the tea set until morning."

"Yes, madam."

Beresford went slowly up the two steps and through the doorway on the left, back toward where the kitchen would be, I assumed, and his quarters above it.

When he had gone, Claire turned once more to the fire in the massive fireplace. And then, as Claire feared, Roger came back. He stepped silently through the door from the entryway and looked at Claire, though she hadn't noticed him yet. His hat and coat were dripping wet as he hung them on the hall tree before moving slowly down the steps toward the center of the room. He paused, his left hand on the back of a green sofa covered in fleur-de-lis. Roger was attractive in a dark, sinister sort of way, with broad shoulders and a narrow, high waist. He was probably in his late forties and had a classic jawline and good cheekbones.

"Hello, Claire. Bloody awful night out there," he said at last, his voice deep and husky.

Claire whirled about and stared at him, her expression changing from one of weariness to one of anger. She walked swiftly toward him. "So, you've come back. I told you to stay away, but you didn't listen. So typical of you."

"And so typical of you, Claire, to try and tell me what to do. Don't you know by now that's a waste of your breath?" He ran his hands over his dark, velvety hair as he leered at her.

"You're a waste of my breath, Roger, and a waste of my time."

He laughed bitterly. "You think you can get by without me? Without my money, Lochwood is finished, and so are you."

"You're wrong, Roger. I've only just begun. You cheated on me with Charlotte, my own sister, you drove my brother to suicide, and you forced me to do things I'm ashamed of, things I don't even want to think about. I'm over you once and for all."

He opened his mouth to speak, closed it again, then opened it once more. "No, you're not."

"My God, you're arrogant." Claire said.

"Maybe, but I'm also cold and wet. I could use a warm shoulder," he said, his words suddenly almost tender.

She glared at him. "My shoulders are ice. So is the rest of me."

"A little heat and friction can melt ice," he said, running his hand up and down her arm.

"You have little heat to spare, Roger, and I have none. At least not for you," she said, shaking off his hand and moving away.

He smiled broadly. "You never change." He glanced at the coffee table in front of the sofa. "What about the tea I see there? Is it fresh?"

"Yes, Beresford's just brought it. But there's only one cup."

"I only need one cup," Roger said.

"Then what am I supposed to use?"

"You shouldn't drink tea this late at night, Claire. It keeps you up, as I recall." He walked around the sofa to the coffee table to pour himself some. He took a sip. "You're weak, Claire." He made a face as he swallowed. "And so is your tea." He set the cup down and walked over to the fireplace to warm his hands.

"You're despicable, Roger. You shouldn't have come back."

"But I did, Claire," he said, looking back at her. "And I'm not leaving. Not until I get Lochwood."

"Because you want to tear her down and put up your tacky little houses."

"Tacky little houses are what England needs right now. Big estates like this are out of date, useless, old, just like—"

"Like me?" She finished his sentence as he faced the fire once more, almost as if he couldn't look her in the eye. So, he didn't see the glass vial she extracted from her pocket. It was beautiful, with a jewel-encrusted gold stopper. A shiver went down my spine as I watched her pour its contents into the teapot.

She put the now-empty vial back into her pocket. "Is that what you were going to say? Look at me."

Slowly he turned and stared at her. "I didn't say that, Claire. You did."

"I only said what you were going to say." She picked up the teapot and poured more tea into his cup. "Here, have some more. The first cup is always the weakest."

He took the cup and saucer from her hand. "Thanks. You may be older, and you're certainly not a girl anymore, but that's all right. You're a big, mature woman."

Claire opened her mouth to speak, but he held up his hand in front of her.

"Don't take offense. A mature woman doesn't play hard to get, and I like that."

She glared at him. "You're right, I don't play hard to get. I *am* hard to get. And you're not getting it."

He took another drink. "Oh, Claire. I thought better of you. I really did."

"Really, Roger? I never thought better of you. You disgust me." Another clap of thunder and flash of lightning. The storm seemed to be getting worse.

"No, I arouse you. I can tell. I always could tell."

"Don't make me laugh even more. You're not getting Lochwood, or me, or anything else. Not tonight, not ever."

Now he laughed, but it morphed into a coughing fit. Clearly something was wrong. Though I knew what was happening, I still gripped the edges of my seat, feeling helpless as my eyes went from Roger to Claire and back to Roger.

"Something the matter, Roger?" Claire said, arching her painted-on brows. From the window on the landing, another bolt of lightning flashed, followed by another clap of thunder. A bit much, I thought.

"My head, it's suddenly pounding. And my stomach is cramping. What did you do, Claire? What did you do?" He bent over, dropping the teacup and saucer, which shattered across the floor as he slumped to the ground, writhing in obvious pain.

Suddenly, I felt a presence heading toward the stage. It was Oliver, his white hair standing out in the darkness as he waved his hands and shouted.

"Cut! Hold it! Turn up the house lights and stop the damned lightning and thunder! Shelby, I told you not to drop the cup!"

The main lights in the theater came on as Shelby got up off the stage floor and dusted himself off. "For crying out loud, how do you expect me to die convincingly if I put my teacup and saucer down before I fall to the floor?" His English accent had completely disappeared.

"Just set the damned thing down after you've taken a drink and before you start to convulse. It's not hard, Shelby. We've been over this. We can't go spilling tea all over the audience members in the front row!"

Shelby tossed his head back. "Fine, have it your way. Get that idiot Dick to clean this mess up, and we'll do it again. I'll set the cup down as delicately as a butterfly, if that's what you want, but don't blame me when the reviewers skewer your direction."

The woman who had been playing Claire scowled at Shelby. "Dick is not an idiot, and if you could follow direction, he wouldn't have to be cleaning up after you!"

Shelby whirled around. "If this was Broadway, they'd have me drop the cup every time. It's realistic. A man dying from poison doesn't stop to gently set his cup and saucer down first."

Oliver rubbed his temples. "This is Milwaukee, not Broadway, Shelby. Set the cup down first, then die. Got it?"

"*If* you insist. You're the director, for better or worse."

"And stick to the script!" the woman playing Claire boomed again, her voice even louder and no longer English. "The line is, 'You're certainly not a girl anymore, but that's all right. You're a mature woman.'"

"That's what I *said*."

"You said, 'You're a *big*, mature woman.' I don't like you making cracks about my weight."

"Well, Jazz, I can't help it if you've put on a few pounds since I last saw you," Shelby said, looking her up and down. "Frankly, I find it laughable Roger is supposed to find you attractive, and the audience won't believe it. Even from the balcony, they can see you're old and fat."

She moved closer to him. "How dare you? So help me, if you improvise your lines when we're in front of an audience…"

"Oh, don't be so sensitive." He waved her off and turned to Oliver again. "I'll be in what passes for my dressing room. Call me when we're ready to continue." He walked upstage and off, shaking his head and muttering.

I had moved to the aisle as Oliver looked back at me. "Hello, Heath. I'm glad you could make it."

I smiled as I went toward him and shook his hand. "I'm sorry I'm late. Traffic was unbearable. It's hard to get away in the middle of the day."

"It's okay. Most of the action is in the second act, anyway."

"I can't stay long. The chief is having a tirade today, and I have a counterfeiting case I need to work on some more," I said, "though I would like to see—"

"Oliver! I want to talk to you!" the woman playing Claire called out, her voice echoing throughout the empty auditorium and bouncing off the walls and ceiling.

"Speaking of tirades, brace yourself, Heath."

She came across the stage, heels pounding down the stairs on the left side of the orchestra pit, with a scowl on her face that cracked her pancake makeup. "Did you hear what Berkett just said to me?"

"He didn't mean it, Jazz," Oliver said. "That's just Shelby. Ignore him."

"I will not be insulted like that." Her accent was now Midwestern, and her voice boomed.

"I know he can be difficult, but he's a good actor and a big name."

"I'm a big name. I'm the star of this show, aren't I? Berkett is insufferable, rude, and egotistical."

"So you've said many times, Jazz."

"Apparently, it bears repeating. And he's nasty to poor little Dick. It infuriates me the way he treats him, always calling him an idiot."

"You're not exactly warm and fuzzy to Dick yourself." I could tell he instantly regretted his comment.

Jazz looked indignant. "Dick's my responsibility, my ward. I've raised him all by myself, I got him this job, and I take care of him the best I can."

"I'm sorry, that was uncalled for," Oliver said. He looked quite uncomfortable now. "But Mr. Berkett *will* sell tickets." He wiped the sweat from his brow with his handkerchief.

"Oh really? How have ticket sales been so far?"

"Well, a little slow, but it's early yet," Oliver said, now mopping the back of his neck.

"Early? We open in two days, in case you've forgotten. Obviously, he's not that big a name."

Oliver shifted his weight from one foot to another, looked at me, and then back at her. "He's a big enough name, believe me. It was a coup for the show to sign him. After all, he's from New York."

"He's not *from* New York, he only lives there. He grew up right here, as you well know."

"He tried to be friends with you and Jasper when he first arrived, but you'd have none of it. You couldn't put the past behind you."

"Why should I? I didn't ask him to be in this play. I didn't ask him to come back after all these years. He left Milwaukee in February, 1926. I remember it well," Jazz said. "I have a constant reminder with me always."

"What reminder?" Oliver said, shoving his now-damp handkerchief into his back pocket.

Jazz's face took on a strange expression. "The scar from where he stabbed me in the back. And Jasper, well, he has his bad leg as his constant reminder."

"That was a long time ago, Jazz."

"As Jasper would say, some wounds don't heal, but that heel certainly wounds," she said, shaking her head. Her wig slipped a little. "I wouldn't have have agreed to do the play if I'd known he was going to be in it. And what Shelby did to Alex back then…"

"Allegedly. Nothing was ever proven. We've been over this many times," Oliver said.

"You weren't around in the twenties, you don't know. I still can't believe he had the nerve to come back, and that you had the nerve to offer him the role," Jazz said, seething.

"You're really quite good in the role of Claire," I said, hoping to take some of the heat off Oliver.

She looked at me then, for the first time acknowledging my presence, her expression softening a bit. "Thank you, Mr…?"

"Ah, er, Miss Monroe, this is Heath Barrington. Heath, this is Miss Jazz Monroe, our female lead."

"The *star* of this show, Mr. Crane, *not* the female lead."

Oliver cringed just a little, but I don't think she noticed. "Right, Jazz, sorry. The star of our show."

"That's better," she said, shooting him another look before turning back to me, her voice a little softer and calmer, but still agitated. "How do you do? You're that policeman fellow Mr. Crane said was working on the script, is that right?"

"That's right, though I'm a detective, actually." Up close, she appeared much older than her character, probably in her late forties. Her makeup was heavy, and her painted-on eyebrows arched up almost to the hairline of her blond wig. She reminded me of a bulldog, with short, stocky legs, small brown eyes on either side of a rather large nose, and chins that hung down in small folds. Her figure was ample, with almost no waistline.

"Mr. Barrington was kind enough to be my consultant, making sure all the little police details are correct, especially with Henry's Inspector Bloom character. Heath's a friend of mine from way back."

"That's right. Today is the first time I've gotten to visit the theater to see the set. Oliver sent me the script a while ago, and I read-through it and made a couple minor changes."

"How interesting," Jazz said, though she didn't seem interested in the least.

"I was happy to do it, though I'm afraid I'm not all that familiar with English police proceedings."

"Neither will anyone in the audience be, so don't worry about it."

"I suppose you're right. I was late getting here, but the scene I just saw was spectacular, Miss Monroe. I was on the edge of my seat. You were excellent."

She smiled, and I could tell she was eating up my words. "Thank you so much, Mr. Barrington. Of course, you read the script. You know what's going to happen."

"Yes, of course. But seeing it acted out live is entirely different. It's kept me completely captivated. It feels so real, like I'm a part of it. And the set is magnificent."

The three of us glanced up at the stage.

"It did turn out rather well, considering the meager budget. We reused a lot of the sets from last year's *Dracula*," Oliver said.

"Well, it looks like jolly old England to me, or at least what I would imagine an old English country estate to look like," I said.

Oliver smiled. "Good. Theater is illusion, you know, Heath. Make-believe, smoke and mirrors. It's my job, all our jobs, to make you believe."

"So far so good. That fire in the fireplace looks real, too," I said.

"All fake. Fire codes won't allow for the real thing. Colored bulbs and papier-mâché. And the marble staircase? Just painted plywood."

"Amazing. And thanks again for giving Alan a part in all this."

"Who's Alan?" she asked, looking from me to Oliver.

Oliver couldn't hide his exasperation. "Alan Keyes. He plays the policeman who arrests you at the end. Geez, there are only six people in the whole show." He turned back to me. "Jazz plays Claire, of course, and Shelby Berkett is Roger. Eve Holloway plays Claire's sister, and Eve's husband, Peter, plays the butler."

I raised my eyebrows. "Really? The butler is so much older than she is."

Oliver laughed. "Eve likes older men, I guess," he said. "Anyway, Henry Hawthorne has the part of the detective and of the brother who dies at the very beginning of the second act. He also has a small role as the deliveryman."

"Yes. Alan's told me a lot about Henry Hawthorne, and I must say I'm curious to see him in person. I wish I'd gotten here sooner."

"He comes on again as the detective shortly after the murder," Oliver said.

"Henry and I have a wonderful scene together coming up, where he grills me about what's happened. He's quite dashing, and I think he favors me," Jazz said. "He's such a flirt."

"Henry's a good actor. He can make people believe all kinds of things," Oliver said, but the comment went over Jazz's head.

"Is he married?" I said.

Jazz laughed. "That skirt chaser? Not hardly. Any woman who would settle down with him would be just asking for heartache. I don't mind a little flirtation, but that's it. Never marry a man prettier than you, as my mother used to say."

"A wise woman, I'm sure."

"So, Alan's the kid. The tall cute one who replaced Nick when he broke his arm. I thought his name was Paul. Why didn't anyone correct me?"

"Mostly because you always refer to him as the kid. I've never heard you call him Paul," Oliver said.

"Well, he is a kid, a newbie. He and Henry have become quite chummy."

"I know Alan is enjoying his small part immensely," I said, annoyed by her statement.

"Henry's taken the kid under his wing," she continued. "They share a dressing room, you know. Anyway, I'm glad you're enjoying the show. *Death Comes to Lochwood* is a decent play. Not great, but decent. No offense, Mr. Crane. I know your brother wrote it."

"None taken, Jazz. It's Wally's first attempt, and I think he did quite well."

"Good enough for summer stock, anyway. Something to keep me busy until the season starts again. Besides, my part isn't bad. I get to kill Shelby Berkett, so that's a big plus."

"Honestly, Jazz, you really need to get along with him better," Oliver said.

She tossed her head to the side, and the wig slipped again. "Why? You don't like him any better than I do, but you won't admit it."

Oliver put his hand to his forehead as if he had a headache. "Fine, have it your way. Make sure Dick cleans up that teacup mess, and tell Jasper we'll need another cup and saucer. Have him refill your poison vial and the teapot, too. Tell everyone to take ten, and have Hilda touch up your greasepaint and secure your wig better."

Jazz scowled and pushed her wig back into place. "Whatever you say, boss. But if Berkett makes any more cracks, I'm going to smack him into next week."

"I'll talk to him. Again."

"Good, see that you do, and see that it does some good this time. Nice meeting you, Mr. Barrington." And she turned and climbed the stairs once more, rather laboriously, before exiting stage left.

I looked over at Oliver, who had a worn-out look on his face. He was only in his late thirties, but his hair was already the color of an early frost. His skin was like fresh buttermilk, and he had a smattering of freckles on his thin nose. His eyes were the brightest blue I've ever seen, the color of cornflowers, bluer even than Alan's. I'd been attracted to Oliver once upon a time, but of course he never knew that and never would.

"She's certainly something!" I said.

"Yes. Yes, she is. She's like a freight train that can't be stopped. She's loud, brash, obnoxious, and conceited. But she also hits her marks, knows her lines, projects and takes direction. And audiences seem to love her. Her costars, not so much."

"Especially Shelby Berkett, it appears."

"You said it, Heath. Those two are oil and water."

"Why does Miss Monroe dislike Mr. Berkett so much and vice versa?"

Oliver scratched his head, causing his white hair to tumble

over his beautiful blue eyes. "Ugh, actors. Come on, we have a few minutes before we start up again. I'll show you around, and we can have a drink in my office."

"Sounds great." I sensed he didn't want to discuss his two stars in public.

We climbed the stairs on the right side of the orchestra pit up to the stage as I glanced again at Lochwood. It didn't appear so real up close, but it was still impressive. Oliver led me across the set, up the two stairs to the landing of the house and to the right, toward what was supposed to be the entrance to the manor.

"Past the wings here is the stage door. Thirty minutes or so before showtime, Jasper will put the tea set, vial of poison, and other items on this table. The worst thing that can happen to the prop guy is for a prop not to be ready when the actor gets their cue. If they have to go on without it and improvise, it's not good."

"I'm sure it's not. Jasper's the prop man? The one Miss Monroe mentioned?"

"That's right. Jasper Crockett. He used to be an actor a long time ago."

I looked about. On the far wall was a black metal fire door I assumed led out to the back alley. Next to the door was a wooden stool with a newspaper folded on top of it. A lopsided fire extinguisher hung on the left wall, and on the right was a pay phone, its black paint scratched and nicked.

"Those stairs there go to the basement, of course," Oliver said. "Besides the other dressing rooms, the green room's down there along with the boiler room and more storage for old sets, backdrops, and whatnot. The costume shop is in the basement, too. You can access it from either side of the stage. Past the stairwell on this floor is the lavatory, followed by Jazz's, Shelby's, and Eve's dressing rooms, and in here is the makeup department."

Oliver opened the door for me and flipped on the lights as we stepped inside the rectangular room. There were several tables along the wall, each with its own stool, and a mirror above each of the tables. "Some of the actors do their own makeup here or in their dressing rooms, but Hilda's our girl for more involved jobs, like transforming Peter into the butler. She's probably in with Jazz at the moment."

He walked over to one of the tables and poked about a bit at the various tubes, containers, powders, and brushes, and then he picked up a large, round tin. "This is the makeup putty she uses for noses, wrinkles, and whatnot. It's pliable but dries quite hard."

"Interesting," I said. "I find it all fascinating. To play a part, to act a role…"

"Don't we all do that to some extent or another, Heath? Isn't that a part of life, of getting along?"

I glanced over at him, and I knew he was right. I was playing a part right now, keeping my true self hidden, and that was indeed a part of life. Of my life, anyway. And it was necessary for my survival. "What's on the other side of the stage?" I said, changing the subject.

"I'll show you." He put the tin back, and we walked out of the room and down the hall onto the set again, where a small, dark-haired fellow was almost finished cleaning up the shattered teacup and saucer.

"Be sure and get all the broken glass up, Dick. I don't want Shelby or anyone else getting cut," Oliver said.

"Okay."

We entered the doorway that was supposed to lead to Lochwood's dining room, library, and kitchen, but in reality just led to the other side of the stage.

"Who was that?"

"That was Dick, Jazz's ward. He's the janitor here now," Oliver said.

"He looks young."

"He does, but he's actually twenty-one, I think. It's his small stature that's deceiving. Anyway, the prop room, Jasper's home away from home, is just here, next to the basement stairs. Across the hall from that is the supply room, the lavatory, and my office at the end of the hall." I glanced up at the transom windows above each of the four doors as we walked down the dim, narrow hall.

Oliver unlocked his office and ushered me in as he flicked on the overhead light and closed the door again. "Small, but it works," Oliver said.

The little room was occupied mainly by his large oak desk, which sat like an island in the center, upon which was a green banker's lamp, telephone, blotter, ink pen, inkwell, a glass ashtray full of butts, and a battered typewriter. Stacks of papers, flyers, and posters were strewn about. A couple of armchairs faced the desk. Behind Oliver's leather chair was a row of large wooden filing cabinets, along with a console radio and a massive iron safe. On three of the walls were posters of previous shows, some framed reviews, and photographs of people I mostly didn't recognize.

Oliver sat down in his chair with a thud as I took a seat opposite. "Care for a drink? I just have bourbon, no ice," he said, opening a drawer and removing a bottle and a couple of glasses.

I shook my head. "I'm okay for now, Oliver, but please go ahead."

"I think I will. Mama told me never to drink alone, but since you're here I'm not alone." He poured a couple of fingers' worth into one of the glasses and leaned back, breathing in the contents.

"So, what happened between Miss Monroe and Mr. Berkett, Oliver? What's the story?"

He looked at me over the top of the glass. "It was before my time here, but I've heard tales. He said, she said, he said."

"And the truth is a mixture of it all, I suppose," I commented.

"Right. Jazz, Shelby, Jasper Crockett, and a fellow named Alexander Lippencott were doing a show here, and it was getting rave reviews, critical acclaim. All four of them were in their early to mid twenties back then, and this was their first big hit."

"I remember you saying Mr. Crockett used to be an actor."

"That's right, and I hear he was pretty good. They all were," Oliver said.

I fanned my face with my hat, as it was warm and stuffy in his office.

"Word had gotten out that a New York producer had heard about the show and was coming to town, looking for a fresh face, a headliner for a new production he was doing on Broadway."

"Friendly rivalry, then, between the four of them," I said.

Oliver nodded. "Yeah, but it got unfriendly quick. Shortly after they heard about the New York producer, Jasper and Alex were rehearsing their big fight scene onstage, trying out something different they thought would spice it up. Somehow, the trap door in the floor got tripped. Lippencott was standing dead center on it, and Jasper was partially on it. Both fell through to the basement, Jasper on top of Lippencott. Lippencott broke his neck and died instantly. Jasper fractured his leg and knocked his head pretty good. He's been a bit slow ever since, physically and mentally, if you know what I mean."

"Good Lord, that's awful. How did the trap door get opened?"

Oliver picked up the glass again and took another drink, finishing it before setting it back down and dropping his cigarette butt into it. "That, my friend, is something no one will ever know for sure, but fingers were pointed at Shelby, who was near the release at the time. Nothing was ever proven, and Shelby claimed he was innocent."

"Do *you* think he did it?"

Oliver shrugged. "If he did, I don't think he intended to kill anyone. But we'll never know for sure unless Shelby talks. The New York producer showed up a couple weeks later, and of course, at that point only Jazz and Shelby were left. They brought in replacements for Alex and Jasper's parts, but it wasn't the same show, and the director at the time was criticized for not closing after Lippencott's death."

"I imagine that was a tough decision for him, a hit show on his hands and all," I said.

"I agree. I wouldn't have wanted to make that call. Sadly, Jasper's leg never healed properly, and his acting career was pretty much over. He took over as prop manager the following year and has been at it ever since."

"I remember Miss Monroe mentioning Mr. Crockett's leg earlier. But what about her and Shelby?"

Oliver sighed and rubbed his eyes. "Jasper tells me Jazz and Shelby were close back then. They even dated. But this thing with the trap door put Jazz over the edge. They stopped speaking to each other except during the show. Then the producer ended up choosing Shelby over Jazz for his New York show, and that really sealed it between them. Shelby left Milwaukee and never came back."

"Until now," I said. "And he and Miss Monroe are working together again, along with Mr. Crockett."

"Yes. I thought it was water under the bridge after all this time, but the water washed that bridge completely away, apparently." Oliver scratched the back of his sweaty neck. "When Shelby first got back he actually seemed to be trying to make amends with Jazz and Jasper, but they wanted nothing to do with him. So, he has replied in kind, rude and uncalled for or not."

"Old grudges," I said. "How has Shelby been to work with?"

"Shelby's a good actor, but he doesn't like to be directed. At least not by me. All through rehearsals, he's been giving everyone direction contrary to mine, stepping on their lines, ignoring his blocking, and arguing, especially with me and Jazz. He throws his weight around and rubs everyone the wrong way, and of course, he's extremely egotistical. He's also insecure, vain, arrogant, and temperamental. Those are his *good* points."

"How *did* he end up playing Roger, then?"

"He almost didn't. The entire play had been cast except for the roles of the butler, the detective, and Roger. I had to have someone spectacular for Roger, someone who could stand up to Jazz."

"A tall order, I'm sure."

Oliver smiled. "Eve Holloway worked with Henry Hawthorne on the Canteen and USO circuit during the war, entertaining the troops. She suggested Henry would be perfect for the role of Roger, so I gave him a call. He told me he was heading to Hollywood in the fall to try out for a new movie, but he had the summer free and could use the money. He's working part time at Lempke's Pharmacy in West Allis just to pay the bills. Acting is a tough way to make a living."

"I imagine so. So what happened?"

"He read brilliantly for the part of Roger, and he was in my price range, which isn't much. I was all set to sign him to a contract when out of the blue, I got a long-distance collect phone call from Shelby Berkett in New York. He'd received a telegram telling him about the show and the role of Roger and asking him to call me."

"Who sent the telegram?"

Oliver looked at me with an odd expression. "That's the funny part. Shelby told me it was signed by Alexander Lippencott."

"The actor who died?"

"That's right. Our friendly neighborhood ghost."

"Ghost?"

Oliver shrugged. "Yeah. Jasper believes Lippencott's spirit is still in the theater. Some say on the anniversary of his death, the blood stain reappears on the basement floor beneath the trap door."

"Have you ever seen that?"

He shook his head. "No, but I've never looked, either. I don't put much stock in things like that, but I will say ever since his death there have been sightings and reports of strange occurrences, going way back to before I ever took over."

"Anything you've ever witnessed?"

Oliver picked up a folder from his desk and fanned himself with it. "Oh, you know. Sometimes when I'm here alone I hear strange noises, and I think I see things, but then I tell myself it's just my imagination. Occasionally when I'm in my office the door will seemingly close on its own, but it's an old building, and buildings settle."

"Interesting. So, Mr. Berkett claims he got a telegram from this ghost?"

"That's what he said, and I can't imagine why he'd make something like that up. He thought someone was playing a joke on him and he sounded upset. As you can guess, he's sensitive when it comes to Mr. Lippencott."

"Who really sent it?"

"I honestly don't know. I certainly didn't. I'd never even met him before. When I finally convinced him I didn't know who had sent the telegram, but the part of Roger was available, he seemed interested."

"But you were all set to sign Henry."

Oliver looked sheepish. "I know, but business is business. Shelby's not a big star, but his name is known here in Milwaukee. Local boy makes good, you know? The *Journal* and the *Sentinel* have run a few stories on him through the years. He's gotten good press. The accident has been all but forgotten over time."

"What did he say?"

Oliver leaned back, balancing the chair on its two rear legs, his feet on the desk, and stretched, still fanning himself. "After more talking, all on my dime as he'd called collect, remember, he surprisingly agreed to do the show if I paid him what he was asking. It was more than I was going to pay Henry, but I gambled his name would sell tickets."

"He agreed without even seeing the script? And you wanted him without an audition?"

"I didn't see the need to waste time auditioning him, especially since he was in New York and I was here. He said he was between shows. I wired him a contract, and he signed it and sent it back. He was on the train west the next week in time for the first read-through."

"How did Miss Monroe and Mr. Crockett react to Shelby coming back?"

Oliver groaned. "As you can imagine, neither of them were pleased. Jasper even threatened to quit. They both believe the trap door incident was intentional, and they blame Berkett for killing Lippencott. They were angry with me for signing him without consulting them first. To be honest, I didn't even think of their feelings when I signed Berkett. I just thought Shelby would be good for the show and the bottom line. At this point, I truly regret that."

"And Henry?"

"I still had the role of the detective open, so I offered that to him, even though he was all set to play Roger. I sweetened the deal by giving him the role of the brother and the deliveryman, too. Those parts were originally written to go to the person playing the policeman, Alan's part, but again, business is business."

"I understand, and I'm sure Alan does, too."

"Well, Alan's role belonged to someone else at that point."

"Yes, I remember. The man you had cast ended up breaking his arm a couple weeks into rehearsal."

Oliver took his legs off the desk and brought his chair down with a thud. "Right, Nick Schultz. He fell off the stage, but some suggest Jazz pushed him when he blocked her, including Nick Schultz."

"She wouldn't really do that, would she?"

Oliver raised his eyebrows. "I wouldn't put it past her, but she said she accidentally bumped him, and he fell into the orchestra pit."

"Wowzer!"

"Right. Accident or not, a few weeks into rehearsal, I was left without anyone to play the policeman. When you suggested Alan, it seemed a perfect fit. Of course, it's a small part with no lines."

"But he makes it his own," I said.

"He *does*. And Henry's doing a fine job as the detective, though Peter Holloway wanted that role."

"How did Mr. Holloway take the news the part he wanted went to Henry?"

Oliver shook his head. "Not well. Peter is Eve's husband, as

I believe I mentioned. Eve plays Charlotte, and she's wonderful. She had suggested Henry for the role of Roger, and her husband for the detective part. Peter is a talented actor, and he fit the role of the detective physically."

"So why didn't you sign him for it?"

Oliver sighed. "He drinks too much. He's not reliable, and he takes a colorful variety of pills with alarming frequency. It's sad, really."

"I see. So Mr. Berkett got the role of Roger, Henry took the role of the detective, and you moved Peter to the role of the butler."

"That was Eve's idea, too, and I wanted to appease her. The initial cast read-through was pretty tense, and I started to have second thoughts about the whole thing right then and there, but I couldn't do anything but forge ahead. I've been forging ahead ever since."

"I'm sorry, Oliver."

"Thanks, but I guess it's my own fault. I hope the reviewers will be kind."

"They will be, I'm sure of it. How bad is the financial situation, if you don't mind my asking?"

Oliver looked pained as he set the folder he had been fanning himself with back down and rubbed his eyes again. "Pretty bad. I have a lot invested in this show. I borrowed some money from a few backers, hoping to make it back and then some so I could do a bigger show in the fall. I just don't understand it. I really thought signing Shelby Berkett would be a coup for the bottom line. I printed posters and flyers, took out ads in the morning and evening papers—hell, I even signed a contract for some radio ads this morning, though since it was so last minute, the first open slot was this Saturday at 6:13 p.m. on the Opera Hour."

"Oh my, Oliver."

He threw his head back and glanced briefly at the ceiling, and then at me. "I know, but I'm desperate, and that's what I get for waiting. Hopefully, it will do some good, though I'm not sure who all listens to the Opera Hour besides Jasper. He's a big fan, or at least his dog likes it."

I laughed, but then I realized he was serious.

Oliver smiled. "It sounds crazy, but it's true. Jasper has a radio in his prop room and he plays the *Opera Hour* for his dog. It's the only radio I allow in the theater besides the one in my office here."

"Why is that?"

"They're too much of a distraction, and people miss their cues. Plus, if I'm doing a musical, I want the players focused on the music in the show and not what's on the radio."

"Makes sense, I guess."

"Yeah, I find it helps. Anyway, I'd appreciate it if you would help spread the word about the show, Heath. I can give you some flyers if you would be so kind as to put them up at work, in the lobby of your building, and anywhere else you think they may do some good."

"Sure thing, Oliver. I'd be happy to. I don't know how you manage to do it all. You're the stage manager, the director, and the producer."

"Don't remind me, Heath. But it keeps costs down. And I got used to wearing many hats during the war, when manpower was in short supply. Jasper used to do props *and* janitorial, but Jazz pressured me into hiring Dick, so now he's on the payroll, too."

"Prop manager sounds like a big enough job on its own."

"It is. Jasper makes sure everything is where it needs to be when it needs to be. The tea tray and service, the tea in the teapot, the poison in the vial, the rainwater for Roger's hat and coat, the list goes on and on."

"The poison is fake, of course."

"I should hope so! The poison and the tea are all just tea and more tea. Shelby likes it extra sweet, so Jasper always adds a lot of sugar. We've gone through a whole bag just during rehearsals, and it's not cheap. We're lucky we can even get sugar since the rationing on it ended not long ago."

"Yes, it's one of the last items to stop being rationed. In some parts of the country, it just ended this year."

"And Shelby eats it up like nobody's business."

"You certainly have your hands full," I said.

"And how. Something's gotta give. On top of everything else, Peter's pillbox is now missing."

"Missing?"

"As I said before, Peter takes pills to get him going in the morning, pills to calm him down during the day, and pills to help him sleep."

"That's a lot of pills, Oliver."

"I know. He calls them his happy pills. He found a doctor that keeps him well supplied for a price. I don't like it and neither does Eve, but he's a stubborn man."

"All those pills must get expensive."

"Eve's been getting the prescriptions filled from Lempke's Pharmacy."

"The place where Henry Hawthorne works?"

"That's right. He and Eve have been friends a long time. I think Henry gets her some kind of a discount."

"Interesting. Was the pillbox valuable?"

"According to Peter, it was sterling silver and gold. He said someone took it out of his dressing room while he was onstage. And last week, Eve said a small compact framed in ivory that had belonged to her mother had disappeared from her dressing room. Before that, Hilda the makeup lady told me one of her jars of putty had gone missing."

"Putty?"

"The stuff I showed you earlier that she uses to age actors, add wrinkles, elongate noses, that type of thing."

"Any idea who's behind it all?"

Oliver shook his head. "None. At first I put it down to items just being misplaced. But three items within days makes me wonder. Jasper thinks it's the infamous Alexander Lippencott."

"I wasn't aware ghosts stole things, or sent telegrams, for that matter. I can't say I put a lot of stock in spirits."

"I don't really, either, Heath, but Jasper and Alex were friends, and he says he can sense Alex's presence."

"Who has access to the dressing rooms and the makeup room?"

"The dressing rooms don't lock from the outside, and the makeup room is always open, so it could have been anyone, really."

"Curious. The pill case and mirror I can see, as they sound like they were worth something, but the putty?"

"I know, it's baffling."

"Has anyone supposedly ever seen this Lippencott ghost?"

Oliver looked surprisingly serious. "Not directly, but Eve mentioned feeling like someone was watching her when she was in her dressing room the other day, even though no one was there. She's had that sensation several times recently."

"Hmmm. Do you keep your office locked at all times when you're not here?"

"Yes, just as a precaution, of course. About the only rooms we keep locked are my office, the box office, the supply room, and the prop room. Why?"

"Just wondering."

At that moment there was a knock on the door.

"Come in," Oliver called out.

I turned to see a tall, almost gaunt man about forty-five years old, with a small black and white pup wagging an active little tail.

"We're all set. Miss Monroe and Mr. Berkett are waiting onstage."

"Thanks, Jasper. I'll be right there. Leave the door open, please."

"Yes, sir," Jasper said. He turned and walked slowly back down the hall with a pronounced limp. The dog trotted behind, his tail still swishing about like a propeller.

Oliver looked back at me. "That's Jasper, the prop man."

"So I gathered. He totally ignored me, as if I wasn't even here."

"That's just the way he is. I'm used to it. His life hasn't been easy, and he's not one to trust many people. He and I are friends, but I'm one of the few. He has taken a liking to Alan, though. Alan's helped him out a lot backstage."

"Not surprising, knowing Alan."

"Here's some of those flyers to put up if you're sure you don't mind?" He handed me some from a stack on his desk.

"I absolutely don't mind, glad to." I rolled them up and put them in my inside jacket pocket as we exited the office. I waited as he turned out the light and locked the door. I followed him back down the dark hall into the wings. He picked up a megaphone from a small desk and strode onstage.

"Places, everyone! Starting from the death scene. Shelby, take it from: 'No, I arouse you, I can tell. I always could tell.' And this time, set the cup and saucer down before you convulse."

We went into the seating area as Shelby and Jazz took their places onstage, but seeing the infamous Henry Hawthorne in person would have to wait.

"I wish I could stay for the rest, Oliver, but I really have to go. I'll see it all Saturday night." I nudged his shoulder. "The show will be great. It will all fall together."

"Or fall apart," Oliver said with a sigh. He took out his damp handkerchief again and mopped his brow before shoving it back into his pocket.

"You'll hold it together."

"I hope so. I'll put a ticket aside for you at the box office."

"Any chance you could make it two?"

"You've been holding out on me, Heath. I thought you said you weren't dating anyone."

"I'm not. What about you?"

"I've got my eye on a pretty blond millinery clerk at Schuster's, but we'll see. So, who are you bringing?"

"My Aunt Verbina. She loves the theater."

"Ah, okay, two it is. Unfortunately, I can spare the seats."

"Thanks, Oliver, I appreciate it. Tell Alan I'll call him later."

"Will do. You're coming to the cast party tomorrow night at my apartment after the final dress rehearsal, aren't you?"

"Sure. Alan mentioned that, but aren't cast parties usually after opening night?"

"Yeah, normally, but Berkett apparently has an engagement Saturday night after the show, and I can't have the party without him. Jazz may be the star, but he's the featured attraction."

I shrugged and rolled my eyes. "Actors. See you tomorrow night, then."

"If I live that long. Actors."

I heard Oliver yell, "Action!" as I turned and walked up the aisle and outside to Third Street and the late afternoon sunshine. The fog from earlier had lifted. The sky was now azure blue, and groups of puffy clouds had gathered overhead, bumping into each other as they rolled gently over the city on their way to the lake. I smiled to myself as I put my gray fedora on and hurried back to my car and the police station.

CHAPTER TWO

Thursday evening, July 10, 1947

I was able to slip back to my desk mostly unnoticed. The chief's mood had apparently lifted like the fog, so I turned my attention to my counterfeiting case. I reviewed the file again. A Mr. and Mrs. Frank Feltcher and their son and his wife had been the latest victims at their small business on Farwell Avenue. I made a note to contact them on Monday, sent some paperwork down to research, and then, well past my normal quitting time, signed myself out and headed home to my apartment on Prospect Avenue.

I live in the Atwater, a classic, three-story brown brick building built in the Twenties. It has no elevator and no parking, but I found a good spot on the street in the shade of an ancient elm tree I referred to as the Great Grandmother Elm. I left the car windows open an inch or two for ventilation, as the heat and humidity had increased substantially as the day wore on.

The lobby of the Atwater was relatively cool and dark, the few lights burning reflecting dully off the tile floors. Still, I felt a bead of sweat run down the back of my neck as I stopped to check the mail in the boxes located to the right of the stairs. There wasn't much, the monthly telephone bill and a letter from my cousin Liz, who was on holiday in Paris.

I fanned my face with the bill and opened the letter from Liz, the highlight of my day. She wrote breezily about what she had been doing and seeing, and it buoyed my spirits considerably. When I had finished, I put it back in its envelope to reread later, locked my mailbox, and climbed the two flights of stairs to my apartment on three.

I'd gotten halfway up when I remembered the flyers in my jacket pocket, so I went back down and pinned one up on the bulletin board next to the mailboxes. I started the climb again, only to run into Mrs. Murphy from the second floor, who was descending rather slowly, step by step. She was wearing a short-sleeved blue print summer dress, white gloves, and a white hat set at a rakish angle, a dark blue ribbon around the brim. She was so big she blocked my path, so I had to stop and chat with her.

"Oh hello, Mr. Barrington. You're home late," she said, tucking up a strand of dyed brunette hair that had fallen below her hat into her eyes.

"Yes, I had a busy day today. How are you, Mrs. Murphy?"

"Oh fine, fine. I'm off to visit my sister, Edna. She lives over on Oakland, you know."

"I seem to recall you mentioning that. How is Mr. Murphy?"

"He's good, same as always. Grumpy. Indigestion, Can't stand this heat. I did get him to agree to take me to the movies tomorrow night, though. They have conditioned air, and it's dish night, you know."

"Oh?"

"Yes, just for buying a ticket you get a plate, glass dish, or a bowl. Of course, the larger pieces like serving trays or pitchers cost two admission tickets, which is why I want Herbert to go with me. I've got my eye on a pitcher. Just the thing for iced tea or lemonade, and like I said, it's been hot this summer."

"Yes, it has."

"I've almost got a complete set. Green's my color, but they have pink, blue, and red, too."

"How interesting. Well, good that Mr. Murphy can go with you, then."

"No easy task, I tell you, Mr. Barrington. He doesn't care much for the movies these days, ever since Lois Moran gave up acting."

"Lois Moran? Wasn't she a silent film star?"

Mrs. Murphy batted her eyes. "The one and only, so that shows you how long it's been since Herbert's been to the pictures. Anyway, Miss McBain is thinking of coming with us tomorrow night. She's been collecting the pink dishes."

"How nice for you," I said, wishing I could squeeze by her and be on my way as I needed to use the bathroom.

"We could make it a foursome," she said, her cheeks flushing as she giggled. "You could help her get a platter or a pitcher."

"That's awfully kind of you, Mrs. Murphy, and I would love to help her complete her set, but I have a party to go to tomorrow night."

"You do?"

"Yes, a friend of mine is directing a play and another friend is in it. They're having a cast party tomorrow evening."

"Oh, how fun. I'm so glad you're getting out. You spend too much time at home alone, Mr. Barrington."

"I work a lot, Mrs. Murphy."

"All work and no play, you know. We can't have that now!" She giggled again. "I do love the theater, but Herbert doesn't. That's why I was so happy when he agreed to go with me to the pictures tomorrow. *Possessed* is playing at the Oriental. I've heard it's quite good."

"The new Joan Crawford picture?"

"Yes, she's so beautiful, isn't she? And such a talent. Miss McBain is a big fan of hers. Poor Miss McBain, all alone, you know."

I resisted the urge to roll my eyes. "Yes, so you've mentioned before."

"Have I? Well, she's such a sweet young thing. Her fiancé was killed in the war, you know. So tragic."

"Yes, you've mentioned that, too."

She laughed again, and her whole body shook. "Oh, I suppose I have. Perhaps she and I can take in your friend's play one night. I know I'll never get Herbert to go. What's it called?"

"*Death Comes to Lochwood*. It's at the Davidson Theater."

"The Davidson? Fancy. It must be quite a show. Are they giving anything away?"

"Not that I'm aware of. It stars Jazz Monroe and Shelby Berkett."

"Oh, I never miss Miss Monroe in her Christmas show. And Shelby Berkett was in that big show on Broadway a few years ago. I remember reading about it in the papers. I had heard he was back in town."

"Yes, that's right."

"Oh my, oh my. A Broadway star right here in Milwaukee. What's the play called again?"

"*Death Comes to Lochwood*. I put up a flyer downstairs next to the mailboxes."

"Oh, that *does* sound interesting. I'm sure it will be a wonderful show. Well, I must be off. My sister will be waiting for me. Ta-ta!"

I flattened myself against the railing and hoped it wouldn't break as she squeezed by me and continued down the stairs. "Goodbye, Mrs. Murphy," I said as I exhaled.

At the bottom of the stairs, she called up once more with a wave of her hand. "Ta-ta!"

I gave a half-hearted wave in return, climbing up to my apartment, glad to be home. Once I had used the bathroom, changed my clothes, and locked my service revolver in the nightstand next to my bed, I decided to see if Alan had made it home yet. I picked up the phone in the hall near the door and dialed his number, letting it ring as I studied myself in the mirror. I was about to hang up when I heard it click.

"Hello?"

"Hey, Officer, I was beginning to think you weren't home."

"Oh, hi, Heath. I just got in. Rehearsal ran late, and then Hank and I stopped for a bite to eat before he dropped me off."

"Hank, as in Henry Hawthorne from the show."

"Yeah. He lets me call him Hank."

"Big of him. You should have called me. I could have given you a ride home tonight and we could have eaten together. I got stuck late, too."

"Oh, I didn't want to bother you. Hank's place is just a short distance from my place."

"It wouldn't have been a bother. I like having dinner with you."

"Thanks, Heath. It was just a spur-of-the-moment thing, you know?"

"You sure seem to like him a lot. You've been spending a lot of time together."

There was a noticeable pause. "Hank's a nice fellow. Everyone likes him, not just me. Well, everyone but Mr. Berkett, that is."

"Why is that?" I was glad to know I had at least one ally in the anti–Henry Hawthorne camp.

"Oh, Hank's up for a big part in a new Alfred Hitchcock movie out in Hollywood. Apparently, the casting director, somebody by the name of Marshall, saw him in a play in Iowa last summer and was really impressed. He told Hank to come see him in Hollywood this fall to try out for the film."

"Bully for him."

"Yeah, but when Mr. Berkett heard about it, he said he and this Marshall go way back."

"I think I may see where this is going."

"You probably do. You always have been good at figuring things out. Anyway, Mr. Berkett sent a telegram to this Marshall fellow and told him he'd be interested in the part Hank is up for."

"That's pretty low, I must admit."

"I thought so, too, but Mr. Berkett claims it's strictly business, and the better actor will prevail. Hank's really upset about it."

"Understandable. So Hank's going to Hollywood right after this show, then?" I said, trying not to sound too hopeful.

"Yes, but he did say if he got the part, I could come visit him out there any time. Can you imagine, Heath? Me in Hollywood?"

"It's a big city, Alan. I'm not sure you'd like it." I decided to change the subject. "By the way, Oliver mentioned some things have gone missing from the makeup and dressing rooms. Have you heard anything about it?"

"Oh yeah, sure. I forgot to tell you about that. It doesn't make much sense to me."

"Nor to me. Maybe Jasper's right about Alexander Lippencott."

"Don't joke about that, Heath. I know you're a non-believer, but that theater is a pretty spooky place sometimes. Jasper told me and Hank what happened. He's convinced Mr. Berkett pulled that lever on purpose, and he says people who die suddenly and tragically like that often haunt the place they died. Jasper believes it, and I think maybe I do, too."

"Why? Have you seen Mr. Lippencott floating about?"

"You're funny. But I feel his presence sometimes, I think. And once when I was onstage alone, I felt a cool breeze on my face and couldn't determine the source. There have been odd noises, too. And Mrs. Holloway says she's sensed someone watching her when she's alone in her dressing room."

"Maybe someone was," I said.

"I don't see how, Heath. Mr. Crane checked carefully for peepholes, but he couldn't find any. And the doorknob doesn't have a keyhole."

"What about the transom over the door?"

"That's almost seven feet off the floor. The last time she felt like someone was watching her, she opened the door and looked out in the hall, but she didn't see anything. Someone would need a chair or ladder to peek in the transom, and no one would take the chance of being seen in the hall. Too many people come and go."

"I suppose. So you think the spirit of Mr. Lippencott has been watching Mrs. Holloway? And is behind the missing pill box, putty, and mirror?"

Alan paused. "I know you're joking with me, and I don't really think he is, but I can't say for certain, to be honest."

"Fascinating. Are you enjoying being in the show, mysterious spirits notwithstanding?"

"Gosh, it's wonderful. Of course, I don't have a big part, but that's almost better. I get to be there, to experience everything, to watch from the sidelines, and I don't have to remember any lines."

"That's the spirit, so to speak. Oliver told me you're doing a fine job."

"Really? Did he really say that?"

"He did, and you are."

"Well, all I do is walk on, stand there, then walk off again with Miss Monroe's character."

"Just be sure not to block her. Always stand upstage."

Alan laughed. "Yeah, I heard about what happened to Nick Schultz, but that's just a rumor."

"Nonetheless, don't take chances. I don't want you getting pushed into the pit and breaking any bones."

"I won't, I promise."

"Good. Listen to Oliver, and you'll do just fine."

"Mr. Crane's been great, but Hank's really been a mentor to me."

I bristled. "I look forward to meeting him."

"You will at the party tomorrow night."

"I can't wait."

"Did you know he also plays Claire Clarington's brother? Then later, he comes on as the detective. In the first act, he plays the telegraph boy. Can you imagine juggling three parts?"

"Well to be fair, the telegraph boy only has one line, if I remember correctly from the script."

"Technically, he has two lines. Mr. Crane told me you were at rehearsal today."

"I was, but I got there late and only saw the death scene. I had to leave shortly after that, so I didn't get to see Mr. Hawthorne perform. Oliver seemed to agree with you that he's attractive."

"I'll say he is. He has a Clark Gable mustache, and those big brown eyes, wavy hair, cleft chin, dimples…"

"So you've said. He's older than you, isn't he?"

"Maybe a little. I think I remember him saying he was thirty-nine."

"Everyone in the theater is thirty-nine, Alan. He's probably really in his mid forties."

"Oh, I don't think so. He wouldn't lie to me, I can tell."

"Regardless, you're only twenty-eight. That's a big age difference."

"He seems younger. And he's really talented. He even sings. Did you know he rides a motorcycle?"

"How fascinating."

"Yeah, he's something. He's been coaching me on my part, too. How and where to stand, how to turn, all that stuff. There's more to it than you realize."

That's what I'm afraid of, I thought. "Isn't that Oliver's job? He's the director."

"Oh sure, Oliver directs me in the general blocking, but Hank helps me with the nuances. By the way, the final programs came out today. I'm listed as 'policeman.'"

"Well, you're the tall, cute one, as Miss Monroe described you."

"Gosh, did she really?"

"On my honor, cute one."

"Gee," Alan said softly. "But Hank's the one with the looks."

"So you've said multiple times. I understand he's a bit of a skirt chaser."

"Oh, he's just a big flirt, Heath. He talks about a few girls."

"Talk is cheap, as you and I both know."

"You sound jealous."

I gripped the phone receiver a little too hard. "Do I have a reason to be?"

Another noticeable pause. "He's just a nice guy. Everyone has been swell, I guess, but I haven't gotten as much of a chance to get to know them like I have Hank. Jasper's a character, I've talked to him a lot. And Dick and I have had a few conversations. He's the janitor."

"Right. I understand Miss Monroe is his aunt."

"Sort of. They say his folks died in the great Mississippi River Flood of 1927 when he was just a baby. Miss Monroe took him in."

"I remember Mom and Pop talking about that flood. How horrible."

"Dick told me he doesn't remember either it or his parents. Miss Monroe is all he's ever known."

"And she is unforgettable. What time should I pick you up for the cast party tomorrow?"

"Oh, I'm getting a ride with Hank right after the final dress rehearsal, so I'll meet you there."

I gripped the phone even tighter. "Oh, I see. Really, it's no bother for me to swing by and get you."

"Don't be nuts, Heath. That's way out of your way. Besides, it might look funny if we show up together, especially since you're not even in the show. Hank's happy to take me."

"I'm sure he is. Not on a motorcycle, I hope."

"No, he drives a car that belongs to the woman who owns the rooming house where he's living. She gives him a good deal on it."

"Okay, if you're sure. I'll see you at Oliver's about seven?"

"We'll be there."

"And so will I, your biggest fan."

One more pause. "You don't like Henry much, I can tell. You haven't even met him."

"Call it my instinct. Maybe I can at least drive you home, huh?"

"Maybe. We'll see how it goes. I need to get going here, I have a few things to do before bed yet."

"Oh, well, all right. I'll see you tomorrow night, then, I guess. Good night, Alan."

"Night, Heath."

I hung up the phone and checked my reflection in the mirror once more, wondering what I'd look like with a Clark Gable mustache, and if I could learn to ride a motorcycle.

CHAPTER THREE

Friday evening, July 11, 1947

After another long day at the precinct, I was glad to finally be home. In some ways, I wished I hadn't agreed to go to Oliver's party, especially since Alan would be there with Henry Hawthorne. But I had to go to size up my competition. That being said, I figured I'd better look my best.

I ate a light dinner, showered and shaved again, put my best hair tonic in, and then got dressed. I decided to wear my navy double-breasted jacket with the peaked lapels, a wide, short tie with red and cream zigzags, and my loose-cut pleated gray trousers. Garnet cufflinks and tie pin, a cream pocket square, freshly shined black cap toe shoes, and a black leather belt completed my ensemble. I studied myself in the full-length mirror on the back of my bedroom door and was satisfied overall. It would have to do, anyway.

It was already six fifty and the party started at seven. I could have been there in less than five minutes if I'd taken my car, but I felt the walk would give me time to think. At five after seven, I grabbed my gray fedora, left a note for the milkman for the morning, and closed and locked the door of my apartment behind me. Mrs. Ferguson's cat was prowling the hall, so I stopped to scratch him behind the ears before heading out into the humid evening air. I put my hat on, gave a nod to some children playing kick the can in the small space next to my building, and walked south on Prospect Avenue.

When I reached Juneau Avenue, I headed west, away from the lake, and picked up my pace the five remaining blocks until I arrived at the Blackstone apartment building on the corner of Juneau and Van Buren. It was seven forty-five, so I was fashionably late as I pressed the buzzer for Oliver's apartment. I heard crackling and static, and an unintelligible voice, then the sound of the door being opened, so I pushed on through to the lobby, pausing in front of a mirror on the wall to adjust my tie and make sure I was presentable.

Satisfied, I rode the elevator to the seventh floor and turned right to 706, which was a two bedroom in the corner. Oliver himself opened the door, dressed in a natty blue blazer, blue and white tie, gray slacks, and black penny loafers. His white hair was combed neatly back and his cornflower blue eyes sparkled. He looked much more relaxed than the last time I had seen him, and still damned attractive. Oh, what could have been if he had been born like me, I thought.

"Hello, Heath. Glad you could make it. Come on in, we got started early." He smiled broadly, a cigarette dangling between his lips, as he motioned me inside. Many of the guests, most of whom I didn't recognize, were already sprawled on the sofa and chairs or standing about drinking, smoking, and chattering.

The open French doors at the far end of the living room allowed for a slight breeze, which came in off a small balcony. In spite of that, the apartment was full of cigar and cigarette smoke, and the air around me felt quite warm and stuffy. The noise level was considerable. I glanced at the kitchen doorway tucked up in the corner of the apartment and saw it was also wall-to-wall people. No room to breathe.

"I think you know some of the cast, the others you'll meet tonight. My brother Wally's here, too, playing the piano," Oliver said, gesturing out toward the crowd. "I'll introduce you later."

"Sounds good, and thanks for having me, Oliver. Who are all the rest of these people, though? I didn't think the cast was this large."

"Oh, you know how it goes. You invite one, they invite two, each of them invites three. Any chance for free booze, right? I also had to invite some of the neighbors to keep them from complaining about the noise. Let me take your hat. I'm putting them on the bed in the guest room."

He took my hat and disappeared briefly into one of the doorways to my left. When he returned, he pointed across the living room to where a skinny woman in a pink feathered hat stood laughing at something. "The bathroom's through the door on the other side, where Hilda is standing, next to the main bedroom. Oh, and your friend Alan's here already with Henry. They're in the kitchen fixing drinks."

"Great. I could use one of those."

"Go on in, if you can fit. Quite a crowd already. There's some food Brenda made over there, too. Help yourself." He took a drag on his cigarette and blew the smoke over my head.

He pointed at a large oak sideboard with a white cloth, filled with various plates of cookies, cakes, and finger sandwiches. A metal fan buzzed back and forth on the left side, keeping flies at bay and moving the smoke around some, but not much.

"Right, thanks," I said.

"Some nice-looking single ladies here, too," Oliver said with a wink, "including the fabulous Fontaine sisters, Lyric and Meadow."

I forced a smile and winked back. "Sounds like it will be a fun night. I'll talk to you later, Oliver." All I could do was plunge in, so I started bobbing and weaving through the people to get to the kitchen. Being tall, however, has its advantages. Alan caught sight of me as I was rounding a short little chap in a tweed blazer and met me halfway, a big smile on that handsome face and a beer in his left hand.

"Hey, Heath! You made it!"

I smiled back and shook his hand, though I wanted to embrace him. "Yes, sorry I'm late. I walked over. Looks like most everyone is here, and then some." Alan had taken off his suit coat and was just in slacks and a white dress shirt, the sleeves rolled up. A green necktie hung loosely about his neck. He looked quite comfortable.

Alan glanced about. "There's a few missing yet, but they'll be here. Mr. Crane said he has a big surprise for us."

I arched my brow. "Oh?"

"Yes, but he won't tell us what it is, he wants to wait until everybody's present."

"I see. The master of suspense."

"Yeah, it's his theatrical background, I guess," Alan said. "Anything new down at the station?"

"The infamous gangster Benny Ballentine was shot today at his girlfriend's house."

Alan whistled. "Wowzer, who shot him?"

"Word is it was the girlfriend. He's not dead, surprisingly."

"Well, that's something, all right."

"I'll say. Is the famous Shelby Berkett here?" I didn't feel like talking shop.

"Oh, sure. He was one of the first to arrive, right after me and Hank. He grabbed a drink and then said he wanted to make a phone call. He made a beeline for the master bedroom, closed the door, and I haven't seen him since."

"How sociable. And where is this Henry, or Hank, as you call him?"

"Right here," a man said, sidling up to Alan and placing his left hand firmly on Alan's shoulder. He was about five feet ten, and clean-shaven except for that Clark Gable mustache above a cleft chin. He had large, dark brown eyes and long lashes that curled up, almost touching his brows. His wavy, sandy brown hair was un-parted, his shoulders big and broad, his waist and hips narrow. He wasn't wearing a tie, and his short-sleeved white shirt, which showed off his bulging biceps, was unbuttoned just far enough to reveal dark brown curly hair spread out across a broad chest. I must admit I took my time taking him all in.

Alan beamed. "Oh, hi, Hank. I'd like you to meet a friend of mine, Heath Barrington. Heath, this is Henry Hawthorne."

"How do you do, Mr. Hawthorne? Alan's told me so much about you," I said, extending my hand.

Henry looked at my hand doubtfully, but then grabbed it in a firm and forceful grip that hurt my fingers. "I do quite well, if I say so myself. Funny, Alan hasn't mentioned you at all."

I raised my eyebrows and looked at Alan. "You haven't?" I said, retrieving my hand from Henry's.

Alan seemed embarrassed. "Well, I'm sure I mentioned you at some point, Heath. You must have just forgotten, Hank."

Henry shook his head. "No, I don't think so. Your name never came up, and Alan and I have spent quite a bit of time together in our dressing room. We share one down in the basement at the theater."

"Yes, I heard."

"So, who are you, exactly? You're not in the play," Henry said in an unfriendly tone.

"I'm a friend of Alan's, and I'm a police detective. I did some research on your part for Mr. Crane."

"Oh, right, Oliver mentioned that, Mr. Barrington."

"You can call him Heath. We're all friends, right?" Alan said. I noticed he was sweating, but so was I. It was stifling.

"All friends, right," Henry said.

"So, Mr. Hawthorne, you're just in town for the summer?" I said.

"That's right, though I may stick around a little longer, you never know. I just have to get out to California in time to audition for a new Hitchcock movie."

"I heard about that. I understand Mr. Berkett is interested in that same part."

Henry flinched and looked pained. "That's right, he is. He's an ass."

"Gee, Hank, you shouldn't say that," Alan said. "Not here, anyway."

Henry rubbed Alan's shoulder casually but firmly. "You're too kind, Alan. Adorable, just adorable. You're like a big puppy, with those big puppy dog eyes. But Shelby Berkett is an ass." He looked at me again, a scowl on his face. "Yes, we're up for the same part in that movie. A part he heard about from me, and so help me I'll kill myself if he gets it."

"That seems a bit drastic, Mr. Hawthorne, but clearly you must do what you think best," I said, staring him in the eye.

He took his hand off Alan's shoulder and stared back at me. "I beg your pardon?"

"Heath's just kidding, Hank. He's got a funny sense of humor."

"I'll say," Henry said, still staring at me. "I guess I should have said if he gets the role, I'll kill *him*."

"That, Mr. Hawthorne, is against the law. I'd have to arrest you."

"You'd have to catch me first," he said, "and you don't look that fast." Then he glanced at Alan. "I'm going out on the balcony for some fresh air. Come with me?" He put his hand back on Alan's shoulder, and it annoyed me greatly. He seemed a little too familiar.

Alan shook his head, but didn't seem bothered in the least by Henry's hand, which annoyed me even more. "Ah, no, I'm going to stay here and talk to Heath, if you don't mind. He just got here."

"Suit yourself, kid, I'll see you in a bit. Nice to meet you, Mr. Barrington."

"Likewise, I'm sure."

"I'm sure." He turned to Alan. "Remember the house party afterward, and don't forget who's taking you home, pup." He let his hand drop off Alan's shoulder and trail slowly down his back before he turned and waded into the crowd toward the French doors.

"What house party?" I said.

"Hank invited me to a private house party over on the west side. *Very* private. You have to have a password to get in."

I raised my eyebrows. "You're aware of what goes on at those, aren't you, Alan? The police raid them with alarming frequency, as you should know."

"I didn't say I was going. I just told him I'd think about it."

"Well, think twice, or even three times. If you get caught there, it would be the end of you on the force. Besides, I thought I was going to take you home."

Alan looked at me. "We never decided that for sure. Besides, you said you walked over."

"Oh, right." I wished I had brought my car.

"Hank doesn't live far from me. It just makes sense for him to drop me off."

"Sure it does. Mr. Hawthorne seems awfully casually dressed for a party."

"Oh, that's just Hank. Rehearsal ran late again, and he didn't want to run home to change."

"Of course he didn't, though Oliver said you two were among the first to arrive. I should think he would have had plenty of time."

"Yeah, that's true, but Hank likes to be comfortable."

"Comfortable is not the word I would have chosen. So who's not here yet?"

Alan looked around the room. "Mainly Jazz Monroe and Dick Cooper. I guess he's her escort tonight, or at least her driver. She owns the car but doesn't drive, so she relies on Dick to chauffeur her around."

"And she's waiting to make a grand entrance?"

Alan grinned. "Naturally. How about a drink?"

"I thought you'd never ask. I could use one. Or two."

"Bar's in the kitchen. It's a bit crowded in there, so I'll bring it out to you. Vodka martini with a pickle, right?"

"Of course, but I can come with you."

"Not to worry. I've become adept at dealing with this crowd. Back in a flash, more or less!" He laughed, and I admired the view of his backside as he walked away, weaving through the people with a slight bounce in his step. Soon, all I could see was his head and shoulders, and then I lost sight of him.

I turned my attention to the corner by the balcony where Oliver's brother, who looked a lot like him, was playing the keys, and a vibrant blonde with a pert little mouth like a strawberry was doing her best to sing over the noise. I moved alongside her and joined in on a few bars. She didn't seem to mind. As the song ended and Wally started some ragtime, she smiled at me, her chin low, her green eyes deep and narrow over a slightly upturned nose.

"Nice voice," she said huskily.

I grinned. "Thanks and likewise. I'm an old glee club chap from way back. And my mother made me sing in the church choir."

"You don't look like the churchgoing type."

"I'm an infidel, but don't tell my mother," I said with a wink.

She laughed. "Your secret's safe with me."

She eyed me up and down slowly, and I did the same to her. If I had to guess, I'd say she was in her mid twenties. Her ample breasts bulged from her low-cut emerald green strapless dress. It hugged her waist and hips and flowed down in a straight line to just below the knee. I had to wonder how she ever managed to use the bathroom or even sit down in that thing. Her full, straw-colored hair, parted at the side, hung loosely about her bare pink shoulders, which looked as soft as a baby's bottom. If I went for that sort of thing, she'd be the sort of thing I'd go for.

"So, you are?"

"Barrington. Heath Barrington. I did some technical advising for Mr. Crane, and I'm a friend of Alan Keyes."

She bit her lower lip. "Oh. I see. You're the policeman fellow they've been talking about."

I sighed. "Wherever I go it seems someone's been talking about me." Except Alan to Henry, I thought.

"Hazard of the trade, I suppose. And of being handsome."

I blushed. "Uh, thanks, Miss?"

"Mrs., actually. Mrs. Peter Holloway. But you can call me Eve."

I nodded with sudden recognition. "You're Charlotte Clarington, Claire's younger and prettier sister!"

She laughed. "Don't let Jazz hear you say that. But yes, I play her sister, in this reincarnation, anyway. Being an actress is a bit like being reborn many times."

"I didn't recognize you out of character. I saw you at rehearsal on Thursday."

"The magic of makeup. Charlotte is a bit more naïve than I am, if you know what I mean. I like to show off my assets." She ran her finger around the top of her glass and looked up at me, her pink nail polish sparkling in the light.

"Yes, so I noticed. Those heels you're wearing are really something, but how do you walk in them?"

Eve glanced down past her breasts at her feet and then back up at me.

"Practice, Mr. Barrington."

I smiled. "Your husband is the chap that plays the butler, right? Peter Holloway?"

"That's right. You sound surprised."

"Well, he's so much older than you."

"Nearly eighty, the dotty old man," she said, her eyes laughing.

I opened my mouth to speak, but then closed it again.

"He's over there, by the kitchen door now. The one in the blue plaid sport coat," she said, nodding.

I looked where she directed and was surprised to see a handsome man, roughly in his mid thirties. His hair was parted on the right, his jaw solid below a Roman nose tinged a soft shade of red. He had high cheekbones and nicely set eyes and was a far cry from the elderly, shaky butler I had seen in the play. He was chatting up the handsome Dave Bergstrom, a fellow I've known a long time, but I couldn't hear what they were saying.

"That's the butler?"

"The magic of makeup, Mr. Barrington, as I said earlier."

"I guess so. You can't believe your eyes."

"Things and people aren't always what they seem."

"Apparently not."

She laughed. "Makeup is a girl's best friend, and sometimes a fellow's. You'd be amazed at what a wig and some putty will do. So, your friend seems nice. Alan, I mean. I haven't gotten to talk to him much during rehearsals, though," Eve said.

"He's thrilled to be in the play. He's even talking about doing more this fall."

Eve smiled broadly. "He's got the bug. It happens, and there's no cure, I'm afraid." She played with her hair, twisting it about with her long fingers and chewing on a strand. It was quite distracting, even for me. "He's easy on the eyes, too. Just like you. Men who are tall and easy on the eyes can go a long way in show business. Take Henry, for example."

"I suppose he's attractive enough, if you go for that type. I understand you and Mr. Hawthorne are old friends," I said.

"Yes. We both did the Canteen and USO circuit during the war, and we've been in a few shows together. He's a talented man. He sings, dances, acts, and as you said, he's quite attractive."

"I believe what I said was he's attractive *enough*, not *quite* attractive. He and Alan seem to be rather chummy."

"I wouldn't worry about it, Mr. Barrington," she said, a twinkle in her green eyes. "Henry will be moving on soon. He always does."

"Why would I worry about it? We're just friends."

She shrugged ever so slightly. "Henry's going to make it big, and I'll be able to say, 'I knew him when.' You know, you and Alan would make a good duo. Too bad vaudeville's dead, but the theater's still kicking. Two handsome men like you could go places."

"I'll take that under advisement, Mrs. Holloway."

"Eve, please. My maiden name was Gabranski, so I took my husband's name professionally when we married. But my friends call me Eve."

"Eve, then. And please call me Heath. But I think Alan and I are both better suited for police work."

"Suit yourselves. But don't begrudge him a little fun."

"Not for me to say. He's just a pal, a coworker, like I said."

She looked amused. "Just friends. Of course, Mr. Barrington. But remember, this is the theater crowd you're in."

"And what does that mean?"

She raised her bare pink shoulders and dropped them again. I thought her dress would plunge with them, but she didn't seem concerned and it magically stayed in place.

"Only that in the theater we see things differently. People aren't all one way or the other. It's not all black or white. Everyone's welcome, and it's all make-believe. That's why so many men, so many men who have men friends, come to this world, the theater world. It's a friendlier, safer place. The theater's a refuge of sorts, and for *all* sorts. That's why I like it."

"I'm sure it is, Eve, but I don't know what you mean."

"Of course you don't. But don't forget it, either. You know, just in case you get tired of your world, Heath."

"Again, I'll take that under advisement."

"Good. It was the comment about my shoes that did it, by the way. Most men don't look me up and down when I'm dressed like this and wonder how I walk in my heels."

I felt my face turning red. "I'm just a curious fellow."

"Quite curious, indeed," she said.

At that point, Alan returned with a fresh beer and my martini, which he handed to me. "Here you go, Heath. Sorry it took a while. I got cornered by the costume lady, who has had a few too many cocktails. She wanted me to go in the bedroom with her and double-check my sizes."

Eve laughed. "Oh, that would be Beth. She does have roving hands when she drinks too much."

"I noticed," Alan said, blushing a bit. "Even when she doesn't drink. I thought she was awfully attentive when I had my first costume fitting."

"Don't worry, darling. She doesn't bite, she just likes to nibble," Eve said.

"On my ear, apparently. Anyway, savor your drink a while, Heath. They're running dangerously low on vodka, but I think Hank's going to make a run for more. May I get you another, Mrs. Holloway?"

She shook her head. "Not right now, and I'm Eve, not Mrs. Holloway. I think we can be on a first-name basis at this point, don't you?"

He looked extremely pleased. "Gee, sure. That would be swell."

Behind Alan, Shelby Berkett flung open the master bedroom door, framing himself dramatically against the doorjamb, a cigarette dangling from his right hand. In his other hand, he held the remains of a mysterious-looking green drink. He also had a fairly good-size bruise below his left eye.

"My goodness, it's gotten crowded in here since I first locked myself in," Berkett said to no one in particular. Then he saw the three of us and a peculiar expression came over his face. "Hello, Eve. Nice to see you," he said. "I wasn't sure you'd come."

Eve's expression also changed as she nodded in his direction. "Peter and I are here together."

Shelby put his left hand to his ear. "What? I honestly can't hear a thing over all this noise. I've been trying to place a call to Hollywood on the bedroom extension, but the volume in here is ridiculous. Can't you people keep it down?"

The piano player, as if on cue, started in on a loud jazz number as Shelby rolled his eyes dramatically. "Oh. My. God!" He straightened himself up and moved within earshot of us. "On top of that, Oliver has a party line. I must have waited fifteen minutes listening to two women gossip about the mailman. Did you know he keeps a bottle tucked in the potted plant in the lobby?"

"You're not supposed to listen in on other people's conversations, Mr. Berkett. It's against the law," I said.

"Well, how else was I supposed to know when the line was free? I finally got the Hollywood call placed, but as I said before, the noise level out here is ridiculous."

"It is a party, Shelby," Eve said. "And I hope you reversed the charges."

"My dear girl, one does not reverse charges when calling a man like Hamilton Marshall Brach. Besides, Oliver can afford it."

"And you can't," Eve said.

"Ouch. You do know how to hurt a man. In more ways than one." He turned to me and Alan. "Mr. Brach is casting a movie set in Australia, of all places, for which I would be perfect in the lead."

"The role Henry's up for. The role you heard about from him," Eve said.

He looked at her again. "Oh, Marshall was *originally* interested in that Hawthorne chap, but honestly, he's just not right for the role."

"So, they don't want someone handsome and talented? In that case, you're a shoo-in."

"Ha ha, you're so, so amusing, Eve," Shelby said.

"Some people think so. Isn't it up to Mr. Brach to decide who's right for the part?"

"Oh, of course, of course," Shelby said, waving his cigarette around. "Let the better actor prevail, though Marshall and I go way back, and I am the better actor, if I do say so myself."

"And you do say so frequently. I really should go check on Peter, if you'll excuse me."

"Oh, Eve, don't go running off each time I appear. You'll give me a complex."

"What's one more?"

"Ouch again. If you keep talking like that, I'll think you don't like me."

"I think I've made it clear how I feel about you, Shelby."

"Apparently, to know me *isn't* to love me. But don't go running off just yet, please. This is a party, after all."

"How did you get that bruise, Mr. Berkett?" Alan said.

He looked at Alan and then glanced at Eve. "Ugh, beastly little accident. I was in my dressing room. I thought I had closed the door but it must not have latched. I heard a noise in the hall and when I got up, I slipped on some water I'd spilled on the floor. I ran right into the edge of the door." Shelby gingerly touched his cold glass to his face. "I could have been severely injured, but this is bad enough."

"Will you be all right for tomorrow night?" I said.

"Oh, yes. The show must go on, you know. Besides, our makeup girl can cover this bruise up so no one will ever notice. Of course, it's my own fault. Water is dangerous in general. I try to avoid it, unless it's in the form of ice." He swirled the remaining cubes in his glass and then finished it. Shelby looked at the three of us one by one, and then settled on Alan. "You there, fix me another drink. A green dragon."

"The bar's in the kitchen, Mr. Berkett. Help yourself," I said.

Alan put his free hand on my shoulder. "It's all right, Heath. I don't mind. Mr. Berkett's been on Broadway."

I resisted the urge to groan. "So I've heard."

"And you are?" Shelby said, giving me an appraising look.

"Heath Barrington. Detective Heath Barrington of the Milwaukee Police. I'm a friend of Mr. Crane's."

"Well, please don't arrest me for eavesdropping on the phone. The show would be ruined without its star."

"Don't worry, Mr. Berkett. I'm letting you off with just a warning," I said with a smile. "Besides, I thought Jazz Monroe was the star of the show."

He sighed heavily, his gray-blue eyes cast toward the ceiling. "Oh, please. Put me in a wig and a dress, and I could play Claire Clarington better than that old bag. As initially written, Claire Clarington is supposed to be in her mid thirties and attractive. Jazz Monroe is pushing sixty, she's fat as a cow, and she sags more than a hammock."

"I think you're exaggerating. And besides, as Eve has pointed out, makeup does wondrous things. She looks to be in her thirties when she's onstage," I said.

Shelby took a drag on his cigarette, the green eyes of the lion's head ring he was wearing sparkling in the light. "You, sir, are far too kind. There was a time once, but not anymore. And she's just plain vicious. I tried to be friendly to her when I got to town. I tried to make amends, even brought her flowers, but she'd have none of it. And then there's Peter…"

"What about him?" Eve said, irritation growing in her voice with every sentence.

"Oh, my dear. He can't even remember his two or three lines, and he almost dropped the tea tray today. My God, if he drops it when we're in front of the audience…"

"He won't drop it, Shelby. He's promised not to drink during the show."

"Promises, promises. Ever the protective Eve."

"That's enough." Eve's voice was quiet but firm as she stared at him.

He held up his hand, the ashes from his cigarette dropping unnoticed to the floor. "All right, fine. I'll behave and not talk about Peter. But then we must talk about Henry." I admit my ears perked up.

"Don't start on Henry, either, Shelby. You're just jealous. He's a talented man," Eve said.

Shelby raised his brows and stared back at her. "He's just

a pretty boy with a mustache and dimples. Typical sullen, silent type."

"He's a friend of mine and a superb actor," Eve said, her teeth clenched.

"If you say so. But I don't recall *him* ever doing a show on Broadway, much less four," he replied.

"Maybe not, but I wouldn't bet against him winning that movie part away from you."

Shelby ignored her and turned to me once more. "I remember you now. You were at the theater yesterday. I must say you dress rather nattily for a policeman."

"Thanks. I manage."

"Heath's one of the best dressed men I know," Alan said.

"Then clearly you don't know me, my boy," Shelby said, taking another drag on his cigarette and blowing the smoke almost directly at Alan.

I looked at him. He was in his mid to late forties, with large, deer-shaped eyes on either side of a long, narrow nose. The nasty bruise was just below his left eye. Up close, I could see he was indeed sporting a toupee, and he had a cleft chin beneath pouty dark lips. He was wearing a gray sport coat with a garish yellow and red polka dot tie and a silk lavender pocket square. His uncuffed trousers were dark green.

"Fashion is in the eye of the beholder, I suppose, Mr. Berkett," I said. "That kind of outfit you're wearing doesn't really fit in here in Milwaukee."

"People in the Midwest seem to think fashion is coordinating your overalls with your flannels, Mr. Barrington. At least the theater people understand how I dress."

"Yes, I suppose they're used to some pretty wild costumes," I said, and Eve laughed.

"If you're trying to be amusing, my good fellow, you're failing miserably."

"I thought it was funny, Shelby."

Shelby looked at Eve. "I didn't." Then he glanced back at me. "So, you're a friend of Oliver's."

"Yes, we go back a few years. Oliver is a good friend and a good director."

"I don't know about the former, but the latter could certainly be argued successfully, Mr. Barrington." He looked at Alan. "Now then, young man, about that drink? It's not going to make itself, and you definitely don't want me cranky."

"Right, Mr. Berkett. What's in a green dragon, anyway?"

Shelby rolled his eyes again and took another long drag on his cigarette, which was almost down to nothing. "Oh, good grief. You small-town hicks need to get out more. One and a half ounces of dry gin, a half ounce of Kummel, a half ounce of *green* crème de menthe, lemon juice, green mint, and four dashes of peach bitters. Shake, strain, and garnish with a lemon peel, please. And use the good gin in the cabinet next to the stove, not that schlock Oliver has sitting out on the counter."

"Where would I find kummen? I'm not even sure what that is," Alan said.

"It's Kummel, and it's a sweet, colorless liqueur. I knew Oliver wouldn't have any, so I brought my own bottle along with peach bitters. They're on the counter, next to the bread box." He dropped his cigarette butt into his empty glass. "And take this with you."

"Yes sir. Kummel, peach bitters, lemon juice, gin, green mint, right. Back in a few." Alan turned and made his way through the crowd toward the kitchen, muttering the ingredients and directions to himself as he did so.

"Wouldn't it be easier, Mr. Berkett, if you just got it yourself?" I said.

Shelby smiled at me. "The little people love doing things like that for the stars. It makes them feel important."

"And you are *such* a giver, Shelby," Eve said.

He turned to her as he lit another cigarette. "Eve, darling, here we've been chatting away, and I haven't even commented on your dress. Don't you look lovely tonight? I am so glad you didn't run off when I came out. And did you just get here? You weren't here earlier."

"We got here about forty-five minutes ago, Shelby. You've been on the phone in the bedroom a long time."

He threw his head back as if suddenly stricken and I was afraid his toupee would fly off, but it was glued down securely. "Ugh, those two women on the party line, don't remind me. And you know those long-distance operators are so difficult. Marshall Brach is hard to get hold of on a Friday night."

Alan returned and handed Shelby his green dragon. "Here you go, Mr. Berkett. Sorry some of it spilled on my way back. Mr. Roberts bumped my elbow. I'm afraid he got some of it on his jacket."

Shelby took the drink from Alan. "Best thing that will happen to that jacket. Tweed. How revolting. I thought Geoffrey had better taste than that." He took a sip of the green dragon and looked at Alan, who was standing by for approval. "Not bad, my boy, not bad. But I don't think you got the proportions just right, and you didn't use the good gin. I told you it was by the stove."

"I couldn't get near the stove, Mr. Berkett. The kitchen is packed, I'm sorry."

Shelby sighed and put the back of his hand to his forehead dramatically. "I'll just have to suffer through."

"Yes sir, I am sorry."

"I'll forgive you, perhaps," he said.

"That's big of you, Shelby," Eve said, her voice tightening. "But I think you're the one who should be asking forgiveness. Alan's not your servant. And you've been rude, pushy, condescending, and obnoxious to just about everyone in this room ever since you got to town."

He glanced around and rolled his eyes. "I hardly think so. I don't even know most of these people."

"The people in the cast, then, and everyone at the theater. I've witnessed it firsthand, and you need to stop it."

He looked at her appreciatively. "You're a strong woman, Eve Holloway. There aren't many women or men who stand up to me the way you do. I'm not used to being told no."

"Jazz certainly tells you no, among other things. She's not intimidated by you," Eve said.

"She'd stand up to Hitler and beat him at arm wrestling given the chance, but you're different. You're forceful yet still feminine, independent but still soft. You know, you could make a name for yourself with me in New York someday, if you ever change your mind. Jazz, on the other hand, is a bulldozer. She's a big name in Milwaukee, but she'd never make it anywhere else."

"Some say that's due to you, Shelby. Because of what happened back in 1926," Eve said.

He looked cross. "Jazz and Jasper do like to talk, don't they? Well, there are two sides to every story, you know. It's true I happened to be near that switch, but I never touched it. My conscience is clear. If I was guilty, do you think I would have come back here?"

"They say criminals often return to the scene of the crime," Eve said.

"I am not a criminal. And whatever became of Jazz after I left is her own fault. She likes being a big fish in a small pond. In New York, she'd be nothing more than a guppy in the ocean, and she knows it. You, on the other hand, have star potential, except Peter is holding you back."

"Peter is my husband, for better or worse."

Shelby laughed. "Certainly the latter with that one. He's more like a big leech in a small pond. He'd be nothing without you. He lives by your success, but unfortunately he's also dying from it," Shelby said.

"What do you mean by that?"

"Isn't it obvious? He needs you to be successful so you can pay the bills and find him work. But when you're successful, it kills a part of him. He's slowly dying, bit by bit. You'd be doing both of you a favor by letting him go. Where is the cretin, anyway?" Shelby asked, looking about as he sipped more of his green dragon between puffs on his cigarette.

"Peter is over there, by the balcony, and don't call him a cretin, a leech, or a drunk."

"Certainly not, not to his face, anyway. You certainly cry an awful lot over that drunken whatever you want to call him."

"How about we call him my husband? And how about it's none of your business?"

"Where are you staying while you're in town, Mr. Berkett?" I said.

Shelby glanced at me as he finished his cocktail. "The Wisconsin Hotel on Third Street. It's convenient to the theater, and they have been most accommodating."

"And cheap," Eve said.

He waved her off with his free hand. "Affordable. I need another cocktail."

"I think you've had enough. You're a mean drunk, Shelby. In fact, you're just mean," she said, her voice softer now.

"Oh, Eve, I suppose I have been rather harsh. I must buy you something pretty to make up for what I've done," Shelby replied.

She looked at him sharply, her green eyes squinting. "Jasper told us you're nearly broke, living out of a suitcase, leaving a trail of bills and creditors behind you. If I did want something from you, which I *don't*, you couldn't afford it."

Shelby's face turned an interesting shade of red. "Jasper has a big mouth. And how dare you? I am a *star*. I was a star on Broadway. I may owe a bill or two, but that will all be corrected when I star in the new Hitchcock movie. Jasper will still be nothing but a prop man, Jazz will still be a fat fish in a small pond, and you'll still be nothing little Eve stuck here in Milwaukee with an alcoholic loser of a husband." He laughed harshly. "You at least had a way out, but you threw it in my face, didn't you, when you found out I'm *temporarily* without funds. And now you're stuck here for all eternity with him and the rest of these hicks."

"The fact that you're broke has nothing to do with how I feel about you. I was friendly to you when you started rehearsals because no one liked you, and I felt sorry for you. But it's clear now that you've brought it all on yourself, and how *dare* you say those things about Peter and me?"

Shelby looked aghast as he dropped what was left of his cigarette into his now-empty glass again and handed it once more to Alan, who in turn set it on a nearby table. "Oh, my dear, you're absolutely right. I've gone too far. Too, too far. Forgive me. I was just lashing out at you after...well, you know. I mistook your kindness for something else, and I'm sorry about that, but to have you curse me, avoid me, treat me like yesterday's news when we used to be friendly..."

Eve raised her chin and looked him in the eye. Her eyes were moist. "You are yesterday's news, Shelby. And Henry *will* get that movie role."

"Now who's being cruel?" Shelby said. "I understand, Eve. More than you think I do."

"Well, that makes one of us, then," Alan said.

Peter, dressed in a blue plaid sport coat, appeared at Eve's side. "Hey there, buttercup, what's old Shelby done now that's gotten my little wife so upset looking?"

"Oh, apparently I was an absolute beast, Peter."

"No argument from me," Peter said.

Peter slurred his words a bit and I wondered just how many cocktails and pills he had consumed at this point. Up close, his nose was even more red and veined.

"Oh, go take another pill," Shelby said.

Before Peter could reply, Oliver raised his voice and tapped a metal swizzle stick against his highball glass.

"Attention, everyone! Our star, Jazz Monroe, has entered the party!"

The room fell relatively quiet as the piano player stopped and people turned in Oliver's direction. Claire stood in the doorway, only it was Jazz Monroe, larger than life in an off-the-shoulder teal satin cocktail dress, white pearls, and black pumps. Her hair was too black and clearly from a bottle, but she wore it up and she wore it well. Atop her head sat a small, white satin hat with a black veil that came down just over her dark eyes. Behind her was Dick Cooper, her ward and escort for the evening, in a suit a size or two too big for him.

A few people applauded, and Miss Monroe looked appreciative as she smiled and nodded.

"Someone get Jazz a cocktail. What will it be, Jazz?" Oliver said.

She looked at him, still smiling. "A champagne cocktail with a sugar cube."

"Right, right. Tony, get Miss Monroe a champagne cocktail."

"Yes sir." A mustached man in a dark suit to match hurried through the crowd toward the kitchen, which had noticeably emptied of most of its people.

"I could use a beer, Mr. Crane," Dick said from within Jazz's shadow.

"What? Oh, hello, Dick. I didn't see you there. Fine, beer's in the kitchen."

"What should I do with my hat and keys?"

"Hats go in the guest room over there, and you can put your keys on the dresser." Oliver motioned to a door on the left side.

"Okay." Dick took off his hat and went to the bedroom as Jazz surveyed the gathering and continued to smile.

"Now that everyone is here, I think it's time for my surprise," Oliver said to the group.

"Hold it, Mr. Crane. If you're going to make some big announcement, I want my drink first!" Jazz said, and everybody laughed appropriately.

"Oh, sure, sure, Jazz. Tony! Hurry up with that drink."

Dick had deposited his hat in the guest room and was now

headed for the kitchen, presumably to get his beer. As Oliver caught sight of him, he called out.

"Dick! Go find out what's keeping Tony!"

"Will do, Mr. Crane."

After a few minutes, Tony returned with Jazz's champagne cocktail and handed it to her. Dick was nowhere in sight, but presumably in the kitchen.

"Jazz has her cocktail, Oliver, so what's the big announcement?" Shelby said. "I could use another drink myself, you know."

"Sorry, Shelby. It will have to wait just a few more minutes," Oliver said. "Gather round, folks, over to the cabinet here, the one with the tablecloth over it. Someone get those glasses off there, for God's sake!"

We moved closer to the other side of the room and stared at the rectangular shape beneath the floral tablecloth as various people picked up their drinks from the top of it. Henry had reappeared and taken a place on the other side of Alan.

"Can someone give me a drum roll, please?" Oliver said.

Wally pounded out a "da, da, da, daaaaaa" on the piano. Oliver pulled the tablecloth off a beautiful walnut cabinet with two doors in the front and what appeared to be a speaker panel below.

The room was silent as everyone gazed at it curiously. Finally, from the back of the room, a voice called out, "Did you get a new radio, Mr. Crane?"

Oliver laughed. "No, not a radio. It's a television!" He swung open the doors dramatically to reveal a ten-inch dark green glass rectangle.

Collective gasps were heard throughout the group.

"How much did that set you back, Mr. Crane?"

"I saw one on display at the Boston Store for three hundred fifty-two dollars," a woman said.

Several people whistled and some gasped. "That's about seven weeks' worth of wages!"

"Yeah, but you can buy it on time," someone else said. "Of course, once you get it paid off, it will be history." The crowd chuckled.

"Laugh all you want, but television is here to stay. Mark my words, ladies and gentlemen, you have seen the future," Oliver said. "I'm going to turn it on now, but the screen is small, so come up just a few at a time!"

I caught Alan's eye. "Let's go see about some more drinks."

"Don't you want to see the television?"

"It's a passing fancy. We can see it later."

"Okay, sure."

"Won't you excuse us?" I said to everyone nearby and no one in particular.

"Need a drink, Hank?" Alan said.

Henry stared around Alan at me. "No, I'm fine. I did a run for vodka and sampled some when I got back a few minutes ago. You've been monopolizing Alan, Mr. Barrington."

"Have I?"

"It's okay, Hank. Heath and I are close friends."

"I gathered that. And you need him to help you make two drinks, Mr. Barrington?"

I bristled. "If he wants to stay here with you, that's his prerogative, Mr. Hawthorne. Alan?"

Alan looked from me to Henry and then back to me as if trying to decide. Finally, he said, "Let's, uh, get some drinks. We'll be back in a bit, Hank."

"Sure, I'll be waiting."

"Don't do us any favors," I said. Alan and I easily navigated the crowd, which had dispersed somewhat as many of them had gone up to get a closer look at the television or to ask Oliver questions about it.

The kitchen was beginning to fill up again with those more interested in booze than television, such as Dick Cooper, who we found nursing a beer. He was indeed a slight fellow, and his brown suit bagged on him like a sail without wind. On his right wrist was a watch the size of a child's. He stood maybe five feet two and couldn't have weighed more than a hundred pounds. He was clean-shaven, with round, light brown eyes, a long, thin nose, and a little mouth surrounded by full lips. His limp, black hair was parted down the middle. He looked up at us as we entered.

"Hey, Dick! You missed Mr. Crane's big announcement," Alan said.

"I heard from in here. He got a television," Dick said. "I imagine everyone will have one eventually." His voice was almost a monotone, unaffected, a bit nasal.

"Not at those prices," Alan said.

"It will never last, so don't throw out your radio," I said.

"Eh, it's a changing world, Mr..."

"Barrington."

"Oh, I'm sorry. Dick, this is my friend, Heath Barrington. Heath, Dick Cooper."

"Pleased to meet you, Mr. Cooper."

"Sure. Alan's mentioned you a few times."

"Oh? I'm glad he's mentioned me to someone, at least. You're the janitor at the theater."

He shrugged his small, bony shoulders from within the oversized coat. "That's right." He took a drink of beer and looked up at the ceiling for a moment. "I only do it because Jazz wants me to."

"Oh?"

"She likes me within arm's reach in case she needs something or wants to go someplace 'cause she doesn't drive. Anyway, it's a job, I guess. Photography is what I really enjoy. I've studied Arnold Newman, you know. He was commissioned by *Life* last year, takes wonderful pictures. I even have a darkroom set up in the spare bathroom, but Jazz doesn't like it. She hasn't brought it up lately because she's too distracted by Mr. Berkett being back in town."

"Yes," I said. "They don't seem to care for each other much."

"With good reason. Jasper told me what happened back then. Jazz has, too," Dick said.

"But there are at least two sides to that story, according to Mr. Berkett," I said.

"Maybe," Dick said. "I kind of thought so when Jasper first told me about him. I figured Jasper was just bitter. But then I got to know Berkett, and I realized it wouldn't surprise me in the least if he pulled that lever intentionally."

"That seems to be the consensus," Alan said.

"Jazz and Jasper hate him, and Mr. and Mrs. Holloway don't like him much, either."

"Why is that?"

"Mr. Holloway's jealous. Mr. Berkett and Mrs. Holloway hit it off when he first got to Milwaukee, and Mr. Holloway didn't like it one bit."

"I imagine not," I said. "Did something happen between Mr. Berkett and Mrs. Holloway?"

"I saw him make some improper advances toward Mrs. Holloway the other night, and she decked him. Served him right. I was surprised at how strong she is. Almost knocked him flat."

"She's a strong woman in many ways. What kind of improper advances?"

"He touched her where he shouldn't have, tried to kiss her. He got a nice bruise on his face. Of course, he's telling everyone he walked into a door."

At that moment, Shelby's voice rang out from the doorway. "Dick! Do you know how to make a proper green dragon?"

We all turned to look at him as he entered, shaking another empty glass at us. "No, I don't," Dick said, glaring at him.

"Then you're no good to me, either."

The eyes of the lion's head on his ring sparkled in the light. The lion's mane appeared to be made of sterling silver. The eyes were real emeralds, I was sure.

"Your ring is really something, Mr. Berkett. Jazz has one

like it, only it's a lioness. She rarely wears it, but I've seen it," Dick said, staring at the ring as if entranced.

"Yes, I know. She gave me this ring once upon a time."

"Dicky! What are you doing in here, and why are you talking to him?" Jazz stood in the doorway of the kitchen, arms up, holding on to the door frame.

"I was just talking to Alan and Mr. Barrington, here, and I was also asking Mr. Berkett about his lion ring," Dick said.

Jazz's complexion darkened ever so slightly. She glared at Berkett. "I ought to cut your fat little finger off to get my ring back."

"I'm sure you would, given the chance. Don't worry, I'm going to fix myself a green dragon, since no one else seems capable, and then I'll mingle amongst my fans and give them a thrill." He went to the counter and started to work on his concoction, looking for all the world like a mad scientist as we watched him pour dark, mysterious liquids from various bottles into a shaker.

Jazz, not one to be ignored, cleared her throat loudly, and the three of us turned back to her, still standing in the doorway.

"Do you notice anything wrong with me, Dicky?"

"No," Dick finally said.

"I'm not holding a cocktail. Be a good boy and get me one. And don't forget the sugar cube."

"I never forget the sugar cube. You wouldn't let me," he said as he got a bottle of champagne and Jazz came in. Up close, she smelled of sweat, and her breath was foul.

"You're Heath Barrington, the detective. I met you at the theater yesterday."

"That's right, just after the poison scene."

"Ugh, the one that idiot keeps screwing up." She glared in Shelby's direction.

"I heard that, Jazz. Of course, the entire city probably heard it."

"You were meant to hear it. Get your green dragon and get out."

"I've got it and I'm going. One green dragon coming through," he said as he pushed past us, "and one big-mouthed, fat-assed dragon staying here." He disappeared into the depths of the living room before Jazz could reply.

"Big-mouthed, fat-assed dragon. How dare he. I'm sorry you had to suffer in here with him for company."

"Don't be. I find him rather entertaining," I said.

"I suppose fools generally are. He finally, finally got his death scene right today at the last rehearsal. We'll see how he does tomorrow night."

"I hope all goes well. Do you mind my asking about your name, Miss Monroe? It's unusual," I said.

She smiled, showing the lipstick on her teeth. "It's not so unusual, really. It's short for Jasmine. Jazz just sounds more theatrical, don't you think, Detective?"

"Yes, it's quite catchy. Most memorable."

"Thank you. Are you coming to opening night?"

"Yes, I'm looking forward to it."

"How lovely. Dicky, what's taking you so long? That idiot concocted his green dragon faster than you can make a simple champagne cocktail."

"Sorry," Dick said as he returned with a glass. "I had to open a fresh bottle, and I had trouble with the cork."

"You're such a boy. Never send a boy to do a man's job, isn't that what they say?" she said, taking the glass from him. "Oh look, here's our Eve."

As Eve Holloway entered the kitchen, Dick's face brightened considerably.

"Hello, Jazz," she said dryly.

"Dear Eve. You missed your mark in rehearsal today."

"Did I?"

"You know you did. You're supposed to stand just behind

me when I'm facing the fireplace. You came up and intentionally stood next to me, blocking me from the audience."

"There wasn't an audience. It was a rehearsal."

"Potential audience, then." She smiled thinly over the top of her glass, her dark eyes cold.

"You're so wide I don't think it's possible to block a view of you."

"Careful, Eve."

"Why? Am I going to end up like Nick Shultz?"

"What's that supposed to mean?"

"Just that he broke his arm falling into the orchestra pit when he accidently blocked you," Eve said.

"He didn't fall, I pushed him, is that what you're getting at?"

"Your words, not mine."

"Just don't get in my way."

"Hello, Mrs. Holloway," Dick said.

"Oh, hello, Dick," she said, glancing down at him. "I didn't see you there."

"Can I get you a drink?"

"I could use one. A sidecar, please, and make it a double."

"Sure, you bet," Dick said, going to the counter on the other side of the kitchen.

"Try to remember who's the star of this show, Eve," Jazz said.

"Like you'd ever let anyone forget," Eve said as Dick returned with her sidecar.

"Here's your drink, I hope it's to your liking."

She took it from him without a glance. "Thanks, I'm sure it's fine. Now if you'll excuse me…" She turned to leave.

"There's not much of an excuse for you, darling. You're a passable actress, attractive, and you have a nice caboose, but you have terrible taste in men," Jazz said.

"At least I *have* a man, Jazz. I believe you've never married."

"I don't need a man. I've gotten by just fine by myself, and I've made quite a career for myself. I'm married to the theater."

"With the theater as a husband, I guess you can get as fat as you want."

"Shut up!"

"Did I touch a nerve, Jazz?"

"No more than Shelby Berkett touched yours."

Eve glared at her. "I'm sure I don't know what you're talking about. Excuse me," Eve said. She brushed past us abruptly and went back into the living room.

"Eve Holloway. Pretty little thing, but deadly," Jazz said.

I cocked my head. "What do you mean?"

"Ask Shelby," she said with a smirk.

"She seemed quite nice when we were talking before," I said.

"She is nice, Mr. Barrington. And an up-and-coming actress," Dick said.

"Another champagne cocktail, Dicky!" Jazz's voice boomed through the kitchen, and we all winced. She was starting to slur her words as well.

"Don't you think you've had enough?" Dick said.

"No, I most certainly do not, and I don't recall asking your opinion."

"Your funeral," he said as he fixed another drink and handed it to her. "They're out of sugar cubes."

When she threw her head back, her satin hat shifted and her veil turned sideways. "Goddammit. Leave it to Oliver to run out of everything." She took a large swallow anyway and then continued on her tirade, ignoring her now-cockeyed hat and veil. "Eve Holloway. She and Shelby were quite intimate when he got to town, you know."

"Oh? I heard she was just being friendly," I said.

"That's one word for it," Jazz said, smirking as she wiped her mouth with the back of her hand.

"That's the only word for it," Dick said. "Berkett mistook her kindness for interest."

"Oh don't be naive, Dicky," she snapped. She let out a hiccup and a burp, wiped her mouth again, and then continued. "You follow her around the theater like a puppy. It's embarrassing."

"So, you believe Mrs. Holloway and Mr. Berkett were intimate?" I said.

"I know so. We were all angry at Shelby coming back here and we wanted nothing to do with him. Eve didn't know him before, so she was friendly to him. And he, lying snake that he is, made out like he could get her a role in a big show on Broadway, maybe even in the movie out in Hollywood, and so she warmed up to him rather nicely. But then he put the moves on her, and she decked him but good. I'd say they both got what they deserved."

"Does Peter know about this?" I said.

Jazz shrugged. "I have no idea. And I really couldn't care less. Or, as Shelby says, 'I could care less.' God that drives me crazy. When he says that I *try* to tell him he's actually saying he *could* care less, but he just gives me one of those droll stares. I hate that man."

"I get the impression Eve and Peter's marriage isn't exactly happy," I said, trying to steer her back on subject.

She took another drink. "Hardly. Oh they may have been in love once. But now she's more like a mother to him, taking care of him, watching over him, nursing him, keeping him supplied in pills," Jazz said, finally straightening her hat and veil. She glanced down at Dick, who appeared to be watching her carefully. "Go get yourself another beer and stop bothering me."

"I'm not the one you're bothered by," Dick said. He got himself another bottle of beer and disappeared into the crowd in the other room.

When he had gone, I turned to Jazz. "Aren't you a bit harsh with Dick, Miss Monroe?"

"That, Mr. Barrington, is none of your concern. If I ride Dick hard, it's only for his own good."

"I see."

"Good. And here comes Eve's worse half. Speak of the devil and he shall appear." She laughed a booming laugh that hurt my ears.

Peter was behind Alan, holding an empty glass, his red eyes matching his nose.

"How do you do, Mr. Holloway?" I said.

"Do I know you?"

"Not really. I'm Heath Barrington, and this is Alan Keyes. He's in the play."

Peter studied Alan. "Is he?"

"I play the policeman at the end, sir. Don't you remember me?"

His eyes looked glazed. "If you say so. I need a drink." He pushed past us and poured himself a large bourbon over ice. He returned with a full glass in hand. "Now then, what were you saying about my wife, Jazz?"

"I was saying you're lucky to have her, Peter," Jazz said. I wondered how much he had overheard.

He arched his brows, making his bloodshot eyes appear larger. "That's funny coming from you. She's the one that's lucky. She's pretty and she's lucky. She's lucky she's pretty. She's pretty lucky!" He laughed almost hysterically at this, spilling much of his drink on himself and the floor, but he didn't seem to notice.

"Good Lord, Peter, you drink too much," Jazz said.

"I don't drink enough. I can still see you, *and* hear you, unfortunately. Besides, you do a good job of drinking, yourself. How many of those champagne cocktails have you put away tonight?"

Jazz ignored the question, possibly because she didn't know the answer. She turned to Alan and me. "Won't you excuse me, gentlemen? I must powder my nose." She didn't wait for an answer but left us standing there as she too disappeared into the living room, weaving just a touch as she held her champagne cocktail above her like liberty's torch.

"There goes the great Jazz Monroe. Big voice, bigger bottom!" Peter laughed again, almost giggling, and spilled still more of his drink. "And the more she drinks, the louder she gets."

"Are you all ready for opening night tomorrow?" I said when he had somewhat composed himself.

He stared up at me, his eyes the color of raw meat. "Oh, I remember you now. You were talking to Berkett and Eve earlier."

"That's right."

"What was the question again?"

"I was wondering if you're ready for tomorrow night."

"How ready do I need to be? I answer the door, I carry a tea tray, I pick up the telephone when it rings. I only have a handful of lines. I should have been playing Hawthorne's role."

"Did you try out for it, Mr. Holloway?" Alan said.

Peter glared at him. "I don't try out for roles, my boy. I'm *offered* roles. And I would have been offered the role of the inspector if Shelby hadn't slithered back into town and spoiled everything. Instead, I got the role of the butler."

"It's still a role," I said.

"Just barely. At least they didn't make me play the idiot policeman who only comes on at the end and doesn't have any lines. He's simply dreadful, so wooden."

"I play the policeman, Mr. Holloway," Alan said, looking hurt.

"And you play your part well," I said defensively.

Peter nodded at Alan. "Oh, that's right. You said that before, didn't you? You do look familiar. Well, no offense. Ah, there's Jasper."

Alan and I followed Peter's gaze to a tall, thin man, about forty-five years old, who had wandered into the kitchen, looking lost. He had light brown eyes beneath a broad, high forehead, and a slender nose. His lips were thin and pale. I could tell he had once been attractive, and he still was in some ways, but the years had not been kind to him. His hair was sparse and gray, combed over the top of his head from right to left.

"Hello, Jasper," Peter said.

The man moved closer, clutching a bottle of beer tightly as he looked at each of us in turn. He had a bandage on his left hand. "Hello, Mr. Holloway, hello, Alan." He moved slowly, his limp impairing his speed.

"How do you do?" I said, extending my hand. "I'm Heath Barrington, a friend of Mr. Crane and of Mr. Keyes here."

Jasper shook my hand firmly. "Jasper Crockett. Any friend of Alan's is a friend of mine, Mr. Barrington. I saw you at the theater yesterday."

"Yes, that's right. I was watching the rehearsal, but I had to leave."

Jasper bobbed his head up and down. "Alan's a nice fellow. Always has a kind word and a smile, and he's real helpful backstage."

Alan looked embarrassed. "Well, I have a lot of time before I go on, so I try to help out."

Jasper's head bobbed again. "I'm just saying. You're nicer than most."

"Looking for something, Jasper?" Peter said.

"No, not really. Just avoiding Berkett. He's on a rant in the living room, and I don't want to be around him any more than I have to."

"That seems to be a common feeling amongst those who know him," Peter said.

Jasper glanced around to see who else might be listening. "It's no secret I never liked him. He's an evil man, and I will never forgive him for what he did to Alex, to me, and to Jazz. I'm still irked at Oliver for hiring him. I wish he'd never come back, stirring up trouble and all. I hoped I'd never see him again."

Peter laughed harshly. "Same here. I'd like to know who really sent that telegram."

"I hear tell it was signed by Alex," Jasper said.

"You don't really believe that, do you?"

He shrugged. "Maybe. I'm not sure really. Alex was a good man, a friend. I sense his spirit in the theater sometimes. I think he may have wanted to lure Berkett back here to face justice once and for all."

"What justice would that be, Mr. Crockett?" I said.

"Justice for what happened those many years ago, for what he did to all of us. Alex was a real talent. Nice looking, too. He could have gone places. As for me, well, I don't think I ever would have made it big, but I feel guilty sometimes, you know? Because I survived that fall and he didn't."

"It wasn't your fault," Peter said, surprisingly soft. "I heard what happened. We all have."

"I guess everyone knows. So, Alex is dead, I've got a bad leg, Jazz never left Milwaukee, and Berkett is up for a movie role," Jasper said, anger rising up in his voice.

"There's a good chance he won't get that movie role, Jasper. Just wait and see," Peter said.

"Someone needs to make sure he doesn't. One way or the other."

"Maybe someone will," Peter said. "Maybe someone will. But right now, I'm hearing the sound of ice in a glass, which tells me it's time for another drink."

Peter wandered off somewhat unsteadily in search of more alcohol, leaving Jasper alone with us.

"What did you do to your hand, Mr. Crockett?" I said.

He glanced down at the bandage. "Oh, I burned it on the stove. Good thing it's my left, or I'd be lost. Anyway, I should get going. Pompom's home alone. He doesn't like it when I leave him for too long, though I always leave the radio on for him. He likes opera, and so do I."

"Well, that's convenient, then, isn't it? Pompom's your dog? The one who was with you at the theater yesterday?"

Jasper grinned, baring gray teeth within his thin lips. The second tooth on the upper left was missing. "Yeah, he's a good boy, all right. The best. He goes with me everywhere, for the most part. But I couldn't bring him tonight, of course."

"Of course."

"He doesn't like being left home alone much, so I'd better get going. Besides, WBSM's Opera Hour ended at seven. After that, it's all classical. Pompom's not big on classical. Nice meeting you, Mr. Barrington."

"Likewise, Mr. Crockett."

He nodded and raised his bottle in salute, and then limped and shuffled along like a tall, thin tortoise.

"Well, Alan, I think I could use another drink. How about you?"

"Definitely, Heath. Some party. I suppose Hank must be wondering where we are. Maybe we should head back out to the living room after we get our drinks."

"I suppose," I said, though I really didn't want to see any more of Hank. The crowd in the kitchen had thinned some, and we helped ourselves, Alan fishing out another bottle of beer from the melting ice in the sink while I made a vodka martini, though they were out of pickles.

Drinks in hand, we returned to the living room, where the skinny lady in the pink hat and carrot orange hair was trying to rhumba with the man with the dark mustache, but they kept bumping into people. On the far wall, a man in a blue pinstriped suit and yellow tie was leaning precariously and looking quite pale. He had unbuttoned his collar and opened his suit jacket, slowly sinking down the wall until he was sitting on the floor. From there he finally tipped over and lay in a fetal position on his right side as people stepped over him.

"He doesn't look too good," I said.

"That's Tony," Alan said. "He'll be in bad shape tomorrow, and Mr. Crane will *not* be happy."

"What does he do?"

"Lights."

"Ah," I said.

Alan surveyed the room. "I think just about everyone here has had a bit too much to drink."

"Me included, I believe. I'm a trifle woozy, and the floor is swaying beneath my feet a tad."

Nearby Eve and Peter were talking to Oliver. Eve had apparently overheard us.

"I think you've had more than enough to drink tonight, too, Peter."

He glared at her. "You always think I've had enough to drink, and you hid my pillbox to punish me, didn't you?"

Eve sighed, exasperated. "I told you I didn't *take* your pill box. You probably just misplaced it."

"Then it was you!" Peter said, pointing a shaky finger at Oliver.

Oliver shook his head. "Sorry, old boy, but I had nothing to do with it."

"Maybe old Alexander Lippencott stole my pillbox. The friendly ghost? The spirit took my pills? The spirited spirit spirited away my pillbox?" He burst out laughing as Eve and Oliver exchanged concerned looks.

"Peter, we open tomorrow," she said softly.

Peter rolled his head around and stared glassy-eyed at her. "Oh, Good Lord, don't you think I know that? But what do you care? My part is meaningless. I have next to no lines."

"The role of the butler is important, Peter. All the roles are, or they wouldn't be in the play," Oliver said.

Peter shook his head slowly and deliberately. "No. That's not true. You know it as well as I do. Even my unfaithful wife here knows it, don't you, love?"

Eve and Oliver both looked surprised and startled. Oliver laughed nervously. "You're joking, Peter."

"I'm not." He hiccupped.

"What do you mean?" Eve said.

Peter grimaced, his eyes even more bloodshot. "Just what it sounds like. You and the great Shelby Berkett."

"Peter!" she cried.

"Are you denying it? You act like you hate each other, but that's all it is, isn't it? Acting. You've been sleeping with him since the day he got into town, haven't you?"

"That's not true!"

"Isn't it? You spent an awful lot of time with him when he first got to Milwaukee."

"I was simply being kind, something you've apparently forgotten how to do. I can't talk to you anymore," Eve said.

"You did more than talk with *him*, didn't you? I've heard the rumors," Peter said, shaking his finger at her.

She looked back at him, avoiding his finger. "I did not do more than talk with him, much to his chagrin. Don't believe everything you hear, and don't shake your finger at me."

"Peter, that's uncalled for," Oliver said.

Now it was Peter's turn to laugh. "Oh, I think it's definitely called for."

"Nothing happened between us, Peter, though he wanted it. He pushed me, but I pushed back. I always push back."

"Oh, I know you do, darling. I know you do. Everyone always says you're the strong one, that you hold me up because I'm weak. Well, I can stand on my own without you," he said, ironically weaving back and forth unsteadily.

"What are you saying, Peter?" Eve looked shocked.

"I'm saying I could have been the detective. I *should* have been the detective. Now I'm nothing. Shelby took that away from me, too. Where is that son of a bitch? He needs to be taught a lesson." He looked about the room rather wildly.

"Peter, I think we should talk about this in private," she said, touching his arm.

He brought his gaze back to her and stared down at her face. "What's the matter? Afraid I'm going to hurt your boyfriend? Embarrass you?"

"Peter, please."

He shook off her hand. "All right, let's go. No offense,

Oliver, but this party is an utter bore. And apparently my wife is an utter—"

"Peter!" Eve cried out again, her face now angry. "I was nothing but friendly to him, and, yes, he was easy to talk to, and I needed that. But I soon realized he wanted more, and he wouldn't take no for an answer. It's all been horrible."

"Eve, Eve, Eve. What's the matter? Couldn't you handle that pompous snake? The great and glorious Eve. Sorely tempted, she bit the forbidden fruit, but it bit back." He chuckled heavily and hiccupped again, almost falling over as he stumbled.

"I didn't bite. I hit him right in the face as hard as I could. Don't you understand what I'm saying?"

He wagged his finger at her again. "Am I supposed to feel sorry for you now? You thought he was a big, rich Broadway star who could take you places, didn't you? Little did you know the joke was on you and, sadly, on me," Peter said, swaying back and forth even more.

Eve put her hand on his arm again to steady him, and this time he didn't shake it off. "We have a lot to talk about, Peter. I don't think you realize everything that's happened."

He laughed again. "Oh, you are good. Yes, go ahead and talk your way out of this." His voice was getting louder, but hers was softer, yet firm.

"I'm not trying to talk my way out of anything. I just think we should go home. *Now.*"

Peter stared at her again. Finally, he spoke, somewhat more quietly. "I must say I agree. There's no point in staying anymore. Here or anywhere else. Tally ho, then. I'll bring the car around, you say goodbye for both of us. I can't stand these people, and right now I'm not too fond of you, either."

"Right now, I'd say the feeling is mutual. Are you all right to drive?"

"Never better, my dear. Never better." He staggered out of the apartment, leaving the door ajar.

"I'll get his hat and my purse," Eve said to no one in

particular, still visibly shaken as she made her way to the guest room.

When she returned, she seemed relieved no one else had overheard their exchange. The piano player was playing some lively music, and the woman in the pink hat and orange hair had given up trying to rhumba and was now attempting to sing, except she kept forgetting the words and starting over.

Peter reappeared, standing in the apartment door, holding on to the frame for support. "Where's Dick? I want to see Dick." He spoke loudly, running his words together.

"I'm here, Mr. Holloway. Something wrong?" Dick asked from behind me.

Peter peered around me and down at Dick. "You've parked me in, son. Give me your keys so I can get my car out."

"Oh gosh, I'm sorry, sir. I didn't realize."

Peter held his hand out in front of him. "Give me your keys."

"They're in the bedroom, on the dresser," Dick said.

"Then go get them."

"Yes sir, Mr. Holloway." Dick vanished into the crowd, only to reappear moments later with a key ring, which he held out to Peter. Peter stared at the ring of keys briefly and then snatched them up. "Back in a flash."

"Yes sir."

"Don't wait up," Peter said with a snide laugh as he weaved and bobbed out the door once more, and I wondered to myself just what Jazz would say if she knew or found out Dick had handed over her car keys to Peter Holloway. True to his word, though, he was back quickly and handed Dick his key ring. "There, no harm done, you see? Now, where is the lovely and talented Eve Holloway?"

"I'm right here, Peter. I got your hat for you. And I'll drive so you can sleep it off."

"How wonderful. Isn't she wonderful, Mr..."

"Barrington. Heath Barrington," I said. "We met earlier."

"Did we? Well, I'm sure I was pleased to meet you, Mr.

Barrington. Do you know my wife? Most men seem to. Eve Holloway. Lovely girl. Handy with a knife, too. But now we must be going. Toodle-oo." He took Eve's arm and guided her out the door without another word.

I turned to Alan. "Wowzer."

"You said it. Wowzer indeed."

Henry reappeared, annoyed. "There you two are."

"We were in the kitchen," Alan said. "When we came back, you were gone."

"I was occupied. I think we should go. I'll drive you home, Alan," Henry said, ignoring me.

"I, uh, just got a beer. Let me finish it, okay?" Alan said, looking from Henry to me.

Henry shrugged. "Bottoms up."

Suddenly the skinny woman in the pink hat, who had started from the beginning of the song for about the fourth time, stopped singing and let out a screech, as if someone had slit her throat.

"Who the hell pricked me?" she said, glancing about sharply, her eyes landing upon Jazz, who was standing just to the side and back of her, hatpin in hand.

"Good Lord, someone had to stop you. How can you forget the lyrics to 'Sentimental Journey'? You call that singing, Hilda? I've heard cats mating that sounded better. And who did your hair? Bugs Bunny?" Jazz faced the crowd, which was now staring at her, as was her intent, I was sure. "Let me show you how it's done. Take it from the top, Wally." Then Jazz started belting out the song, and I could swear the light fixture in the ceiling started to sway from the vibration.

Shelby, who happened to be standing nearby, covered his ears and closed his eyes in full view of Jazz, who then started to sing even louder. Finally he opened his eyes, uncovered his ears, and put his hand over her mouth while shouting, "Shut up!"

She bit him, and he screamed. Wally stopped playing as Hilda laughed.

"You bit me, you bitch!"

"That's what you get for sticking your hand on my mouth."

"Stop screeching like that, and I won't."

"It's called singing, you talentless hack. Maybe I'll bite your finger off and get my ring back."

"If you do, I hope you choke on it. You wouldn't last two minutes in a real show on Broadway. You overact, oversing, overdo everything."

"That's the pot calling the kettle black, Shelby Berkett. In twenty years in New York, you've been in exactly four shows on Broadway, the last two of which were flops, and you're dead broke."

The crowd had fallen silent as all eyes fell upon the two of them. They moved toward Shelby and Jazz, but just close enough to give them room if they started slugging. Hilda looked thrilled.

Shelby puffed out his chest in indignation. "Neither of the last two were flops, the timing just wasn't right. And I've made a good career for myself in New York. Granted, mostly off Broadway, but I'm just now beginning to get started, whereas you're finished."

"How dare you, Shelby Berkett? You of all people to speak to me this way? To come back here, shoving it in my face after all this time. You know I could have been a big star, far bigger than you."

"You were always bigger than me, Jazz, but you've gotten even bigger. You really need to watch what you eat. By the way, you have some of Brenda's cake on your chin, I believe."

Jazz swiped at her chin, glaring at him.

"No, darling, the fourth chin down."

Her voice turned to a low growl. "Why, you worthless, talentless little man. You come back here after all this time, worm your way into a part in *my* play, and try to take over. Do you hear me?"

"The entire apartment can hear you, Jazz. The entire building even. Possibly the planet," Shelby replied, wincing and putting his fingers in his ears again for effect.

"I don't care. Milwaukee is my city now. You left it and you left me. You stabbed me in the back twenty years ago and bad-mouthed me to that New York producer, Otto Granger, to make yourself look good." Jazz was louder than ever and heavily intoxicated.

Shelby removed his fingers from his ears. "Oh, let's dig that up again, shall we? How, Jazz, did I stab you in the back to Otto Granger? Tell me—tell *all* of us. We want to hear it."

"You know, Shelby. You know." This time her voice was softer and lower, but that wasn't saying much for Jazz. She still held the hatpin.

He shook his head violently. "No, I don't know. If I did, maybe I could understand your maniacal rantings. All I know is Otto Granger chose me to headline his show, and you never got over it."

"After you eliminated most of your competition."

"How dare you."

"No, how dare *you*. I never believed for a second that was an accident. And you come back here after all this time, and face me and Jasper and Alex after what you did to us."

"I didn't do anything to him, to Alex, or to you, despite what you believe, and I'm tired of having to defend myself."

"Otto Granger never would have chosen you over Alex, and you know it. Alex was better looking and a better actor, singer, and dancer."

"That's not true."

"So, you got him and Jasper both out of the way, and when it was down to just you and me, you stabbed me in the back."

"Otto Granger chose me over you because you were expecting with Dick." He spat the words out, but I could see in his eyes he instantly regretted it.

For once, Jazz was speechless. She scanned the crowd, her eyes falling on Dick, who was standing just to the left of her.

"Well, the truth is finally out, once and for all. You *were* expecting, Jazz, and I had every right to let Otto Granger know that. You were going to be an unwed mother, and that isn't exactly Broadway material. You can't blame *me* for that."

She looked at Dick for a long time, and then slowly back to Shelby. I couldn't tell if she was going to cry, stab him with the hatpin, or slug him. Finally she took a step toward Shelby and stared him down.

"Fine, Shelby. After twenty plus years, yes, my little secret is out. Yes, I was an unwed mother, and I *do* blame you because you are the father. Only you left me high and dry to run off to New York, and you never came back. All those letters I sent, all those excuses, those promises over the years, they obviously meant nothing."

Shelby looked slightly uncomfortable as he stepped away from her. "Oh, there you go again, claiming I'm the father. I didn't believe it back then, and I don't believe it now. You and Alex were close, too."

"Don't insult me even more, Berkett. Just look at Dick, Can't you see yourself twenty years ago? Oh, he looks a bit like me, too, but he definitely has your nose. Thankfully, he didn't inherit your personality."

"He doesn't look a thing like me. Frankly he doesn't even look like you, thank God. And if you think for one minute I'm going to take responsibility…"

I glanced across the room to where Dick was standing. He looked angry now, his brow furrowed deeply. When he realized people were staring at him, he fled, leaving the door to the apartment open.

"Now see what you've done?" Jazz said, but she made no attempt to go after him. Tears were forming in her eyes, and she swiped at them unsuccessfully before they splashed down her face, taking a good portion of her mascara with it. "Good God, Shelby, you're an ass. I loathe you with every fiber of my being."

"Honestly, Jazz, I could care less."

Jazz's face turned purple. "It's *couldn't* care less, you ignorant blowhard! Stuart, take me home." She grabbed his arm and hurled him toward the door as she shoved her hatpin back into her hat.

"My hat's in the bedroom," Stuart said.

"Oliver will bring it to the theater tomorrow, along with Dick's. Let's go!" She pulled him along through the crowd, which parted accordingly, and out the still open door, leaving Shelby standing by the piano, licking his hand where she had bit him.

"What a bitch," he said.

CHAPTER FOUR

Saturday morning, July 12, 1947

The next morning I awoke to a pounding, persistent headache and a parched mouth. I felt like I had swallowed a glass of sand. I opened my right eye and slowly surveyed my surroundings. I was in my bedroom; that was a good thing. I reached behind me and felt the rest of my double bed. Empty. That wasn't as good a thing, or maybe it was. I closed my right eye again, pulled the covers over my head, and wished I hadn't drunk so much at the party. I suspected a lot of people were feeling this way today.

Dave Bergstrom had driven me home sometime after one in the morning, though I wasn't entirely sure it was Dave, and I wasn't entirely sure about the time. I lowered the covers once more, opened both eyes halfway, and glanced about. Through the roller shade on my bedroom window, I could see the shadows of the treetops outside, swaying in the wind, beckoning me to get up. I opened my eyes all the way, swung my feet to the cool wood floor, then sat up and stretched.

All my clothes were in a pile next to the bed, including my underwear and someone else's tie. Hmmm. I was indeed naked. Oh my, it had been a night. A good scratch, and I stood up, hanging on to my head to keep it from falling off. I stretched again, then walked cautiously to the window and put up the shade, squinting as the bright sunshine flooded the room.

I pulled the shade down again and considered crawling back into bed. Unfortunately, it was twenty after eight, and I needed to be up. I hit the bathroom and took two aspirin with several glasses of water. I followed that with a hot shower before heading to the kitchen, clad only in a towel, to brew some coffee on the stove. From the kitchen vent, I could hear Mrs. Murphy in the apartment below.

"Herbert, do you want your eggs poached or over medium?"

I couldn't hear his response, but her voice boomed up again shortly. "I know you always have them over medium, but it wouldn't hurt you to change things up a bit now and then, you know. I'm going to do them scrambled, and you can eat them or not."

I smiled to myself as I took the pot off the stove and filled my cup, the steam rising up to my nose. I inhaled deeply, but it hurt my head. I vowed never to drink that much again, a vow I vaguely remember making once or twice before.

Cup in hand, I padded over to the telephone in the hall by the door and dialed Alan's number while I glanced at myself in the mirror. Yikes, I looked ghastly. He picked up on the third ring.

"Hello?"

"Hey, Mr. Thespian."

"Hi, Heath. Good morning," he said cheerfully.

I winced as his voice boomed in my ear and echoed around my head. "Morning," I said in a voice just above a hoarse whisper. "Not sure how good it is yet. My head is pounding and someone turned the sunshine on high. Keep the volume low, if you don't mind."

"Ouch. Right. Sorry to hear it. You sound terrible," he said, this time softly.

"Thanks. I don't look so good either right now. My own fault. How are you?"

"I'm feeling pretty good, but I didn't drink as much as you did. And I slept soundly, all things considered."

"Well, that makes one of us. You slept alone?"

Silence for a moment. "What kind of a question is that?"

"Henry drove you home, I presume." He didn't answer my previous question, I noted.

"Yes." I could hear the irritation in his voice. "We all left at the same time, or don't you remember?"

"Parts of the evening are a bit hazy, I will admit."

"Hank wanted to leave. I asked him if he'd drop you home, but you live in the opposite direction. Dave Bergstrom was heading your way and offered to take you home."

"I see. What about the private house party?"

"I didn't go, and neither did he."

"Smart decision. So, what did you do?"

"Went to bed."

"Huh." I decided that line of questioning was going nowhere. "Did you really never mention me to Henry?"

A brief bit of silence. "I don't remember. I mean, you probably just never came up in conversation. We're trying to keep things quiet, remember?"

"Right, quiet."

"Are you jealous of Hank? Or jealous that he likes me and ignores you?"

"Truthfully, maybe a little bit of both. But mostly jealous of Hank. He's awfully good looking."

"True, he is that, and he's really smart. He told me he practically runs Lempke's. Hank says Mr. Lempke leaves him in charge a lot."

"I'm sure he says a lot of things. So did Charles Ponzi." I stuck out my tongue and examined it in the mirror. It felt fuzzy. "What time do you have to be at the theater?"

"Five. Hank's picking me up."

I shook my head and it hurt. "Of course he is." My eyes looked like two puffy red cardinals.

"You should get there by six thirty or so. Curtain goes up at seven."

"I'll be there, but I make no promises as to how I'll look or feel. What about dinner?"

"Mr. Crane is bringing in some takeout Chinese for us."

"Oh, okay. I'll probably grab something at the diner before I pick up Verbina."

"I'm looking forward to meeting her. I haven't met any of your family yet."

"She's one of a kind," I said, "but you'll like her, and she'll like you."

"Good, I'm glad."

"Yeah. So, you ready?"

"For opening night or for meeting your aunt?"

"Wise guy. Both, since you mention it."

"Ready as I'll ever be," Alan said. "Though I'm anxious to see what the mood at the theater will be today after what all happened last night at the party."

"You and me both. I expect a full report."

"The tension is going to be thick as molasses in January, as they say. Perhaps thicker."

"Well, we'll be in the audience cheering you on, buddy."

"Thanks, Detective. Maybe after the show, the three of us can go get a drink together. You, your aunt, and me, I mean."

"Ugh, don't say 'drink' right now, Alan."

His laugh hurt my head again.

"Sorry. Did you take some aspirin?"

"Two. They haven't helped yet."

"Just takes time. And drink plenty of water. But, yeah, it would be nice if the three of us could go somewhere, even if just for coffee."

"What about Henry? Don't you have a get-together with the cast?"

"Jazz is hosting something at the Pfister Hotel, but Mr. Berkett won't be there, and I think I've had enough socializing with those folks after last night."

"Including Henry Hawthorne?"

"Heath…"

"Sorry, sorry. But how do I compete with an actor? With a potential movie star?"

"Hank told me he's taking Patty Perlman to Jazz's party."

"Oliver mentioned her, I believe."

"Yeah, she's a pretty girl. She works the front end."

"So, is that why you don't want to go to Jazz's get-together?"

"No. I don't know. Maybe, maybe not. I'm just done with parties for a while."

"Interesting."

"No, not really. So, do you want to go somewhere after the show or not? You, me, and your aunt? If not, maybe I'll go to the party after all." He sounded annoyed.

"I'll ask Verbina. I'm sure she'll be up for something."

"Okay," he said, his voice louder again.

I winced. "I should let you go. I still need to get dressed."

"I'll see you tonight, then."

"Right." I waited until I heard him disconnect, and then I hung up the receiver and took my empty cup back to the kitchen for a refill. I ate an overripe banana and drank a glass of orange juice, then headed to the bedroom to dress and pick up the mess from last night. No sooner had I put the notch in my black leather belt than the phone rang. Figuring Alan had forgotten to tell me something, I hurried back into the hall and picked up. The ringing was echoing in my ears.

"Hello?"

"Heath?"

"Oh, hi, Mom. Yes, it's me. Who did you expect?"

"You, of course, but you don't sound like yourself at all."

"I'm kinda tired, not feeling the greatest." I wasn't about to tell her I had too much to drink last night. Mom was a teetotaler from way back.

"Oh, dear. In the middle of summer? How odd. It certainly isn't cold and flu season. Would you like me to bring you some soup?"

"No, Mom. I'm fine, really. I didn't sleep that well."

"I see. Were you out painting the town with a young lady?"

"No, I was at a party. And there were lots of young ladies there."

"Oh, how nice. I'm so glad you're getting out and about, Heath. You spend too much time with that friend of yours."

"Alan."

"What?"

"My friend's name is Alan."

She made the clicking sound with her teeth again that meant she was annoyed. "Yes, well, anyway, you spend too much time with him, is all I'm saying. I'm glad you got out. Did you meet a nice girl?"

"Yes, Mother. Her name's Eve. A beautiful blonde."

"Oh, how nice. You'll have to bring her to supper." I could tell she was pleased. "Not too soon, of course. You don't want to rush. But after a while. Your father and I would love to get to know her."

"Sure, Mom. Can her husband come, too?"

"Her what?"

"Her husband. She's married."

"What are you talking about? I thought you said you met a nice girl." Click, click, click.

"Can't married women be nice?"

More teeth clicking. "Honestly, Heath, I don't understand you."

"Clearly, you don't," I said, annoyed myself. "Did you want something in particular this morning, Mom?"

"Hmmm? Oh, yes. I heard you're taking Verbina to the theater tonight."

I grimaced. I was hoping she wouldn't hear about that. Verbina wasn't supposed to say anything. "That's right. A new play. Alan is in it."

"I like to go to the theater, you know. I'm your mother."

"Yes, I'm aware of that. At least that's what you tell me. I was going to ask you if you wanted to go to the matinee tomorrow afternoon. I could only get two tickets for tonight's show."

"If you could only get two tickets, why didn't you take me tonight and Verbina tomorrow?"

"Because opening night is never all that good. They're still working out the kinks, everyone has opening night jitters, and things go wrong. I figured you'd much rather go the second day." Boy, I was getting good at this lying stuff.

"Well, when were you planning on asking me?"

"I was just about to call you when the phone rang. So, is it a date?"

"You want to go to the same play two days in a row?"

"Why not? It's supposed to be good. I've read the script. The matinee starts at one."

"Well, I'd have to get lunch early for your father, right after church. You know he hates eating early."

"So, you don't want to go?"

"I didn't say that. But you'll have to explain it to your father. Pick me up at noon. You can come in and say hello to him."

"Fine, Mom."

"What should I wear? My blue dress has gotten a bit snug, but I suppose I could let it out a bit."

"Great idea, Mom. You look good in blue. It suits you."

There was a noise on the line, then I heard a familiar woman's voice. "Is that you, Mrs. Barrington?"

"Hello, Mrs. Farrell. Yes, I'm just talking to Heath."

"Oh, hello, Heath. How have you been?"

"Fine, Mrs. Farrell. How's your son?"

"He's good. He's taken up photography, you know."

"How interesting. Do you need the line, Mrs. Farrell?"

"Yes, I was going to call my sister to see if she could take me shopping. Are you through?"

"Yes, I think so. I have to run, Mom, but I'll see you tomorrow."

"All right, Heath. I hope you feel better."

"Aren't you feeling well, Heath?"

"I'm fine, Mrs. Farrell, just a little tired today. Say hello to Mr. F. and to your son. Bye, and bye, Mom."

I hung up the phone. Party lines could be annoying, but sometimes they made it easier to end a conversation with my mother. I glanced at myself in the mirror one last time, straightened my tie, grabbed my hat, and headed out the door.

CHAPTER FIVE

Saturday afternoon, July 12, 1947

By the time I reached Gimbels department store on Plankinton Avenue, my headache was almost gone. I rode the narrow wooden escalator to Men's Furnishings on the third floor and stopped at the first glass counter, where a perky blonde stood, wearing a dark green jacket and matching skirt. She had a pink carnation in her lapel that matched her lips. Her name tag read "A. Quinn."

She looked up at me and smiled as I approached. "May I help you, sir?"

"Yes, I bought a pair of gold cufflinks in the shape of stars last week. I left them here to be engraved, and they were supposed to be ready today."

"Yes, of course. Do you have your claim ticket?"

I took my wallet out of my suit jacket pocket and handed her the cardboard ticket. "Here you are, Miss Quinn."

"And the name, sir?"

"Barrington. Heath Barrington."

"One moment, please." She smiled politely once more and went through a doorway. She returned with a small, shiny black box, which she set on the counter. Then, as if opening Tut's tomb, she carefully opened the shiny box and set the cufflinks gingerly on the black velvet cloth she'd laid out. "Here you are, Mr. Barrington. Please take a moment to make sure everything is correct."

I picked up one of the gold stars and looked at it closely. In script were the tiny words, "you're a star in my eyes." I set it back down, then picked up the other, which read in equally tiny script, "A.K. & H.B." Satisfied, I set it back down, too.

"Yes, those are perfect. Nice job."

"We here at Gimbels always strive to make our customers happy, Mr. Barrington. Would you like these gift wrapped?"

"Yes, please."

"Certainly." She returned them to the shiny black box, referred once more to the claim ticket, and said, "The balance due is two dollars and eleven cents, sir," as a severe woman in a green organdy cloche hat and matching suit marched up to the counter next to me.

"I'm here to pick up my watch, Agatha," the woman said, totally ignoring me.

"Good afternoon, Mrs. Christie. I'll be with you shortly," the clerk said. "I just have to finish up with this gentleman."

"I'm in a hurry. I'm lunching with my old friend Miss Crowley," the severe woman said, impatiently drumming her gloved fingers atop the glass case as a middle-aged, thinly built man stepped behind the counter. He was dressed in black trousers and a sport coat the same color and style as Miss Quinn's, with a white carnation in his lapel. He smelled of gardenias. "I'm back from my break, Miss Quinn."

"Oh good, Mr. Collins. Would you please attend to Mrs. Christie? She's picking up a watch she had repaired. It's under the name Julia Christie."

The thin man turned to the woman. "Certainly. I can take care of you, madam. Do you have your claim ticket?" His voice was a bit high and his overall appearance and mannerisms just a touch feminine, I noticed. He was not wearing a wedding ring, but he sported a large diamond on the ring finger of his right hand. His nails were shiny with clear polish.

"No, thank you. I'll wait for Miss Quinn." Her voice was cold and surprisingly harsh.

The man raised his thin eyebrows. "As you wish, madam." He shrugged and moved on to the other side of the work area as I handed Miss Quinn a five-dollar bill.

"I'm almost finished here, Mrs. Christie," the girl said as she counted out my change and gave me my receipt.

"I'll wait. I'm in a hurry, as I said, but I can't stand those kind of people."

I turned to the woman then and addressed her. "What kind of people, madam?"

She looked up at me, surprised. "*His* kind of people." She nodded in the direction of the male clerk. "They're not right. My husband is a doctor, so I should know. Homosexuals are revolting." She hissed her words like a fat snake would.

I smiled sweetly down at her. "Not yet, Mrs. Christie, but they will someday."

Miss Quinn suppressed a giggle as I turned back to her. "Just take your purchase and your receipt to Gift Wrapping on the fifth floor. They'll take good care of you, Mr. Barrington. Thank you for shopping at Gimbels." She gave me that smile again. I smiled back and headed off to the fifth floor, leaving the severe Mrs. Christie looking positively baffled and annoyed.

Once the cufflinks were gift wrapped and securely in my pocket, it was time for lunch. Gimbels has a lovely little restaurant called the Forum on the street level, so I took the marble staircase down and had a turkey club on rye with a cream soda, the lunch special for eighty-nine cents. I also downed three or four glasses of water, which helped a lot. I went back up to the third floor and did a little shopping for myself, settling on some new underwear and a snazzy green and ivory polka dot tie. It was almost three thirty before I finally got back to my apartment, and I was feeling nearly like my old self. I put my new things away, discarded the wrappings, and gave my aunt Verbina a call.

"Verbina Partridge speaking."

"It's Heath, Auntie."

"Oh, hello, dear. How nice to hear from you."

"Thanks. Mother called earlier."

"She was most annoyed about this whole thing with the theater. I'm so sorry I mentioned it, Heath."

"It's all right. I straightened things out. I'm taking her tomorrow."

"Well, good. She's my only sister, you know. I offered to let her go in my place tonight, but she's such a martyr, and she kept making that clicking sound with her teeth. I find that quite irritating."

I laughed. "I agree. Drives me batty. What time should I pick you up tonight?"

"Are we doing dinner first?"

"We could. I was planning on grabbing something at the diner and then picking you up, but we could go to the China Cupboard in your building."

"I'm there much too often. Let's go to the Circle Room in the Hotel LaSalle. Nat King Cole recorded there last year, you know. I just love him."

"So do I. All right, the Circle Room it is. The show starts at seven, so why don't we eat at five thirty?"

"All right, I'll make reservations. Pick me up at five fifteen."

"Yes, ma'am. By the way, Alan was wondering if you'd like to go for coffee after the show."

"Oh, he was, was he?"

"Yes, Aunt 'Bina. He'd like to meet you."

"Well, I should very much like to meet him, too. I'd say it's high time."

"So that's a yes?"

"A firm yes."

"You'll like him, Auntie."

"He's special to you, Heath, and that's enough for me."

"Thanks, Verbina. Truly."

"Of course, my darling. Now I must run. I want to go down to Mary's apartment and borrow some of her new perfume for tonight. I'll see you soon, dear."

"Bye, Auntie."

I couldn't help but smile as I hung up the phone. I had just about an hour before I had to leave again, so I had a quick shave, then settled in to peruse a few chapters in my book on Ancient Greece, with illustrations.

CHAPTER SIX

Saturday evening, July 12, 1947

I picked up Aunt Verbina from her apartment at the Cudahy Towers at 5:15 sharp according to the clock on the dash of my car, as I had inadvertently left my pocket watch on my nightstand, much to my chagrin. She was looking chic in a dark blue pencil skirt, just below the knee, and a dark blue blouse with white polka dots, over which she wore a simple, tailored white jacket. A small hat, low white heels, a cream clutch, a triple strand of pearls with matching earrings, and mid-length black gloves completed the ensemble. I whistled as she stepped out the door.

"You look, smashing, Auntie, as always."

She smiled sweetly. "Thank you, dear. I'm not sure about this hat, but I do try to be considerate of those who may be behind me when I go to the theater."

I opened the passenger door of my car for her, and she slid in. "It's a charming choice. You smell wonderful, too," I said, getting behind the wheel.

"It's Goat de Minute, or something like that. Mary spritzed me. She just got a bottle. It's French, you know."

"Goat de Minute?" I said as I put my car in gear and headed toward the Circle Room in the LaSalle Hotel on Eleventh Street. "French? Do you mean *Goût de minuit*? That means 'Taste of Midnight.'"

"That's what I said. I'm glad you like it. I may have to get a bottle of my own. My goodness, it's warm tonight, isn't it?"

It was indeed a hot July night, and the air hung thick around us. I could smell it and taste it, but Auntie rolled up her window just the same. "Nevertheless, I can't have my hair messed up. The wind and humidity will ruin my permanent. Just the vent window will do."

"Yes, ma'am," I said, dutifully rolling up my window as well.

Happily, we found a place on the street close to the entrance. Verbina would never admit it, but she was perspiring by the time we arrived, and we were both relieved to get inside the conditioned air of the hotel.

The Circle Room proved to be a good choice. The service was excellent, and the food plentiful and delicious. No Nat King Cole Trio tonight, but the music was lively, and the girl singer did a decent job. In fact, I was feeling so much better I even indulged in a couple vodka martinis while I entertained Verbina by recounting the events at last night's party, as best as I could recall them.

In typical Verbina fashion, she was horrified at the behavior of Jazz and Shelby, but she hung on each word. After dessert and coffee, I paid the bill and escorted her back to my car. It was 6:25 as I steered toward the Davidson Theater, located within the Davidson Hotel on North Third Street and Michigan Avenue. I lucked out on a parking spot once more, and we entered the lobby at 6:40.

"I'll get our tickets from Will Call, Auntie. Be right back." The lobby was bustling with people, all dressed to the nines and chattering away like a murder of magpies. I had difficulty in locating Verbina again after I had gotten the tickets, because she was diminutive and had been surrounded by taller people. I finally pushed my way through to see her talking to an older, bespectacled gentleman with a short cigar and a large gray mustache. He was wearing a three-piece suit that seemed just a tad snug on him, and he seemed quite animated.

"I've got the tickets, Auntie."

"Oh, good. Heath, this is Mr. Quartus Finch. Mr. Finch, my nephew, Heath Barrington."

"How do you do?" he said, grasping my hand in a friendly shake.

"How do you do, Mr. Finch?"

"Mr. Finch is the president of First City National Bank," Verbina said, with a twinkle in her eye. "He's a widower."

"Oh, I'm so sorry, sir."

"Thank you," he said, "but Louise has been gone over fifteen years. Not that I don't still miss her, mind you."

"Of course."

"She was a fine-looking woman, just like your aunt here. I was telling her she reminds me of the goddess Minerva in that painting over there."

I glanced across the lobby to a large oil of said goddess in an ornate gilt frame. She was represented as a warrior figure, with a metal helmet and an owl perched on her shoulder as she gazed down at the crowds from her lofty perch. She was indeed quite lovely. "I can see the resemblance, Mr. Finch." I turned to Verbina. "Good thing you left your owl at home tonight, Auntie."

"Oh, Heath!" She smiled broadly and her eyes twinkled even more.

"Minerva is the Roman goddess of wisdom and the sponsor of arts, trade, and strategy," Mr. Finch said, his mustache moving up and down as he spoke. We all gazed at the painting once more. "Yes, a striking woman. Strong, too. I can definitely see the resemblance, Mrs. Partridge."

"I agree on both counts," I said.

Verbina giggled, which I had never heard her do before, and her cheeks were flushed. "Oh, stop! You both flatter me too much. The woman in that painting can't be more than twenty-five years old."

"True, but her beauty is eternal, and I can see that in you."

The lights in the lobby flashed on and off. "Oh, dear. Looks like the show is about to start," Verbina said. "What time is it?"

I felt for my pocket watch before remembering. "I'm afraid I left my watch at home."

Mr. Finch glanced at his wristwatch. "Just seven now. I shall see you at intermission, I hope," he said, smiling down at her.

"Oh, definitely. Enjoy the show." I could swear she batted her eyelashes at him.

"Shall we go in?" I said.

Verbina took my arm as I handed the tickets to an usher in a short red jacket, cap, and black trousers, who gave us our programs and showed us to our fifth row center seats. I placed my fedora on my lap and unbuttoned my coat, trying to get as comfortable as I could within the limited confines of the seat. Eagerly I opened my program and flipped to the cast member page, where I saw Alan's credit in fine print at the bottom. I smiled with satisfaction as I pointed this out to Verbina. She'd left her glasses at home, so she only nodded politely and said, "How nice." The theater was about two-thirds empty. Not good.

The lights dimmed, the small crowd hushed, the curtain went up, and the show began. The first act moved along briskly, and I found myself thoroughly entertained until intermission, when Verbina and I found ourselves back in the lobby amongst the crowd.

"What do you think so far?" I said after we had each returned from our respective lounges.

"Oh, it's wonderful. What do you think?"

"Excellent. Jazz Monroe's makeup is a tad more garish than it was in dress rehearsal, though. I think it's Hilda's revenge from last night."

"Who's Hilda?"

"The makeup lady for the play. Just an observation is all."

"If you say so. Where is Mr. Keyes? You said he plays a policeman, but I haven't seen any policemen in the show yet. I thought at first he was that attractive fellow who plays the messenger and the brother."

"That's Henry Hawthorne. Alan doesn't come on until the end."

"Mr. Hawthorne is certainly good looking."

I shrugged. "He's all right, I guess. If you like the Clark Gable type."

Verbina laughed. "I don't know anyone who doesn't, including you," she said, glancing about the lobby.

"Actually, I prefer Cary Grant. Looking for someone?"

"Hmmm? No. No one in particular, dear. My goodness, there are so many people here, though. The theater seemed half empty."

"About two-thirds empty, by my estimation. But the lobby area is small, and everyone is here at once. Don't worry, he'll turn up."

"I don't know who or what you're talking about!"

At that point, Mr. Finch sidled up to us again, his large gray mustache twitching like a squirrel's tail.

"Ah there you are, Mrs. Partridge. How are you enjoying the show?"

"Hello, Mr. Finch. Oh, I daresay it's quite good. What do you think?" Her face was beaming again.

"I agree. Not bad, not bad at all." He smiled warmly at her, and I felt like a third wheel.

"Do you have a good seat?" she said.

"I'm in the Buchanan box on the left. I came with one of my associates, but he's a terrible bore. I do so appreciate you keeping me company."

"Not at all. It's my pleasure, truly. Our pleasure, I should say," Verbina said, as if suddenly remembering I was even there.

Mr. Finch turned to me. "How are you liking the show, Mr. Barrington?"

"Quite enjoyable. Of course, I know how it ends, as I read the script. I did some advising on it in regard to the police aspect. I'm a Milwaukee police detective."

Mr. Finch raised his eyebrows and his large mustache twitched again. "Well, how interesting. Please tell me more."

Feeling included at last, I filled him in on my minor part in the show, and the three of us traded our thoughts on the plot, the acting, and the set until the lights flickered on and off, and we went in for the second act. Verbina and Mr. Finch agreed to meet in the lobby after the show.

As we took our seats, I leaned over to Verbina. "Perhaps Mr. Finch could join us for drinks later."

"That's sweet of you, but no. I want that to be my chance to get to know your Mr. Keyes. I don't want to be distracted."

"And Mr. Finch is rather distracting, isn't he?" I said, giving her a wink.

"I'm sure I don't know what you're talking about, but he is quite distinguished. And a bank president."

"And a widower."

"Don't be cheeky."

"Just don't let him slip away, Auntie."

"My dear nephew, I've been married twice before, so don't you worry," she said with a wink herself as the lights dimmed and the curtain went up. Verbina put her pocketbook in her lap, and I shifted in my seat to peer around the ostrich feathers in the hat of the lady in front of me, who was clearly not as considerate as my aunt when it came to millinery at the theater. She wasn't sitting there in the first act, so she must have changed seats at intermission. Since the seats to Verbina's right were empty, we both shifted over for a better view.

The second act commenced, and I thought everything was running smoothly. The comments from the audience members that I had overheard during intermission were favorable, so Oliver would be pleased.

Claire was back at Lochwood, standing by the fireplace.

The scene played out just as I remembered from rehearsal. Eve's character, Charlotte, came in and left, then the butler entered with the tea tray. When he had left, Shelby's character, Roger, entered again, wet, miserable, and evil. I could feel the tension in the audience as people gasped. Everyone was silent as they played out their scene, exchanging their dialogue effortlessly. There were more gasps as Claire poured the poison into the teapot and Roger drank it. Then Claire laughed a big Jazz Monroe laugh.

The scene continued, and Roger nodded as he moved toward her, taking the cup and saucer from her hand. "Thanks. You may be older, and you're certainly not a girl anymore, but that's all right. You're a big, mature woman."

Ooh, I thought, he slipped that "big" comment in again. He'd hear about that later.

Claire opened her mouth to speak, but he held up his hand in front of her.

"Don't take offense. A mature woman doesn't play hard to get, and I like that."

She glared at him, "You're right. I don't play hard to get. I *am* hard to get. And you're not getting it."

He took another drink. "Oh, Claire. I thought better of you, I really did."

"Really, Roger? I never thought better of you. You disgust me." Another clap of thunder and flash of lightning.

"No, I arouse you. I can tell. I always could tell."

"Don't make me laugh even more. You're not getting Lochwood, or me, or anything else, not tonight, not ever."

He laughed, but it was a strange laugh that morphed into a coughing fit, and instantly everyone in the audience seemed to know something was wrong.

"Something the matter, Roger?" Claire said, arching her painted-on brows. Another bolt of lightning flashed, followed by another clap of thunder. I made a note to mention to Oliver that the thunder and lightning was too distracting.

"My head, it's suddenly pounding. And my stomach is

cramping. What did you do, Claire? What did you do?" He bent over, dropping the teacup and saucer, which shattered across the floor. Oh, Oliver was going to be mad about that, and Shelby went off script, too, I thought. But it didn't stop there.

Shelby slumped to the ground, writhing and convulsing wildly. Good grief, that wasn't in the script, either. He was overacting, and Jazz and Oliver were going to be furious. I watched Jazz's face and could tell she was really angry as she stared down at him jerking back and forth, his face white, gasping, frothing at the mouth, until suddenly he froze, jerked once more, and then stilled. I had to admit it was a convincing death scene, though I noticed his toupee had come loose and was hanging absurdly to the side.

Jazz crossed to him and put her foot in the middle of his back harder than she should have, but he didn't move. She kneeled beside him and checked for a pulse. Then again. She was supposed to stand up at that point and smile at the audience with an evil grin and say, "Good riddance, Roger," but she didn't. She put her ear to his chest and checked for a pulse again, her face almost as white as his.

"Oh my God, I think he's dead!" she cried out, stumbling to her feet and backing away from him as if he could somehow grab her. This was definitely not in the script. "Oliver! Oliver! I think Shelby's dead! Oh, my God!" She screamed again, so high pitched I reckoned all the dogs in the city were howling.

The audience members started whispering. I heard a man behind me say, "Who's Oliver? I don't remember any Oliver. And who's Shelby?" A woman nearby answered. "Shelby Berkett is playing Roger. I think she made a mistake."

I turned to Verbina, who was also looking confused. "Stay here," I said. I got to my feet and went toward the steps that led up to the stage. At the same time, Oliver came out from the wings looking shaken.

"Lights! Turn up the lights!" he yelled as he approached Shelby. The house lights came on, and the audience grew more vocal. Oliver repeated what Jazz had done, checking for a pulse and a heartbeat. "Is there a doctor in the house?"

I had reached the stage by that time, and most of the cast had come out, each talking to someone else. Alan was talking to Henry, but when he saw me he came to my side.

"What's happened, Heath?"

"I think Shelby's really dead. Better go call the station and an ambulance. I don't like the looks of this. Get the coroner and a lab crew down here, too. Tell them I'm here."

"You think…"

"No time to think right now, Alan. Just do it."

"Yes sir." He moved quickly offstage as two men from the audience approached, one carrying a small black satchel.

I heard the older one say, "I'm a doctor," as he knelt at Shelby's side. The younger man said he was also a doctor, and he kneeled on the other side of Shelby. "Can't say for certain without an autopsy," the older doctor said, "but it doesn't appear natural."

Oliver looked stricken.

"Bring down the curtain! Bring down the curtain!" he yelled, but his voice was shaking as the curtain came down, cutting off the audience's view of the stage.

"Oliver," I said to him, "Alan's calling the police. I think you'd better clear the theater until we can figure out what happened"

"What?"

"Go out front and clear the theater," I said again, slowly and distinctly, as he appeared to be in shock. "Tell everyone to go home. Tell them you'll refund their ticket price."

"Refund? You mean give them their money back?" Oliver looked like he might faint. His milk white complexion was even paler, if that was possible.

I took hold of both of his arms briefly. "Yes, Oliver. Do it now before the police get here, but don't let any of the cast members or crew leave just yet."

"Right, right," he said. He stood there for the briefest moment; then, staring at me, his upper lip trembling, he stepped between the curtain part at the side of the stage to address the crowd.

At that point, Alan returned. "I called the station. They're sending a black-and-white along with a lab crew. The coroner is on his way, too."

"Good. Go out front and explain to my aunt what's happened. Call her a cab and tell her I'll talk to her tomorrow. She can be feisty, but be firm. I don't want her here right now."

"I'll take care of it. How will I find her?"

"She's sitting fifth row center, near the aisle, third seat in. She's wearing a white jacket over a dark blue blouse with white polka dots, and a dark blue skirt. She looks something like the goddess Minerva."

"Huh?"

"Just find her."

"Right."

As he went out front, I surveyed the stage. Lochwood was suddenly full of people. The entire cast was onstage, as well as most of the crew, all chattering away with each other and staring at the lifeless body of Shelby Berkett. The only one missing was the lights guy, Tony, and I assumed he was still up in his booth wondering what the hell was going on.

I got closer to the body. "Everyone stay clear of Mr. Berkett, please. I'm Milwaukee Police Detective Heath Barrington. Move to the wings or backstage, because the police are on their way," I shouted. Some people moved off, but others ignored me. Typical. "Please, everyone clear the stage at once. This is a potential crime scene!" I shouted louder. The remaining people grumbled and shot me looks but obliged and moved to the wings, where they turned to watch what would happen next.

Dick was standing near me. My heart went out to him as I saw him staring at the body. He looked at me then, a shocked expression on his face. "Is he really dead?"

DEATH TAKES A BOW

"Yes, Dick, I'm afraid so. I'm sorry," I said, putting my hand on his bony little shoulder.

"What happened?" he said, his voice small and soft.

"We don't know for certain, but I've called for the police, and I'm going to investigate."

"I can't believe it," he said, still staring at Shelby's lifeless body. "He was supposedly my father, you know."

"I know. This must all be a terrible shock."

He nodded. "I never knew him, though, not in that way. To me, my dad and mom died in that flood when I was a baby. That's what I was always told."

"You still have Jazz," I said.

"Yes, and she still has me."

I felt in my pocket for my watch but remembered once more I had left it on my night table. "Do you have the current time, Dick?" I said, knowing I'd need that for the record and hoping to take Dick's mind off the death briefly.

Dick gave me a blank look, then glanced down at his right wrist. "Eight twenty-seven, Mr. Barrington."

"Thanks." I made a mental note of that as Dick turned his gaze once more to the body, seemingly oblivious to anyone and everything else going on around him. I surveyed the rest of the group nearby. Not far from us, Peter was talking loudly, his words slurred, about how the show must go on, and how they should drag Shelby's body off so the play could proceed.

"He was supposed to die, anyway. So what if he really did?" Peter said, waving his hands about wildly. "It just makes the play more realistic. Let's get on with the show. Those people paid good money to see a show and we have to finish what we started. The show must go on, isn't that what everyone's always saying?"

"Oh, shut up, Peter!" Jazz snarled, her nerves apparently at an end.

Peter glared at her, walked back on the set, picked up the tea tray, and dropped it, shattering the pot across the stage and causing everyone else to jump.

"For God's sake, leave that alone! Shelby is dead! What the hell is wrong with you?" Jazz shouted at him again, her voice almost more loud and disturbing than the breaking of the teapot.

I cringed, knowing the mess would make the investigation more difficult, and I couldn't help but wonder if he had done that deliberately.

"I need a drink, that's what's wrong with me, you loud, obnoxious cow, and I need my pills," he said, walking back to the wings unsteadily. "Where's Oliver?"

"Oliver is on the other side of the curtain, Peter, and I think you've had enough for tonight," Eve said, pouncing on him like a cat on a mouse. "Do you mind?"

He turned and stared at her, a wild expression on his face. "I *do* mind, dear Eve." Then he glanced once more at Shelby's body. "Sorry about your boyfriend." Then he weaved away as Jazz disappeared in the opposite direction.

"Everyone stay off the stage, or I'll be forced to place you under arrest!" I shouted once more, still wondering what had possessed Peter to drop the tea tray. Was it just to get attention and piss off Jazz? Or something else?

I glanced at Dick, who was still standing nearby.

"I really think you should go sit down, Dick. The police will be here soon. They're going to want to talk to everyone."

He looked up at me, his eyes glazed. "Yeah, I guess so. Do you want me to clean up this mess first?"

"No, don't touch anything onstage." Had I not made myself clear?

"You know, I've never seen anyone dead before, not in person. It's like I'm watching a movie, but it's real life. Strange, hard to believe."

"It is strange, Dick. Unfortunately, I've seen my share of dead bodies, and I must say I never got used to it."

"I suppose not. I've seen this part in the play several times during the rehearsals. Shelby's character dies, the curtain goes down, and then he gets up and walks off. But he's not getting up this time, is he?"

I shook my head, my heart aching for him. "No, not this time."

From backstage, Peter called out loud and slurred. "Where the hell is Oliver, goddammit? I need my pills."

"That Mr. Holloway is crazy," Dick said. "I guess it's a good thing Mr. Crane locked his pillbox up. He sure seems to want it bad."

"Oliver locked up his pillbox? I thought it was missing."

"It turned up before curtain. Mr. Crane took it away from him and locked it up in his office."

"Interesting."

Dick shrugged his tiny, bony shoulders. "I suppose. Anyway, I guess I better go check on Jazz. She must be pretty upset by all this, too."

"Right, good idea. Maybe bring her some water," I said.

"Okay." Dick strode off slowly, hands still shoved in his pockets, his head down, and I couldn't help but feel for him.

CHAPTER SEVEN

Late Saturday evening, July 12, 1947

The first uniforms arrived, and I directed them to the stage door, front entrance, and emergency exits, with instructions to keep the press out and make sure no one from the cast and crew left the building. I had the curtain raised, as the theater was empty except for a couple of young ushers standing in a corner, their red uniform coats unbuttoned as they talked to each other. Alan was just coming up one of the side stairs to the stage, still dressed in his English police uniform, which didn't look much different than his actual one except for the bobby hat, the nightstick, and the absence of a gun.

"I got your aunt Verbina into a cab, but she wasn't happy about it."

"I imagine not. Thanks for doing that. I'll call her tomorrow."

"You certainly will. She was adamant about that. Someone named Mr. Finch said he'd share the cab with her."

"Love comes to Lochwood," I said.

"Huh? You're not making much sense tonight."

"Sorry, it's nothing. Or maybe something, but I have other things to think about right now."

"Right, so what's happened?"

"The doctors definitely think Shelby's death was suspicious, and I concur. I believe it wasn't an accident."

"Can't say I'm surprised. Mama always told me not to speak ill of the dead, but he was not a nice man."

"No, he wasn't. Still, he was a man, a human. A small baby, a child, at one time. Somewhere deep within, I think he wanted people to like him. Why else would he be in the theater? Why else would he act? He loved the adoration, the applause, the fans. He couldn't seem to garner that kind of attention in real life."

"Because he was so nasty to everyone."

I shrugged. "I've known others like him. They're so afraid of being hurt, of being rejected, that they lash out first and push everyone away."

"That's quite sad."

"Indeed. But in his case, his mean and spiteful ways may have got him murdered."

"Golly, Heath, here we go again. What a night."

My buddy Fletch, the county coroner, arrived then with his assistant. When he saw me, he gave a nod and approached.

"What have you got for me, Heath?"

"Hello, Fletch. Sorry to drag you out on a Saturday night."

He sighed. "It's all right. I was on call. At least I finished my dinner this time."

"You remember Officer Keyes?" I motioned in Alan's direction.

Fletch nodded. "Right. Right. Always by your side."

"Good to see you, Mr. Fletcher," Alan said.

"Sure, sure, likewise. So, what's going on?"

I pointed in the direction of the body, still lying on the floor of the stage. His face, twisted into an agonized expression, vomit still on the lips, was thankfully facing away from us. "Shelby Berkett, one of the actors, collapsed during his scene. The doctors think it wasn't a natural death."

"What doctors?" Fletch said.

"There happened to be a couple doctors in the audience. I

took their names and numbers if you want to question them," I said.

"Shouldn't be necessary. I like to do my own investigating. I'll have the body taken downtown for an autopsy. Who are the rest of these people?" he said, glancing about at the men and women standing in the wings, watching.

"The cast and crew, stagehands and the like. I don't want to release anyone until I get a grip on what's going on and what's happened."

"You putting yourself in charge on this one, Heath?" Fletch said, raising his brow.

"Why not? I was here at the time, saw it happen, first on the scene."

"Green's on call this weekend. This should be his case, so why isn't he here?"

Alan spoke up. "When I phoned for a black-and-white and for you, Mr. Fletcher, I told them Heath was here and not to bother Detective Green."

"That's not how it works, Officer Keyes, and you know it."

"That was actually my decision, Fletch. I told Alan to tell them I had this."

Fletch scowled. "Did you at least *call* Green?"

"No, but I will. Professional courtesy. I'm sure he'll agree I should be the detective on this one. It just makes sense."

"Have you ever met Alvin Green?"

"Of course I have, Fletch. What are you talking about? I work with him every day."

"Right. So, who is this person you think will just agree to turn over a big murder case to you?"

"I'll talk to the chief if I have to, Fletch. I have a personal interest in this one."

"All the more reason you should hand it over to Green. You can give him your information, but let him do the investigating."

"Whose side are you on, anyway?"

"Yours, but you can be bullheaded and stubborn and you don't always look out for yourself. Why do you want to go and piss off Alvin Green? Don't you have enough trouble down at the station?"

"What kind of trouble?" Alan said, looking from Fletch to me and back to Fletch.

Fletch shot him a look. "Gossip, jealousy, rumors. And don't think you're not a part of that, Officer Keyes."

"Leave Alan out of it, Fletch."

"Gladly, but I'm not the one bad-mouthing you. And there's only so much I can say to defend you."

"I appreciate your support, but this is my case and I'm sticking to it. I already have my theories."

Fletch whistled. "Why do I feel like I've been talking to a brick wall? All right, have it your way. I have my own job to do. I'll send over the autopsy results as soon as I have them."

"Thanks, Fletch." I could tell he was exasperated.

"Right." Shaking his head, Fletch walked off in the general direction of the body, his assistant trailing behind.

Alan looked at me. "What was he talking about, Heath?"

"Gossip, that's all. I've been pretty successful lately, and that makes some people jealous. With jealousy comes envy and the need to strike out, to knock the successful one down."

"You mean the other detectives at the station," Alan said.

"Yes, some of them. And some of the boys in blue. Not all, certainly, but there will always be some. It's human nature."

Alan stared at me. "You can't be taking chances, Heath. You're on your way up. Don't let some petty people knock you down. Maybe you *should* hand this over to Detective Green."

I stared back at Alan. "If I do that, they win. Besides, Alvin's probably sitting at home right now all comfy, having a drink and listening to one of his radio programs. I doubt he'd want to be disturbed. And don't forget he's a family man, as the chief has said multiple times. But fine, I'll call him if it will make you and

Fletch happy. Watch for the lab crew. They should be here soon. Where's the nearest telephone?"

"There's a pay phone on the wall near the stage door. Just go back that way, take a left, then down a few steps," Alan said, pointing. "Do you need five cents?"

"Right, I remember seeing that when Oliver gave me a tour on Thursday." I fished in my pocket for a nickel and held it up. "No, I've got one. Why don't you change into your street clothes while I make the call?"

"Okay, I'll meet you back here."

I headed off in the direction Alan had indicated and quickly found the battered old phone. I dropped in my nickel and dialed Alvin Green.

"Hello?" A woman's voice, faintly familiar.

"Mrs. Green?"

"Yes, who's calling, please?"

"This is Heath Barrington. May I please speak to your husband?"

"Just a moment, Mr. Barrington."

I heard her put the phone down, then a few moments later I heard it being picked up again.

"Green here."

"Hey, Alvin, it's Heath."

"What's happened?"

"I'm at the Davidson Theater. There's been a possible murder of one of the cast members. I was in the audience when it occurred, so I took charge temporarily."

"Christ. A possible murder?"

"Yes, it looks suspicious. He died onstage. There were a couple doctors in the audience."

"I see. I can be there in thirty minutes, I suppose," Alvin said. He didn't sound happy.

"Right. I know you're on call this weekend, but since I'm already here, I don't mind taking the case if you'd rather not come down." I waited, biting my lip, wondering what he would say. I imagined he would decline my offer, and I imagined he would be angry I had already called for Fletch and the lab crew before I spoke to him.

"Why didn't the station call me? How long ago did this happen?"

"Just a few minutes ago. I called for a black-and-white, then asked for Fletch and a lab crew, and I told dispatch I'd call you directly." A small lie, but mostly true.

"Not exactly protocol, Barrington, but I'm relieved. My daughter Janey's come down with a fever and a nasty cough, and my wife and I are worried sick. We're waiting for the doctor to get here. When the phone rang, I was afraid it was the station. If you don't mind taking the investigation, I'd appreciate it."

I let out a breath. I was relieved, too. My imagination had gotten the best of me once again. "I'm sorry to hear about your daughter, Alvin. Keep me posted as to how she's doing. And don't worry about all this down here at the theater. I'll take over the investigation and clear it with the chief. I'm sure he'll understand. He's got kids, too."

"Thanks, Heath. I owe you one. I'm sure Janey will be fine, but I've never seen her so sick before."

"You're welcome, Alvin. She will be fine, I'm sure. See you Monday."

"Right, bye."

"Bye." I hung up the receiver and went back to the stage where Alan was waiting, now dressed in a simple gray suit with a blue and green tie and black oxfords, his hat in hand.

"So, what did he say?"

I couldn't help but smile at him. "He let me have the case. His daughter's sick."

"Still, good you cleared it with him. It just makes it easier."

"I know, I know. I rock the boat too much sometimes."

"Just don't tip it over. There are hungry sharks in the water. Will his daughter be all right?"

"Most likely. Probably just a summer cold or flu, maybe something she ate. The doctor is on the way over to their house. I told Green to keep me posted. Anyway, here comes the lab crew."

Two men in plain clothes approached up the side steps, their hats pushed back on their heads.

"Hey, Heath. I heard you were in this play, Alan," Rick said.

"I'm playing an English policeman."

"Someone mentioned that but I thought they were joking," the one called Darren said. "So, what's happened? You're acting so bad it kill somebody?"

"Funny, Darren," Alan said dryly.

"It looks like we've got a murder on our hands, boys," I said. "Potential, anyway."

"I didn't think you'd call us down here to see the play," Rick said.

I ignored his remark. "There's a shattered teacup on the floor of the stage, near the body. Check it for any traces of poison or anything else besides tea. Check the remains of the broken teapot, too."

"Okay, we'll have to take it all down to the lab," Darren said.

"Of course. Also see Jasper Crockett, the prop man, about a glass vial. Jazz Monroe may still have it in her possession. Check it for traces, too."

"Right. Fingerprints?" Rick said.

"You might as well, but I don't think that will tell us anything. Dust the doorknob to the prop room, and a pillbox Oliver Crane has locked in his office. Take it downtown and check the contents. And anything else you can think of. Of course, I'll want complete fingerprint sets from everyone still in the building, right down to Pompom."

"Pompom?" Darren said.

"The prop man's dog. Just a joke. But seriously, no excuses, no exceptions," I said.

"Him, too?" Rick said, pointing at Alan.

I glanced over at Alan, who was looking back at me with those puppy dog eyes of his.

"No, he's with me."

"No, I want to be fingerprinted, too. No excuses, no exceptions."

I sighed. "Suit yourself. You might as well go first, then."

"Right. Follow me, Keyes," Darren said. "I'll set up in the wings." Darren and Alan walked away, Darren carrying his kit.

"That's a lot of prints," Rick said. "I'll take photos, and we should have results and pictures by tomorrow afternoon."

"Thanks, I appreciate the rush."

"Anytime. Say, I thought Green was on call this weekend."

"Long story, Rick, but I've got this one. Just get me the results as soon as you can."

"Sure, we're on it." Rick went to get his equipment and I scratched my head, wondering where to begin.

Thankfully, Alan was back quickly, his fingertips inky black.

"Where's your hat?" I said.

"I left it backstage for now. This ink is hard to get off."

"You should use a rag. That will never come out of your handkerchief."

"It's all right, I have others. Jeepers, Heath, what a night."

"You can say that again. So, Officer, since I am now acting in an official capacity, mind telling me what happened backstage tonight?"

He scratched his head. "Gee, so much happened, I don't know where to start. Hank and I got here just after five. Miss Monroe and Dick arrived last. Mr. Crane was irritated, as he had gotten Chinese takeout for all of us and it was getting cold."

"What time was it when Jazz and Dick finally showed up?"

"It was about five thirty."

"How was everyone behaving?"

Alan shrugged. "Dick seemed the same as always, but maybe quieter than before. None of us were sure he and Jazz would even show after last night. Mr. and Mrs. Holloway didn't appear to be speaking with each other unless absolutely necessary, and Mr. Berkett made himself scarce. I think he hid out in his dressing room until his cue to go on. Hank was his usual self. Mr. Crane was very nervous and agitated."

"With good reason, I should think. What else?"

"Well, I remember Jasper said he had to make the pitcher of tea for the show, and then he was going to take Pompom for a walk. He does the same thing each night, even during the dress rehearsals. He makes the tea and then takes his dog out. Anyway, Hank and I went down to the dressing room to get dressed."

"Right. So, then what?"

"I finished dressing before Hank, so I went back upstairs. I took a minute to peak out at the auditorium and watch people start to file in and take their seats."

"About what time was that?"

"Oh, about six fifteen. I thought maybe I'd see you, but you must not have gotten in yet."

"No, we didn't get here until about six forty. Dinner ran late."

"Okay. I continued on to the other side of the stage where I saw Jasper and Pompom talking to Dick. Or rather Jasper and Dick were talking, Pompom wasn't, of course."

I smiled. "Of course."

"I think it was about six twenty by that time. Pompom was licking Dick's shoes, which seemed to annoy him. I don't think Dick likes dogs much. He told me he got bit once a few years ago."

"That would do it, I suppose. Where was everyone else at that point?"

"Mr. Crane had just come out of his office, and Mr. Holloway was on one of the sofas by the dock door. As soon as the curtain goes up, Jasper rings a doorbell. That's Mr. Holloway's cue. He goes onstage and answers the door, then takes the telegram from Hank's character and closes the door, just as Miss Monroe as Claire comes down the stairs with the candelabra."

"Right, I remember. Great scene. Really sets the tone."

"Yes. Anyway, as I was standing there, Eve came up behind me, and I noticed Jazz had just stepped out of the bathroom."

"So, pretty much the whole cast was on that side of the stage."

"Except Hank and Mr. Berkett. Anyway, Mr. Crane told Mr. Holloway to get up, and Dick went over to help him. Mr. Holloway appeared to have been drinking again. Then Mr. Holloway's pillbox fell to the floor. Mr. Crane surmised it must have slipped out of Mr. Holloway's pocket and wedged between the sofa cushions the last time he was lying there."

"And Peter was accusing Eve, Oliver, and even the spirit of Alexander Lippencott of taking it," I said.

"Well, Mr. Crane *did* take it at that point. He picked it up, noticed it was empty, and told Mr. Holloway he was locking it up in his office. At that point Mr. H just fell back on the sofa and continued to lie there. Eve sat with him. Jasper got the candelabra for Jazz, and she left to go to the other side of the stage, since she enters from upstairs in the first scene. That means she has to go up the wooden stairs behind the set on the scaffolding."

"Right."

"Then Jasper asked me to help him with the tea set and the vial, so I followed him into the prop room. The Opera Hour was playing on his radio. Did I ever tell you I'm not real fond of opera?"

"It's an acquired taste. Some of it is quite beautiful when performed well. Someday, I'll take you to the Lyric Opera House in Chicago to see *The Barber of Seville*. That's always a good introduction."

"I guess I can be open to new things, and another weekend in Chicago would be nice. We could visit Mrs. Gittings."

"We could. So, then what?"

"Jasper took the tea tray with the cup, saucer, and teapot, and I carried the vial over to the prop table. Then Mr. Crane came back out, and we could all tell he was still pretty nervous. I tried to cheer him up by telling him I had peeked out at the auditorium and it was already filling up, but that didn't seem to help much."

"I would imagine not," I said. "He knew what the ticket sales were. The auditorium was only about a third full."

"Such a shame. He's worked so hard," Alan said.

"Maybe the flyers and the radio ad will help some for the rest of the shows."

"Hopefully. Dick told Mr. Crane he had heard the radio spot, but he also pointed out that the commercial said, "*Starring* Shelby Berkett, *with* Jazz Monroe.'"

"Oh, dear."

"Yeah. Mr. Crane asked him not to mention the ad to Jazz."

"I wonder if he did," I said.

"Hard to say. I wish Dick hadn't brought it up. Anyway, Hank came back upstairs ready for his first scene. He said he noticed a hole in the trousers he wears as Carl, Claire's brother, and suggested he could just wear the same trousers he wears for the delivery boy. Mr. Crane said that was fine. I went back downstairs about ten minutes to seven. Since I don't go on until the end, I sat in our dressing room and played solitaire until intermission. When Hank came back to change clothes again, we both went upstairs to see how it was going. We were in the wings when the curtain went back up and Mr. Berkett died onstage."

"And that's where I came in," I said.

"Yes. It's all hard to believe," Alan said. "What do we do now?"

"Mr. Crockett's over there with his dog. Let's go ask him some questions."

"Okay."

We walked across the stage to where Jasper stood, comforting Pompom, who was a bit distraught at all the noise and confusion. I knelt and scratched the little dog behind the ears, and Alan did the same. Pompom licked both our hands and wagged his little tail.

"He likes you two," Jasper said.

"I'm glad. I like Pompom. I like all animals. I trust them more than most people."

Jasper nodded. "Yup, me too. What happened to Berkett?"

I got back up to my feet. "That's what we're trying to figure out. After you made the tea and put it in the teapot and the vial, were they out of your sight at any time?"

"No, they were both on my prop table. Mr. Holloway picked up the tea tray with the teapot just after the curtain went up on the second act, and Miss Monroe got the vial just before the curtain went up."

"So, before Mr. Holloway and Miss Monroe picked up the tea tray and vial, they were always in your view?"

"Yes sir."

"And no one went near them?"

"Not that I'm aware of. You think there was real poison in that vial? That's what folks are saying might have happened."

I sighed. "People do like to talk, don't they? I will say it's a possibility. I'd keep Pompom away from any of it that happened to spill."

"Oh I have been, believe me. Otherwise he'd be lapping it all up, wouldn't you, boy?"

We glanced down at the little dog Alan was still petting, and he wagged his tail enthusiastically.

Alan stood up and brushed himself off.

"I'd be heartbroken if something happened to Pompom, but Berkett? Well, I'd say justice has finally been served, in my opinion," Jasper said.

"That is indeed a matter of opinion," I said. "Alan will take your statement. He'll need to know your exact whereabouts, what you were doing before and during the show, that sort of thing."

"I've nothing to hide."

I glanced at Alan. "When you're finished, get statements from the rest of the cast and crew, too."

"All right. I'll record my own statement, too."

"If you insist."

"Mr. Crockett, you have a key to the theater and the prop room, don't you?" I said, turning back to him.

"Yes. Right here on my ring."

"May I have them? I want to secure them both."

He looked at me briefly, then struggled to take the keys off his ring before handing them over. "Mr. Crane has the only other set of keys."

"Thanks. I'll be sure and get them. For now, I'll leave you to your statement."

"Yes sir." I couldn't help but wonder what he was thinking as Alan led him off to the side to take notes.

I spied Oliver talking to Miss Monroe and walked up to him as she headed backstage once more, probably to look for Dick.

"Is she all right?" I said to him.

"She's had a shock, Heath. We all have." He looked ghastly.

"Alan will be taking statements from her and everyone else. When he's finished, they can all go home for the night. He'll need a statement from you, too."

"What happened to Shelby?"

"That is the question of the night, Oliver. Who has keys to the theater?"

"Just Jasper and I, why?"

"I want the place locked up tight tonight after everyone leaves. No one in, understand? Not you, not Jasper, not anyone."

"I can do that."

"Good. I already collected Jasper's keys from him, I'd like yours, too."

"Why? Don't you trust me?"

"It's not a matter of trust, Oliver, it's a matter of police work."

Oliver shrugged. "Suit yourself, but you'll need me to show you how to lock up. Lights have to be turned off, the front of the house secured, the alarm turned on—"

"All right," I said. "Once Alan's completed his interviews, you and I can lock up together. Then you give me the keys and go home until I call you, understand?"

"I don't like the sound of that, Heath. I know what happened to Shelby is terrible, but I need to get this show back up and running as soon as possible. Each night dark is lost revenue I can't afford."

"I promise I'll do my best, Oliver."

He sighed. "All right. I suppose that's all anyone can do."

CHAPTER EIGHT

Sunday morning, July 13, 1947

I didn't have a hangover the next morning, but my mind was spinning and I hadn't slept well. After a hot shower and a shave, two cups of strong, black coffee, and a banana, I retrieved the *Sentinel* from my doorstep and glanced at it. Shelby Berkett's death was on the front page. I set the newspaper aside, planning to read it later. I needed to call my mother and let her know there would be no matinee today. Fortunately for me, she had also seen the morning paper and was basically understanding, as long as I promised to take her somewhere nice soon. I hung up and dialed my aunt Verbina. She picked up on the second ring.

"Hello, Auntie."

"Heath, I've been waiting for your call. I couldn't sleep a wink last night. What on earth happened?"

"Did you see the morning *Sentinel?*"

"Of course I did, and I read every word. Shelby Berkett died onstage, and circumstances look suspicious, or something like that."

"Something like that indeed, Aunt 'Bina."

"Absolutely shocking. I suppose you can't talk about it."

"No, sorry. Police business."

"I figured you'd say that. Be careful, dear."

"I always am."

"I finally met your Mr. Keyes, anyway. He followed your orders to hustle me away and put me into a cab."

"I wanted to make sure you were out of harm's way. And from what I hear, you weren't alone in that cab."

"Mr. Keyes likes to gossip, doesn't he?"

"He's just being a good policeman, reporting what he sees."

"Well, Mr. Finch shared the cab with me, but that's all. We said good night out front of my building. We might be having lunch next week at his club. But enough about that—how did this Mr. Berkett die? Was it murder?"

"Circumstances look suspicious, but nothing has been determined at this time."

"And that's all you're going to say?"

"Afraid so."

"Humph. That Mr. Keyes wouldn't tell me anything last night, either."

"Like I said, he's a good policeman."

"He's also quite dashing. I've never seen such blue eyes."

"Oliver Crane, the director, has stunning blue eyes."

"Perhaps, but I bet he can't hold a candle in the looks department to that young policeman of yours. I can see why you find him so fetching."

"Auntie, I have a private line, but you don't," I said.

"Oh, yes. I keep forgetting. But I can usually hear if someone picks up. Anyway, I want to meet Alan Keyes properly soon, do you understand?"

"Yes ma'am. I'd like that."

"Good, so would I."

"I need to get going now. Crime doesn't wait on me."

"All right, dear, but keep me posted. And again, be careful. And tell Mr. Keyes to be careful, too."

I smiled. "I will do that." I hung up the phone, grabbed my hat, and headed to the station.

After checking in at the desk, my first stop was Cornelius Leslie Fletcher's office on two. I knew it was still early, but I hoped he had turned something up.

I rapped on the door and didn't wait for an answer as I went in. His office looked like more of a laboratory, with equipment, beakers, test tubes, and papers of all sorts strewn about in a disorderly fashion that I'm sure made sense only to him. The actual police lab was in the basement, just off the morgue. The morgue wasn't my favorite place, but Fletch seemed to love it down there. He was an odd fellow, but a good friend, and someone I could trust. He glanced up at me as I barged in, setting aside the microscope he was peering into and standing up straight to greet me.

"Morning, Heath."

"Good morning, Fletch. What's new?" I said, closing the door behind me.

"Well, I'm working on a beautiful Sunday morning, for one thing," he said sarcastically.

"Right, but as we always say, crime doesn't punch a clock."

"And neither do we, obviously. I understand you're officially on the Shelby Berkett case now. Nice work."

I grinned. "Thanks, but Green was actually relieved to have me take over since his daughter is sick."

"Yeah, I heard that, too. He called in today. It sounds like she's going to be okay, though. The fever broke early this morning."

"Glad to hear it. So, have you finished the autopsy?"

Fletch pushed his glasses back up his nose and looked directly at me. "You detectives seem to think I can just wave a magic wand and complete all the tests I need. Unfortunately, it's not that simple."

"Sorry. You know, I guess I don't really know. What exactly do you do, anyway?"

He crossed his arms and stared at me. "Well, thanks for

finally asking. Autopsies are time consuming and exact. They can't be rushed, no matter how much you may insist. I have to remove and dissect the chest, abdominal, and pelvic organs, sometimes even the brain, depending on what I'm looking for. Then I remove the rib cage and free the intestines by cutting along the attachment tissue. The connections to the esophagus, larynx, arteries and ligaments have to be severed, too. I also check the colon and test the bodily fluids, along with the blood, urine, and bile, for drugs, infections, and possible toxins and poisons. And I take tissue samples from just about all the organs, which have to be cataloged and tested individually. I also review and catalog the stomach contents. And that's just a small part of an autopsy."

I shuddered and felt a little sick. "Wowzer, I had no idea."

He shook his head. "No one ever does. Keep that in mind the next time you ask for a rush job. Since it's you, though, I did put in some extra hours. I got here early this morning while you slept in."

I smiled, knowing he was teasing me. "I have to get my beauty sleep, you know. I appreciate all you do, Fletch, and no one does it better than you."

"Flattery will get you everywhere, Detective. Of course, Taylor and Williams burned the midnight oil on this one also."

"Rick and Darren are top notch."

"Yes, they are," Fletch said. "By the way, Sargent Standish wants to know if this Berkett had any kin. He's having trouble locating his family."

"He was staying at the Wisconsin Hotel, but he's from New York City. I'd check with the director, Oliver Crane. I'm sure he has an emergency contact on file for him."

"Right. I'll pass that along," Fletch said, making a note on his pad.

"Good. In the meantime, how about telling me what you have found so far?"

"Actually, I was just studying the preliminary test results before you barged in. It was definitely poison."

"So, most likely murder. I figured as much."

"No, you didn't."

"I did. I'm not surprised in the least, Fletch."

"Because those doctors at the theater last night said they thought the death was suspicious?"

"Some, but also because of circumstances and experience," I said.

"Right, and I suppose you know the remains of the teapot and the teacup showed traces of poison, but not the vial."

"No, I didn't figure that. Interesting. So, the poison was in the teapot. What kind of poison was it?"

"Potassium cyanide. It's one of the fastest acting poisons around. It can kill a healthy adult human within a few minutes."

"That would make sense. Shelby did die fairly quickly after drinking the tea."

"Cyanide is nasty stuff, Heath. It works by preventing blood from carrying oxygen to the cells and blocking the uptake of oxygen already in the body."

I shuddered involuntarily. "Sounds like an awful way to die. Where would someone get something like that?"

"It's not restricted in the United States. It can be ordered from any laboratory or chemical supply company, even some pharmacies. It's used in gold mining, jewelry, photo developing, even dentistry."

"So, someone working in a pharmacy might have access to it?"

"Theoretically," Fletch said. "Depending on the pharmacy and what the person did there. Have a suspect in mind?"

"Perhaps. A fellow by the name of Henry Hawthorne. He works in a pharmacy, and he's in the play. He also had a grudge against Berkett."

"Sounds like a strong possibility."

"Agreed," I replied, wondering to myself if I wasn't intentionally trying to build a case against Hawthorne. "Anything else I should know about?"

"Once again, these things take time. Did I not make myself clear before?"

"Sorry. Patience may be a virtue, but it's not one of mine."

"I would never describe you as virtuous, Heath."

"Thanks. So, what else do you need to do?"

"Right now I'm waiting for Taylor to finish with that metal pillbox, so I can have a look at it, too."

"Okay, keep me posted on anything else that turns up, will you? When you find it, of course. No rush."

"Don't I always keep you posted?"

"Yes, you always do. I'll be in the briefing room with Officer Keyes."

"Of course you will."

I winked at him and went out, closing the door behind me. Alan was already in the briefing room, seated at the table in the center. And bless his soul, he had a pot of coffee on the sideboard just waiting for us.

"Morning, Officer," I said.

He glanced up and got to his feet. "Detective. Didn't you say to meet you at nine thirty?"

I looked over at the big wall clock, which read nine fifty. "Sorry about that. I stopped in to see Fletch first to see if he'd gotten any results back."

"And?"

"And we have another murder case on our hands, I'd say. Cyanide was found in Shelby's body, along with the teapot and teacup, but not the vial."

"Hmmm."

"My thoughts exactly. Is that coffee I smell?"

"Yeah, I had Rita brew us a pot. I'm already on my second cup. Want some?"

"Don't ask silly questions, just pour."

Alan smiled and picked up the pot. He turned one of the white ceramic mugs right side up and poured the lovely brown liquid into it before returning to the table. "I hope it's still hot enough."

"I'm sure it's fine," I said as I took the mug from him, took a swallow, and felt it go all the way down.

"So?"

"Hot enough."

Alan laughed. "Good, but I was asking about the poison in the teapot and cup."

"You tell me."

"Fair enough. Well, if the vial was clean, the poison had to come from the teapot."

"Excellent, you may make detective one day."

"I'm learning, Heath."

"You are. You have good instincts, and you're smarter than you think you are. The bigger question is, who put actual poison in the teapot and when?"

"Certainly Jazz Monroe had a motive," Alan said. "She hated Shelby Berkett for what he did to her, Jasper, and Alex twenty years ago, not to mention what he did to her the night of the party. He humiliated her in front of everyone and gave away her secret."

"We can't discount Jasper, either. Out of all the suspects, he had the most access to the teapot at any given time, which in my opinion makes him suspect number one."

"Yeah, I suppose so, it's just…"

I held up my hand. "Don't say it."

"He's such a nice man."

"You had to say it."

"Well, he *is*. He just doesn't seem capable of murder."

"I think we've been down this road before."

"I know. So, Jasper's a suspect, too. I must admit he hated Mr. Berkett enough to murder him."

"He made no secret of that. Who else had a motive?"

"Just about everyone, I'd say. But if they slipped into the prop room, they'd be taking a chance on Jasper catching them."

"Jasper's routine is pretty well known amongst the cast and crew, isn't it?" I said.

"Yeah, sure. Oh, I get it. Pretty much everyone knew he took Pompom out for a walk after he made the tea."

"Exactly. So who else is on our suspect list?"

"Well, Peter Holloway. He hated Berkett for taking the role of Roger away from Henry, which got him bumped down to the role of the butler. And he thought Shelby was having an affair with Eve."

"Eve Holloway is also a suspect."

"Why would *she* want to kill him?" Alan said. "I believe what she said about her just being kind to him and him taking it the wrong way."

"I believe it, too, I think. Maybe she'd just had enough of his type. Maybe she wanted to be sure he never tried anything in the future with a woman who wouldn't or couldn't fight back. Or maybe he did more to her than we're aware of."

"Wowzer. If so, she certainly had a motive," Alan said.

"Yes, and I can't say I blame her."

"Me neither. There's also Oliver Crane. He sure didn't seem to like Mr. Berkett since he was making everyone's life miserable. But that's a pretty weak reason for killing someone, and I know Mr. Crane is a friend of yours."

"Friends are still suspects until proven otherwise, you excluded."

"Okay, so Oliver Crane is on the list, too," Alan said.

"What's your opinion on Dick? He certainly had a motive. Shelby treated Jazz poorly over the years, and he virtually ignored Dick. That had to make Dick pretty angry once he found out who Shelby really was."

"Yeah, sure. But angry enough to kill his own father?"

"It's been done. Ask Shakespeare."

"I guess."

"That leaves Henry."

Alan looked at me with a queer expression, then glanced back down at his coffee cup. "You think so?"

"Why not? Shelby stole the role of Roger away from him, and then was attempting to steal the movie role away, too. Maybe Henry wanted to do away with the competition and even the score."

"That would be a motive, but he just doesn't seem the type."

"Not that again. Certainly not because you think he's too nice."

Alan shook his head. "No. Hank can be a bit mean spirited at times, I admit."

"Then because he's young and handsome, is that it? And because he flatters you?"

Alan looked up at me then, hard. "He doesn't flatter me. He likes me, and I like him."

I didn't say anything for a moment as we stared at each other. "There's something else. You told me Hawthorne works at Lempke's Pharmacy in West Allis."

"Yeah, so what?"

"Cyanide isn't exactly an everyday poison. Someone working in a pharmacy may have had access to it."

"*May* have."

"More so than any of the others, it would seem. So, is Henry Hawthorne a suspect or not?"

Alan slowly came around. "Yeah, I guess he is. He could have done it, I suppose."

"Good, I agree."

"But I don't think he did. He wasn't near the prop room before the curtain went up, remember? Any of the others could have slipped in and added the poison to the teapot before the show, but Hank and Mr. Berkett were elsewhere."

"That's true," I said, as much as I hated to admit it.

"But Jasper always keeps the prop room locked. If the poison was added to the teapot in there, how would any of them have gotten in?"

I rubbed my chin. "Good question. Who has keys besides Jasper?"

Alan scratched his head. "Hmm, well, Mr. Crane does, and Dick, I'm pretty sure. I think that's it. Just those three."

"Just those three. So only Oliver, Dick, and Jasper, huh?"

"I guess that limits your suspect list quite a bit, Heath. Just those three. And Miss Monroe, I suppose, since she could have used Dick's key."

"Right. Unless..."

"Unless what?"

"Hmmm? Oh, I'm just thinking about Dick. Dick, Dick, Dick."

"Huh?"

"I'm trying to remember back to the party Friday night. Something about Dick and his keys."

"What about them?"

"Shh, give me a moment." I closed my eyes. "Dick's keys. Peter wanted Dick to move his car so he and Eve could leave, correct?"

"Yeah, that's right. Dick had parked Mr. Holloway in."

"Yes. And Dick had to get his keys from the dresser in the bedroom."

"Sure, I remember that. Then Peter took the keys and moved Dick's car, or rather Jazz's car."

"Interesting."

"Why?" Alan said, cocking his head.

"Because that means everyone at that party had access to Dick's keys. Anyone could have slipped into the bedroom and removed the key to the prop room without being noticed."

"But wouldn't Dick have noticed the key was missing?"

"I imagine he has quite a few keys on that ring. The car

ignition, the trunk, a key to their apartment, probably, the supply room, and God knows what else. Chances are he wouldn't have missed it. Or maybe someone even took the key and left the party to have a key made and then put it back. There's also that missing putty. Hmmm. Henry made a vodka run."

"Heath…"

"I'm just theorizing, Alan, not accusing anyone. Though Henry did admit to leaving the apartment for a short time, didn't he?"

"Yes, but—"

"You said yourself he's a suspect. So, if someone did take the key or had a copy made…"

"They would have been able to slip in to the prop room easily once Jasper left with Pompom," Alan said. "Except Mr. Berkett and Hank weren't over there before the curtain, remember?"

I looked at him, annoyed. "As you keep saying. Conspicuous by their absence, perhaps."

"Perhaps," Alan said, staring at me, his mouth tight.

"Well, for now we'll focus on everyone else. What exactly were the rest of them all up to?" I said as I poured myself another cup of coffee and took a seat at the table.

Alan sat down across from me and flipped open his notebook. All I saw was chicken scratchings, but I knew it was shorthand.

"According to her statement, Miss Monroe had come to get her candelabra that she uses in the first scene, but she said Jasper wasn't there yet, so she used the bathroom. When she came out, Jasper and Pompom had returned from their walk and were talking to Dick. Per Dick's statement, he had finished cleaning the auditorium and had put his cleaning equipment away in the supply room. He was going to go down to the basement and had just gotten to the top of the stairs when Jasper and Pompom came in from the alley, so he stopped to talk to them. Mr. Holloway said after he finished with makeup and wardrobe, he stretched out on the sofa there and closed his eyes."

"Or passed out."

"More likely, I guess. He did seem pretty intoxicated when Mr. Crane and Dick tried to rouse him."

"It could have been an act."

"You think so?"

"I'm told he's a pretty good actor when he's sober," I said. "What was Oliver Crane up to that close to curtain?"

Alan flipped a few pages ahead, studied the page for a moment, and then read aloud. "He said, and I quote, 'I went to my office to make a phone call. I was only in there five or six minutes.'"

"Did he say who he phoned?"

"No sir, he didn't. I should have asked him, I suppose."

"That's all right. Remind me to follow up on that. And what was Eve Holloway up to? Why was she there? She doesn't come on until later. I would think she would have still been in her dressing room."

Alan consulted his notebook once more. "She said she was coming to check on her husband, as he hadn't looked too well when they first arrived, and it was obvious he had been drinking and/or had taken a few pills."

"Again, *apparently* drinking and/or taken pills. Didn't you say they weren't speaking to each other?"

"Yes. They certainly weren't when they first arrived."

"Yet she took the time to come over and check on him. Interesting. So, that's the lot of them."

"I believe so, sir."

"And Oliver and Dick both helped Peter to his feet, causing his supposedly missing pillbox to fall to the floor."

"That's right."

"You said Oliver surmised it must have slipped out of Peter's pocket and between the cushions when Peter was lying there a day or so ago."

"Yes, it makes sense," Alan said.

"Maybe because someone wants it to make sense. And

Oliver locked the empty pillbox away in his office. Was it empty the last time Peter saw it?"

"He seemed to keep it pretty full. But maybe he forgot he took all the pills."

"Maybe so. Or maybe it's more smoke and mirrors."

"Sorry?"

"Just wondering if everything that happened was smoke and mirrors to cover up something else."

"But what?"

"That remains to be seen. Make a note to ask Oliver and Peter more about that pillbox, too."

"Right." Another shorthand scratch went into the notepad.

"So, in the ten minutes or so that Jasper and Pompom were out in the alley, Oliver, Peter, Eve, Jazz, or Dick could have slipped into the prop room and poisoned the teapot."

"Yes, I suppose any of them could have."

"And I'm still not discounting Henry, whether you like it or not. Even Jasper still could have done it. In fact, Jasper would have had the easiest time of it."

"Fine, sure, I suppose so. Heck, even I could have, I guess."

"Let's leave that out of the official notes, okay?"

"I just don't want to be treated any differently," he said, looking at me with those puppy dog eyes.

I looked at him directly. "Did you murder Shelby Berkett?"

"Gosh, no! I'd never!"

I leaned back. "Good, I believe you."

"Why?" Alan said, a slight smirk on his face.

"Because."

"Because why?"

"Because I know you, that's why."

"And because I'm a nice guy who doesn't seem capable of murder?"

"All right, Officer, touché. But I know you far better than you know Jasper and Henry, so just leave yourself out of the record."

"Whatever you say, Detective."

"Besides, you're innocent until proven guilty, and I have a strong feeling someone else is going to be proven guilty."

"Who?"

"I have my suspicions. And speaking of that, what *was* Mr. Hawthorne doing during all of this commotion, since you keep reminding me he wasn't near the prop room? You said he was probably in the dressing room. Why did it take him so much longer to get dressed than you?"

Alan flipped a few more pages in his notebook and read aloud. "He said he was inspecting his costumes. That's when he noticed the hole in his pants that he wears as the brother."

"And what time was that?"

"Well, I left him about ten after six, so from then until he came up to talk to me and Mr. Crane about the pants, I guess."

"So, about fifteen minutes. Interesting. I believe Oliver said you can get from one side of the stage to the other by going through the basement, correct?"

"Yeah, that's right."

"Hmmm." I drained the second cup of coffee, got up and set it back on the sideboard as the phone on the table rang.

I picked it up on the second ring. "Barrington here."

"It's Fletch, Heath. We've got some more results for you."

"Let's hear them."

"The prints on that metal pillbox are from Oliver Crane and Peter Holloway. And it definitely had traces of cyanide in it."

I raised my eyebrows. "Really."

"You mean you didn't figure it did?"

"Wise guy. How much of a trace, Fletch? Enough to kill someone?"

"I don't think so, but maybe. It doesn't take much."

"Right. Anything else?"

"Not much in the way of prints on the prop room door, just Jasper Crockett's and some that were smudged beyond identification. The vial had Jazz Monroe's, Alan Keyes's, and

Jasper's prints on it, no one else's. We found Shelby Berkett's, Jazz Monroe's, and Jasper Crockett's prints on the teapot fragments. Just thought you'd want to know."

"Always. I owe you big-time for the rush job, Fletch."

"I'm keeping score."

"I know you are."

He laughed. "If anything else turns up, I'll let you know. Oh, and Sergeant Standish reached Oliver Crane at home. Mr. Crane said Berkett's contact info is on file in his office at the theater, and he said you have the keys."

"I do indeed." I checked my pocket watch. "Tell Standish to tell Mr. Crane Officer Keyes and I will meet him in the alley behind the theater at the stage door at twelve thirty. I'll be sure and get the contact information to Standish."

"Will do. See ya, Heath."

"See ya, Fletch, and thanks again."

I hung up the phone and filled Alan in on what Fletch had told me.

"What does it all mean, Heath?"

"I'm not sure yet, but we have just enough time to get to the main library on Wisconsin Avenue and do some research on cyanide before we have to meet Oliver."

"Research?"

"It pays to know what we're dealing with. Ready to roll?"

"As I always say, if you're waiting for me, you're wasting your time!"

CHAPTER NINE

Early Sunday afternoon, July 13, 1947

We finished at the main library and headed to the theater, parking once again on Michigan Street. It was a short walk from there to the alley, which ran through to Everett Street in the next block, a convenient thoroughfare for trash collection, deliveries, and service vehicles. It was well-lit from the afternoon sun this time of day. Alan and I walked to the stage door, where Oliver was already leaning against the rusted metal railing that bordered the stoop on three sides. As we climbed the steps to meet him, he smiled, discarded a cigarette onto the concrete landing, and ground it out with his shoe.

"Nice to see you again, Heath, Alan."

I tipped my hat. "Thanks for meeting us here, Oliver. The station needs Mr. Berkett's contact information and his next of kin."

"Yeah, that's what the fellow on the phone said."

"Are you aware of any family he may have had?"

He shook his head. "He never spoke of anyone to me, anyway. But we didn't talk much off the stage. I've got his file in my office. Shall we go in?"

"Let's." I handed him the keys, and he opened the door, turning on the lights as we stepped into the dark interior. Using another key, he disengaged the alarm bell and closed the door behind us as he pushed his fedora back on his head, revealing a shock of his snow-white hair. It was eerily silent as we glanced about, and it gave me an uneasy feeling, though nothing had changed since the night before.

"My office is on the other side, as you may remember. Probably easier and quicker if we go across the set." Oliver flicked some more levers in a panel on the wall, turning on additional lights before stepping through the doorway onto the stage. "This way."

I removed my hat and followed along behind, with Alan bringing up the rear, his hat also in hand. The spooky set did nothing to allay my uneasiness. We walked past the chalk outline of Shelby's body on the floor, surrounded by dried tea stains and shards of ceramic pieces the lab boys didn't take. We hadn't gone far when I heard Alan gasp behind me, and I turned to find him staring up at the stairs on the set that led to the scaffolding.

"What is it?" I said. He had dropped his hat and stopped dead in his tracks. "You look as shaken as a good martini."

Alan looked at me, clearly startled. "I like my martinis stirred."

"A good martini has vodka and a pickle," I said. "Shaken or stirred doesn't matter all that much."

"You're both wrong," Oliver said. "A good martini has gin and two olives. So what did you see?"

Alan pointed to the stairs of the set. "I thought I saw someone or something on the stairway landing of the set," he said as he picked up his hat and brushed it off.

The three of us looked where he'd pointed, but there was nothing there, at least not that I could tell.

"What did you see?" I said.

"I'm not sure, exactly. It was gray and misty, dark. The size of a man almost," Alan said softly.

I felt a shiver run down my spine.

"It's gone now, if it was ever there. Maybe I'm seeing things," he said.

"Maybe. It's a tad creepy here, especially with only minimal lights on. I'm sure all our imaginations are running wild," I said. As a precaution, I walked back, climbed a few of the steps, and looked about, but I didn't see anything. The prop portraits on the fake walls stared down at us glumly, but other than that the place appeared empty.

"I guess I was mistaken," Alan said, and I could tell he was embarrassed.

"Might have been a shadow or a bird that got in somehow."

"Would have had to have been an awfully big bird," Alan said.

"The shadow of a bird, perhaps, or a bat from up in the scaffolding and catwalks. Or a cloud of dust."

Oliver took a few steps back and looked around. "I didn't see or hear anything, and I don't see or hear anything now. There's no one here but the three of us," he said.

Alan looked at him. "I know. It was just for a moment. I could swear he was there…"

"Who?" I said, instinctively feeling for my revolver but leaving it holstered.

Alan shook his head. "I don't know. I'm not sure why I said that."

"You're thinking of Alexander Lippencott, aren't you?" I said.

Alan looked sheepish. "Maybe. You can't discount those things, despite what you believe or don't believe. But if something or someone was there, it's gone now."

"All right, then, let's keep moving," I said.

Oliver turned around and led us across the stage and down the hall to his office. We waited as he unlocked the door, turned on the light, and ushered us in, placing his hat on a hook next to the door.

I must admit I was glad when Oliver closed the door behind us and we were safely in the coziness of his office. I think Alan was even happier.

"The theater can be an eerie place sometimes," Oliver said, as he went behind his desk to a bank of battered old oak file cabinets.

"Yeah, I noticed," Alan said, taking a seat in one of the chairs as I took the other, our hats on our laps.

"Well anyway, I keep the cast member files in here—their contracts, bios, photos, and legal papers, including emergency contact information." He pulled open a drawer marked "A–C" and extracted a folder he put on the desk. "This is Berkett's," he said, sitting down across from us.

"May I?" I said, reaching for it.

Oliver drew it closer to him. "Sorry, Heath. I can give you the contact information, but I can't allow you to have the whole file, unless you have a court order, of course."

I withdrew my hand. "Fair enough. No court order for now, so tell me what's in there."

Oliver turned on the green glass banker's lamp on the desktop and opened the file, flipping through the first few pages as I did my best to have a look upside down at the contents. I noticed there were headshots and bio sheets on Shelby, lots of legal-looking documents and contracts, and then, finally, the personal information page.

"He lists his permanent address as 422 West Sixty-third Street, New York, New York. For next of kin he wrote 'None,'" Oliver said.

"Gee, really?" Alan said.

"That's what he put. I remember him telling me his parents died when he was a teenager, and he was an only child. The contact person is a Merle Babcock, Shelby's agent. There's a phone number and an address in Brooklyn listed."

"I'll need you to write the phone number and address down if you don't mind."

"Sure, that's fine." He reached into his top desk drawer and took out a piece of stationery and a pencil, and jotted the information down, sliding it across to desk to me. "Anything else I can help you with?"

I put the paper in my suit pocket. "Now that you mention it, I would like to ask you a few questions."

"Oh? What about?"

"Last night, for starters."

"Sure, ask away. Want a drink? I can't manage a martini, shaken or stirred, but I do have this, you may remember." He pulled open one of the bottom drawers of his desk and extracted the bottle of bourbon, a third full. "I still don't have any ice, though. And only two glasses."

I shook my head. "That's all right. It's too early, and we're on official business anyway."

He raised his thin white eyebrows. "I see." He put the bottle back in the drawer and closed it. "I don't think I like the sound of that."

"Not sure how else to say it, Oliver. I know we go back a ways, but this is business. You can understand that."

"Of course. But what's this about? You both seem so serious."

"We *are* serious. Alan's going to be taking some notes as we talk, if you don't mind." Alan had put his hat on the desktop and extracted his pencil and notebook from his inside pocket.

Oliver looked from me to Alan and then back to me. "Talk about what?"

"Last night."

"You said that already. What about it?"

"You told Alan you went to your office here about six fifteen to make a phone call."

"That's right, I think. Only it was more like six ten. Besides making the call, I wanted to listen to my radio spot at thirteen after."

"Who did you call?"

"My brother, Wally. He hadn't shown up yet, and I was getting worried."

"Where was he?"

"He had car trouble. I didn't reach him, but he showed up just before curtain."

"How long were you in here?" I said.

"I don't know. Five minutes, maybe. Why?"

"Just curious. Did you close your office door?"

"Yes, I always do. Habit, I guess."

"But you said before that sometimes when you're in the theater alone, the door seems to close on its own, meaning it was left open. You attributed it to the building settling."

Oliver appeared flustered. "Well, sure, sometimes when I'm here alone I leave the door open. The theater can be spooky, as we said before. But I always close it when there are people about. For privacy, you know. Just like it's closed now."

"Right. Were there people about last night? Did you see anyone on your way to your office?"

He shook his head. "No, not exactly. Everyone was getting ready for the show, I suppose. I'm not sure where they all were."

"I see. And what about Peter Holloway?"

"What about him? Peter was passed out on the sofa when I came back out of my office."

"So, he wasn't there when you went in?"

"No, I don't think so. I didn't notice him, anyway. I had been up front in the ticket office, hoping for some last-minute sales. That's when I realized Wally hadn't shown up yet, so I decided to go to my office and call him. I went into the auditorium, up on the stage, behind the curtain, and back here. I guess I didn't really look toward the dock door. Peter may have been lying there. He kind of blends in with his black butler livery."

"But you did notice him when you came out of your office," I said as Alan scribbled away.

"That's right. In the short time I was in here, it seems the whole cast materialized."

"So, you and Dick tried to help Peter to his feet, his pillbox fell to the ground, and you thought it fell from between the sofa cushions?"

"Yes, that's right. Where else would it have come from?"

"Maybe one of Peter's pockets?"

"Maybe, except Peter told us it had disappeared, and he seemed amazed to have it turn up, so why would it have been in his pocket? Unless he was putting me on."

"A possibility. So, you picked it up after it hit the floor."

"I wasn't going to just leave it there. I opened it and noticed it was empty and had an odd odor about it. Peter wanted it back, but I figured it would be better locked in my office until after the show."

"Even though it was empty?"

"I didn't want him dropping it onstage. He did that once during one of the rehearsals. It makes quite a noise when it hits the ground."

"I imagine so."

"Alan can tell you it's quite loud. Right, Alan?"

"That's right, Mr. Crane," Alan said, looking up briefly from his notebook, pencil still on the page.

"I'm not disputing that, Oliver. Was the pillbox empty when it went missing?"

"Apparently not. When I opened it, Peter asked what had happened to all his pills. Of course, he may have taken them all and just forgotten."

"That's possible. The lab reports were conclusive that Shelby died from poisoning, by the way."

Oliver's white face looked ashen. "So the rumors are true. I kept thinking it must have been a heart attack or a stroke. Who would poison him? I mean, he wasn't well liked but...hey, wait a minute, is this what this is all about? Do you think *I* killed him?"

"I'm not saying that, but since you brought it up, did you?"

He laughed nervously. "You're kidding, right?"

"Unfortunately, I'm not."

"Everyone's a suspect, is that it?" he said.

"Yes."

"Including me." He looked nervous and paler than usual, his skin the color of milk. He undid his shirt collar and loosened his tie.

"You had opportunity and motive, Oliver. I can't play favorites, I'm sorry."

"But it doesn't make sense, Heath. Think about it. Why would I kill my star performer on opening night? I told you before I have a lot invested in this show. Without Shelby Berkett, I'm not even sure I *can* reopen. I may be crazy, but I'm not insane. Sure, I admit I didn't care for him, but I don't think that makes for much of a motive."

"Right, right. I thought about that, but as I said, I must consider everyone until proven otherwise."

"Well, I can think of several other people who had the opportunity and a much stronger motive than mine."

"Such as?"

Oliver took out his handkerchief and wiped his brow. "Jazz Monroe, for one. I should think that would be obvious."

"Yes, and Jasper, of course."

"That's true, but I've known them both a long time. Jasper hated Berkett with a passion, but I just don't see him killing anyone, no matter how much of a motive he may have."

"But you could see Jazz doing it?"

"I didn't say that."

"Not directly," I said. "I would like to pay Jazz a visit and talk to Jasper. Do you have their addresses?"

He wiped his neck next, then put his handkerchief back in his pocket. "Sure, sure. Jazz lives on the east side, not too far from my place, and Jasper only lives a couple blocks from the theater." He went back to the file cabinets, got the information, and handed it to me.

"Thanks. We're all finished here, I think," I said, putting their addresses in my other coat pocket.

"I hope I'm not," Oliver said, turning off the banker's lamp on his desktop. "I'm picking up Jasper after I leave here, since he lives close by. We're going to go back to my place and run through some ideas."

Alan and I got to our feet and Oliver followed suit. He put Jazz's folder away and closed the cabinet drawer before walking us to the door.

"Ideas for the show, you mean?" I said.

"Yes, he's my friend and sounding board. I take care of him. He doesn't have much." He opened the door and the three of us stepped into the darkened hall as he turned off the overhead light and took his hat off the hook. "If we can keep the show going, it will be easier to keep him on payroll."

"What happens to *Death Comes to Lochwood* remains to be seen," I said. "A lot depends on who killed Shelby Berkett."

Oliver locked the door behind us. "I have a lot invested in this show, Heath. Not just money, which is considerable for me, but my time and my heart. Besides, it's my brother's first play, so that makes it even more personal, if that makes any sense."

"It makes a lot of sense," Alan said.

"Thanks. I'm glad *you* understand, Alan." He shot me a look that hurt, but I ignored it as best I could. Being a police detective was hard sometimes.

The three of us headed back down the hall single file, but we hadn't gotten far when we were stopped suddenly in our tracks by a loud, piercing noise. Alan covered his ears with his hands as the three of us glanced about, trying to determine the source.

I took a few steps forward. "What's in there?" I said, raising my voice above the noise as I pointed to a door on my right. "It seems like that's where it may be coming from."

"The supply room," Oliver said, "and there is a radiator in there. It may just be air in the pipes."

"Is the door locked?"

"Always, but I have a key."

"Open it," I said.

I took my revolver from its holster beneath my sport coat as I nodded to Alan. Alan moved Oliver off to the side once Oliver had unlocked the door. I turned the knob and pushed the door open, flattening myself against the hall wall. The noise stopped as abruptly as it had started. I paused and waited, my eye on the doorway, but nothing was forthcoming, so I felt for a light switch.

I flicked it on and swung into the door frame. I dropped to a crouch, my gun in both hands in front of me, but there was no one in the room. I got to my feet and holstered my gun.

"All clear," I said. Alan released Oliver, and they both stepped into the light and looked into the room with me. It was more of a large closet, maybe six by ten, with shelves on the left side filled with bottles, jugs, sponges, toilet paper, and toweling. On the right side stood a row of brooms, mops, and buckets. I walked over to the iron radiator at the rear of the room and felt it with the back of my hand. "Ice cold," I said.

"The heat's off," Oliver said.

"Right, so what caused that noise?"

"Old building, odd noises. It happens all the time," Oliver said. "Might have been rats fighting inside one of the walls."

I was doubtful but nodded just the same as I glanced about. One of the brooms seemed out of place, set closer to the front door than the rest. I examined it and noticed something sticky on the end of the handle.

"Curious," I said, putting it back carefully. "There's a sticky substance on the end of it."

Alan had a look. "Sticky? From what?"

"Not sure. Glue or tape maybe." I smelled my fingers, but that test was inconclusive.

"I wonder," I said, more to myself than to either of them.

"What do you wonder?" Alan said.

"Did the lab crew check this room?"

"I don't think so, it's just a supply closet."

"Still, this seems odd to me. I think you better call the station and get the boys down here again. I want to make sure nothing has been overlooked."

"Yes sir. May I use your phone, Mr. Crane?"

"Certainly," he replied, unlocking his office door once more as I continued to inspect the closet, inch by inch.

Alan and Oliver returned momentarily. "Crew's on the way," Alan said. "Shouldn't be more than twenty minutes."

I looked at my pocket watch. "I sometimes marvel at the efficiency of the Milwaukee Police Department."

"I agree. Find anything else?"

"No, but maybe they will. Who all has the key to this room, Oliver?"

"I do, of course, along with Jasper and Dick. It's the same key that opens the prop room."

Alan and I exchanged looks.

"Interesting. Let's go back out to the stage door and wait for the lab crew. I think I've seen enough here." As I turned to leave, something shiny caught my eye, wedged between two paint cans on a shelf near the door. I extracted it carefully.

"What's that?" Alan said.

"A hand mirror, a compact. Look familiar, Oliver?"

Oliver gave it the once over as I held it gingerly. "Seems to fit the description of the one that went missing from Eve's dressing room."

"Hmmm. And it's sticky, just like the broom handle. Curious indeed."

"What do you think that means?" Alan said.

"I don't know, but let's go let the lab crew in." We all stepped out into the hall and I closed the door, leaving the mirror behind on the shelf where I found it.

"What are you thinking?" Oliver said. "What's it all about? Or maybe I don't want to know."

"Maybe *you* don't, Oliver, but I do."

The three of us headed down the hall then and back onto the stage.

"I'm sorry about all this, Oliver, I really am. I know you had a lot invested in this play, and I'm sorry all this happened. Sorry for Shelby, sorry for you, sorry for whoever the murderer is."

"Thanks, Heath. I appreciate that. I wasn't sure I could reopen without Shelby, but I think I can still make it work. I'm sure Henry will be more than willing to take over the role of Roger, and Peter can take over the role of the inspector. Alan, maybe you could take over the role of the butler. I can find someone else to play the policeman."

Alan grinned as we walked across the stage, the mystery vision on the stairs from earlier apparently forgotten.

"Before any of that can happen, we have a murder to solve," I said, "and if it's one of your other cast members, I'm not so sure you'll be able to reopen."

"You always were the voice of reason," Oliver said glumly.

"Just doing my job. I intend to find the murderer no matter who it is." I swallowed hard, avoiding his gaze. *Even if it's you*, I added silently to myself.

True to their word, the lab boys showed up not more than fifteen minutes later. We retraced our steps to the supply room as I filled them in on what had transpired. I asked them to give the room the once-over, specifically the broom handle and mirror, which I wanted dusted for fingerprints. As they went to work, I decided to poke my head into the prop room directly across the hall.

"You said it's the same key for this door as the supply room?"

"Yes. It just makes it easier," Oliver said.

"Open it up for me, will you? That noise might have been coming from in there. The hall is so narrow it was hard to tell."

Oliver unlocked the prop room door and stepped back as I turned the knob. The overhead light was already on. A musty smell hung in the air. The room was much larger than the supply room, filled with shelves and drawers full of all sorts of odd things, including clocks, telephones, books, boxes, vases, artificial flowers, glassware, cups, saucers, and small statues. On the left was a slop sink, a glass pitcher resting inside it. The faucet's slow drip plunked steadily down into the now-full pitcher. A large container of sugar rested on a shelf above the sink. On the far wall stood a small metal desk. On the desk's surface were a green felt blotter, large notebook, a pencil to the left of the notebook, and a radio, which was softly playing. Oliver and Alan had followed me in, leaving the door ajar.

"Maybe that noise we heard before came from the radio," Alan said, looking at me.

"Perhaps." I walked over to the radio and turned up the volume knob quite high. The sounds of a big band came booming out, followed by a man's voice.

"This is WBSM, the WB network. And now, a word from today's sponsor, Spritely Travel. Let Spritely Travel take you away to sunny Orlando, Florida, this winter." As the commercial began, I went back out into the hall and closed the door. Then I stepped back in and turned the volume down.

"I couldn't hear it out there at all, even with the sound turned up, so I don't think that was the noise we heard. I'm mystified as to what it was," I said.

"Old buildings, like I said before," Oliver said. "Maybe rats. I have seen a few here and there. Jasper sets out traps, but they don't do much good. He's worried Pompom will get into them, so he only puts them in out-of-the-way places. I should get a cat or two."

"Right. Cats are good company, too. Does Jasper keep the radio and the light on all the time, Oliver?" I said.

"No, he usually turns them off before he goes home. But you took his keys last night, so he couldn't get back in here."

"I left his keys at the station for safekeeping. What's in the notebook on the desk?"

"Jasper keeps track of all the props, including what shows they were used in, who used them, all that stuff, and where they're stored. It may look like organized chaos in here, but he has his own unique system."

"Does anyone else make notes in the ledger besides Jasper?"

Oliver shook his head. "He's pretty territorial about those things. Besides, no one else would even know where to begin."

"I see." I flipped through the notebook but, as Oliver had said, it might as well have been written in a foreign language. I set it back down and noticed a small wicker basket on the floor next to the desk, filled with a small, plump green and blue plaid cushion. "Pompom's?"

"That's right. Always by his side. The radio is more for Pompom than Jasper. Jasper says it soothes him."

"The things people do for their dogs. Where did Jasper normally keep the teapot when the play wasn't going on?"

"On the shelf right here by the door."

The wooden shelf had a small ring the size of the teapot lid to the left of where the teapot must have been sitting. "That must be where the murderer set the top down when he or she filled the teapot with the poison."

"What makes you think that?" Alan said.

"I imagine when Jasper put the teapot away after each performance or rehearsal, he would rinse it out and place it on the shelf here. When he filled it before each performance, he would fill it at the sink, where the sugar is, removing the lid over by the sink, not on the shelf. Something to ask him about, anyway."

I looked about once more but couldn't see anything out of place, so I turned off the radio and left, Oliver and Alan following, just as one of the lab guys was coming out of the supply closet.

"We're all finished, Detective. We dusted the broom handle and mirror for prints and took a sample of the sticky substance for analysis downtown. We photographed everything, too, just in case."

"Good, thanks. Did you notice anything else?"

"No sir. Just your usual mops, buckets, soap, sponges, brooms, and whatnot."

I fished the contact information from Oliver out of my

pocket. "Okay, give this to Sergeant Standish. Tell him it's from me, and he'll know what's it for."

"Yes sir." The other lab tech came out of the closet carrying the sample in question, along with his camera.

"One more thing," I said. "In the prop room, there is a ledger with a pencil to the left of it on the desk against the wall. Take the pencil and ledger downtown and give them the once-over."

The one with the camera looked at the other one, then back at me. "Sure thing, Detective. Have something in mind?"

"Maybe. Too soon to tell."

The one with the camera shrugged as the other fellow entered and carefully retrieved the pencil and book. When he had them secured, I turned out the light and closed the door, instructing Oliver to lock both rooms up.

The five of us exited the building. "I'll expect a full report as soon as you have it, boys," I said.

"Will do, Detective. Shouldn't take long," the taller one said as they put on their hats and got in their car.

I turned back to Oliver. "Thanks again for meeting us here."

"You're welcome. Please keep me posted. You know where to find me," he said, handing me back the key ring.

"I do. See ya."

"See ya," Oliver said. He looked worried and tired.

When Alan and I were back in my car, I turned it toward downtown. "Let's get some lunch before we visit Jazz. I'm feeling a bit peckish."

"Good idea. I'm starved!"

I laughed. "Hardly starved, but I know what you mean."

CHAPTER TEN

Later Sunday afternoon, July 13, 1947

Art's diner was just over the bridge downtown on Water Street. I found a parking spot almost directly in front, since most of the businesses and shops are closed on Sundays.

As we approached the door, Alan and I tipped our hats to two elderly women walking arm in arm down the broad sidewalk, probably on their way home from church. A bell jingled when we entered. We had the place to ourselves, so we hung our hats on a hook near the jukebox and chose a booth by the large plate glass window. The smell of burnt coffee and bacon grease hung heavy in the air, moved about slightly by a rusting ceiling fan hanging down precariously.

Eventually, a tired-looking waitress whose name tag read "Betty" came over with a pot of coffee, a bead of sweat on her brow, her apron stained and worn.

Alan and I turned over our cups, which she filled accordingly before handing us menus.

"Cream, sugar?" she said without emotion or inflection.

"No, we both take it black," Alan said.

"Fine by me. The last fella in here left his newspaper behind. You want it?"

"Sure," I said, smiling. She didn't smile back.

"Right." She shuffled away, returning after a while with the morning *Sentinel*. She handed it to me and put two glasses of water on the table. "Here's the front page, anyway. The evening *Journal*'s not out yet. Ready to order?"

I glanced at Alan and he nodded. We both ordered the tuna fish sandwich on rye and a slice of cherry pie, made fresh from Door County cherries, according to the menu.

"Anything else?"

"No, thank you, Betty, that will do it," I said, swatting a fly away with my menu.

She gazed blankly at me, order pad in hand, chewing her gum. "I'm not Betty. My name's Alane. Betty quit last week, and I lost my name tag. So I wear hers."

"I see."

"Alane," she said. "Not a road, not a street, but Alane, get it?"

"Got it, Alane."

"Good." She picked up our menus and walked away, her pencil tucked back behind her ear.

Alan smiled at me as I raised my eyebrows and shook my head. I took a sip of my coffee and opened the newspaper on the table, wiping away a drop of grape jelly the previous customer had spilled on it.

"I didn't have time to read it this morning, but I saw the headline," I said. "Below the fold, but still front page."

"What's it say?" Alan picked up his cup and blew on it.

I read the headline aloud. "'*Death Comes to Lochwood* comes true. Actor Shelby Berkett dies onstage in front of audience in a real-life death scene at the Davidson Theater last night.' There's a big picture of Mr. Berkett, too, though it looks a few years old."

"Jeepers."

"Yup. It goes on to say the cause of death is being investigated, but circumstances seem unusual. Well, they're right there."

"Yeah."

I glanced again at Shelby Berkett's face in the paper. "I see someone blacked out some of his teeth with a pencil. Probably the same chap with the grape jelly."

Alan peered at the picture from the opposite side of the table. "Suits him."

I laughed.

"He was a nice-looking fellow, though," Alan said. "Except for that bad hairpiece."

"True enough. By the way, my aunt thinks you're pretty dashing."

He blushed. "She didn't get a good look at me."

"Oh, don't be so modest. My auntie has superb taste in men. It runs in the family," I said quietly so as not to be overheard by Alane.

"That's sweet of her, and of you, thanks," he replied shyly.

Alane brought our sandwiches and pie over and shuffled away once more, her right hand on her lower back as she groaned and moaned.

We ate in silence for a while as I read the rest of the newspaper article to myself. When Alan was finished with his sandwich and had started in on his pie, I set the paper aside.

"How was it?" I said, brushing the persistent fly away again.

"The sandwich? It was okay, a little dry. Yours?"

"The same. You going to eat that pickle?"

Alan smiled. "My pickle is your pickle, Detective."

I smiled back as I reached over and took it off his plate. When I had finished that, I started on my pie too, as Alane came by with more coffee.

When she had shuffled away again, still groaning, Alan spoke. "So, I've been wondering. Why did you want them to investigate the pencil and the journal?"

"Just a hunch. According to what I read at the library, potassium cyanide is an innocent-looking white solid, a crystal similar in texture to sugar."

"Not a liquid."

"So, how would the killer transport the poison? It's lethal, even in small doses."

"The pill case!"

"Yes, we know it had traces of the cyanide in it."

"But what does that have to do with the pencil and journal?"

"I was just thinking if I was in the prop room with the clock ticking, what would I do? I'd take the lid off the teapot and set it on the shelf next to it. Maybe I'd pick the teapot up and look into it."

"Why?"

"To make sure the tea was in it."

"That makes sense."

"Yes, and if it was, I would set it back on the shelf and drop in the cyanide crystals."

"Go on," Alan said.

"But if the tea was cold or even room temperature at best, the crystals might not dissolve fast enough, so I'd look around for something to stir the tea with. Time is of the essence, and the opening of the teapot is small. I glance about and spot the pencil on the desk."

"I see, of course. The killer would have stirred it with the pencil."

"Perhaps. It's one of my working theories at the moment, anyway."

"But what about the journal?"

"Still thinking about that."

"So, who do you think did it?"

I leaned back in the booth. "Kill Shelby Berkett? That's a good question. Certainly there are several suspects. And like it or not, Henry is moving up the list."

"Why?" Alan sounded slightly perturbed as he leaned back and folded his arms across his chest.

"Because he would have had access to potassium cyanide because he works in a pharmacy, and if he'd made a copy of the prop room key, he would have had access to the supply room, too."

"*Might* have had access to potassium cyanide, is what I believe you said. You don't know that for sure."

"It's a strong possibility, anyway. Though I admit Oliver Crane is still on my list."

"But Mr. Crane doesn't have a motive, remember? With Shelby Berkett dead, his play is in serious jeopardy, and he stands to lose a great deal of money. I know he didn't care for Mr. Berkett much, but it doesn't make sense he'd kill him."

I wrapped my hands around my coffee mug. "True. All true. Whereas all the others easily could have poisoned him, with nothing to lose on their end."

"Right, and they all had access to the prop room and supply room, except for Henry," Alan said.

"Henry would have had access if he'd copied the key," I said, irritated. "I just said that."

"But he wasn't near that side of the stage. I'm simply stating the facts the way you taught me to do."

I frowned. "He wasn't near that side of the stage that we know of, but he could have come across the basement and up the stairs."

Alan shrugged and frowned. "Maybe."

"So, what's your theory, then?"

He uncrossed his arms and picked up his fork once more, pushing the remains of his cherry pie around the plate. "Well, I was just thinking, about the broom and mirror from in the supply room. Well, remember how both the broom and the mirror were sticky?"

"I do. The end of the broom and the back of the mirror."

"I read once where spirits leave behind sticky substances, something called ecto plasma or something. You know. And ghosts sometimes take small things. Mischievous. Things go missing, a pillbox, a mirror, the putty."

"And the spirit in question again is Alexander Lippencott, I presume."

Alan's cheeks turned rosy. "I mean, it's a possibility, isn't it? He had a personal stake in this, seeing he knew Shelby, Jasper, and Jazz back in the day. And doesn't it make sense he would want to see Shelby dead after what he did?"

I sighed and stared into his eyes. Such strength, such intelligence, such innocence that I hoped he would never lose. "After what Shelby *possibly* did. Remember, nothing was ever proven."

"Right, *possibly* did, then. Still, Lippencott would have known the truth, wouldn't he? It just makes sense."

"You seriously think a ghost murdered Shelby Berkett?" I said, finishing the last of my pie. "You'd believe that over Henry Hawthorne?"

Alan looked sheepish. "I don't know. Not everything has a reasonable explanation. You don't think it's possible?"

"I think everything's a possibility until proven not so."

"I think so, too. And I think *you* have a personal grudge against Hank."

"I'm just stating facts, too. Mr. Hawthorne had motive and opportunity."

"Possibly had opportunity. I think him running through the basement and up the stairs, unlocking the door and slipping in and out of the prop room unseen is a bit of a long shot."

"Perhaps, but I think the idea of a ghostly murderer is even more of a long shot, so let's look at the earthbound suspects more closely for now, okay? *All* the suspects."

"Sure, fine by me."

"Fine. What else you got?" I said.

"My other working theory is they were all in on it together. All the suspects killed him, providing alibis for each other."

"That's the theory I thought you were first going to propose, the one you've proposed for every case we've had since you read about it in that book a few years ago."

"Well, this time it is more of a possibility, don't you think, Heath?"

"Yes, it's more of a possibility, and I admit not out of the question, just yet. But back to that sticky ecto whatever mirror. How did it get in the supply room? And why? And why was it left behind?"

Alan cocked his head. "Maybe Mrs. Holloway left it there and lied about it being stolen."

"Why would she leave it in the supply room?"

"Maybe she left it behind because someone was coming."

"Maybe, but she still could have easily taken it along."

"True, but her costume didn't have any pockets and the curtain was going up soon."

"Valid theory. But, Alexander Lippencott notwithstanding, why was the mirror sticky in the first place and why was it in the supply room?"

"Hmmm. I'm not sure. But if Eve is the murderer she may have had something sticky on her hands, and she went in the supply room to find something to clean them off. While she was in there, she checked her makeup using the mirror, then set it on the shelf and forgot it. Maybe she spilled something she had to sweep up, so she got the broom handle sticky."

"Perhaps."

"But where would she have gotten the poison?"

I scratched my chin. "I've been thinking about that. Eve and Mr. Hawthorne have been friends for some time, I understand."

"That's right. They were in the USO together and they did the Canteens during the war."

"And Eve gets Peter's pill prescriptions filled at Lempke's Pharmacy, where Henry works."

"Sure," Alan said. "He probably gets her a discount."

"What if Eve and Henry were in on it together? He gets her the poison, she does the deed."

"Gee, Heath, I suppose that's possible. I mean, both she and Hank had motives."

"Yes. I'm surprised Berkett would have attempted to assault Eve where there was a possibility of him being seen."

"He probably thought they were out of sight."

"Yes. And she murdered him to prevent him from attacking other women in the future. Who knows what he actually did to her beyond the groping."

"It makes sense."

"It's all quite interesting. But someone other than Eve Holloway might have left the mirror in the supply room."

"You mean someone may have indeed stolen it, just as she said? But why?"

"That remains to be seen," I said. "But whoever stole it might have been trying to frame Eve Holloway. Remember the missing pillbox?"

"Yeah. It presumably fell from the sofa cushions when Mr. Crane and Dick attempted to rouse Mr. Holloway."

"Given the fact that it had traces of cyanide in it, it's more likely it was on Holloway all along, and he lied about it being stolen, and about being drunk. If that's the case, it probably fell out of his pocket accidently. He would have had plenty of time to poison the tea after Jasper and his dog left and then plant the mirror in the supply room."

"But why the supply room? Wouldn't it make more sense for him to leave it in the prop room?"

"Thinking logically, yes, but I get the impression Mr. Holloway isn't always logical. I think it's possible Peter killed Shelby and then tried to frame his wife, killing two birds with one stone, so to speak."

"Golly, that's cold."

I leaned forward again. "Truly, if that's what happened. But I've been mulling over another possibility."

Alan raised his brows, his blue eyes sparkling. "Care to share?"

I smiled. "Always, with you. I was just thinking about Shelby Berkett. He was conceited, difficult, probably insecure, troubled, financially strapped, and completely alone. No family, no real friends. Failed plays and shows, middle-aged, and no real prospects."

"Pretty sad."

"Yeah. Not even a person to notify in case of emergency except his agent. So, what brought him back here to Milwaukee?"

"The chance to make some money in Mr. Crane's show," Alan said.

"Yes. He needed cash desperately, and his East Coast prospects were apparently nil. So, he followed up on that ghostly telegram, perhaps curious as to who really sent it. I'm sure it must have stirred up old, painful memories, and he wanted to find out what all was behind it. Maybe he wanted to see Jazz and Jasper again, too. Make amends, ease his guilt. Perhaps he was also curious to see how Dick had turned out."

"Only Shelby turned out to be far from paternal once he met Dick, and Jazz and Jasper wanted nothing to do with him."

"Yes, but on a brighter note, Shelby did meet Eve Holloway. She was kind to him, and Shelby Berkett was an attractive enough man, surely attentive. They spent time together, but she fought back when he tried to carry it too far."

"Why would she ever be friendly with someone like that in the first place?"

"I'm not sure. I think a big part of it was she felt sorry for him, like she said. But certainly a so-called Broadway star with a chance at a movie role would have his appeal to someone like Eve. And he flattered her and gave her attention. But he wanted more and she didn't, especially after she found out he wasn't what he pretended to be."

"And he wouldn't take no for an answer, so she hit him." Alan said. "He was certainly hostile to her at the party."

"His ego was bruised along with his face, I suspect," I said. "Faced with Eve's rejection, the realization that his future is bleak, and the fact that his son was not what he'd hoped, what would a man like that do?"

Alan set his fork back on his plate and stared at me, wide eyed. "Suicide?"

I looked at him over the top of my coffee cup. "It's possible. His death was theatrical in every sense of the word. It's all over the papers this morning, just as he would have wanted. To die in front of fans, to go out in glory onstage—what could be better in his opinion?"

"Gee," Alan said softly. "The death of a star."

"He could have stolen Eve's mirror and planted it in the supply room for some as yet unknown reason, in an attempt to frame her as an act of revenge for rejecting him or for fighting back."

"Jeepers, I could see him doing that."

"Yes, but there's a problem."

"What?"

I set my now-empty cup down on the table. "Again, why was the mirror left in the supply room and not the prop room? Maybe I could see Peter doing that, but Shelby was sharper, more intelligent. Also, he had that movie role to look forward to, so his future wasn't entirely bleak."

"That's *if* he got the role, if he even really was up for it. And if he was, he had to compete against Hank for it, and Hank is pretty charming and talented."

I groaned. "Don't remind me. But there's one other thing. How would Shelby have gotten the poison into the teapot? He and Henry were about the only two *not* near the prop room before the show, as you constantly point out."

"Couldn't he have dropped it in onstage, when he poured that first cup?"

"That is a possibility. But why would the cyanide be in Peter's pillbox?"

"Maybe Berkett wanted to frame Peter," Alan said, "to get back at Eve. So, he stole the pillbox and the mirror, hid the pillbox in the sofa cushions, and tucked the mirror in the supply room to make it look like Peter killed him."

"Maybe. I'm still puzzled as to why the mirror was in the supply room, though. We need to talk to Jazz about all this. I guess it's high time we get over to her place. You about ready?"

He pushed his plate away and wiped his mouth with his napkin. "If you're waiting for me, you're wasting your time!"

I smiled at him as I called the waitress over for the check, gave her the money, and told her to keep the change. The fly, I noticed, had settled down on the windowsill next to a few of his dead brethren.

We gathered up our hats, Alan downed the last of his coffee, and we headed out the door, the bell jingling once more.

CHAPTER ELEVEN

Later yet, Sunday afternoon, July 13, 1947

With our stomachs satisfied, we headed for Jazz Monroe's apartment on Van Buren Street on the fashionable east side. I parked in the shade of a large old oak tree, and Alan and I mounted the steps to the front door of the four-story Cream City brick building, ringing the apartment of J. Monroe. When we were buzzed in, we climbed the two flights of stairs to 3D at the back of the building. I knocked twice, and then we waited for what seemed a long time, considering we had already buzzed from below.

Dick opened the door and looked up at each of us in turn, not saying anything.

"Hello, Dick. Is Jazz home?" I said, breaking the awkward silence.

He motioned with his head and stepped back, allowing us to step inside the entryway and into the living room, which was colorful, to say the least. We took our hats off and set them on a mirrored hall table as we looked about.

The sofa was grass green, the drapes pink, and the rug on top of the wood floors sunny yellow. The overstuffed easy chair and ottoman were upholstered in a green and yellow stripe. Opposite the sofa was what appeared to be an antique Queen Anne side chair, but the fabric had been redone in hot pink velvet, and the frame painted silver. The chair sat in front of a white brick fireplace, above which was a portrait of Jazz in her younger, thinner days, smiling down at us in a low-cut red satin dress.

The obligatory baby grand piano, painted a shiny, glossy white, engulfed a corner by the window. The living room windows were open, and the pink satin drapes billowed in and out with the breeze.

"How are you, Dick?" Alan said.

"Okay."

"We'd like to talk to Jazz," I said.

"She's in her bedroom. Want me to get her?"

"Not just yet. I have a couple of questions for you. I seem to recall you left your keys on the dresser in the guest room Friday night at Oliver Crane's apartment, is that correct?"

"Yeah, I carry around all my keys, including the ones for the theater. I don't like them in my pocket."

"And you have keys to the supply room and the prop room?"

"Sure, they're the same key. Opens both locks, why?"

"Just curious. You, Mr. Crane, and Jasper are the only ones with that key, correct?"

"That's right. But now you mention it, when I went to use the key to get in the supply room on Saturday, it was hard to open. Bits of clay or something were stuck in the ridges."

I raised my eyebrows. "Oh?"

"Yeah. Made it hard to unlock the door. I was gonna use a toothpick or something to clean it, but I haven't got around to it yet."

"That may be a good thing, Dick. Do you have your keys handy?"

"They're in the drawer of the hall table, right here." He got them from the center drawer of the console and handed them to me. "What do you want them for?"

"Just curious. Which one is the supply and prop room key?"

"The gold one in the middle. It's marked with an 'S' and a 'P,' like salt and pepper, only for 'supply' and 'prop,' get it?"

"Got it. Makes it easy to identify." I examined the key closely. There did indeed appear to be traces of clay stuck in the ridges. I removed it from the ring and then placed the ring back in the still-open drawer. "Mind if I borrow this one?"

He shrugged his tiny shoulders again. "Fine with me. I got no use for it right now. The theater's been shuttered."

"I know. I'm sorry about that," I said, wrapping the key in my handkerchief and putting it in my pocket. "And I'm sorry again about what happened to Shelby Berkett."

"Thanks."

"This all must be quite a shock to you," Alan said.

Dick rolled his eyes around to look at Alan. "I guess I always wondered about it. Some things Jazz has said over the years never really made sense, but I learned early on not to question her."

"Still, to find out he was your father and then to have him die the next day must be hard," I said.

"My father died shortly after I was born, Detective. So did my mother. Jazz is all I've got, all I've ever had. Mr. Berkett, well, I never got the chance to really know him."

Alan and I exchanged looks. "Maybe we'd better talk to her now," I said.

Dick shrugged his thin, bony shoulders a third time. "Fine by me. Like I said, she's in her bedroom." He walked away from us down a hall toward what I assumed was Jazz's bedroom.

"Are we supposed to follow?" Alan said quietly.

"I think not. Jazz isn't the type of person who entertains in her bedroom, at least not in this respect," I said as we moved farther into the living room and looked around.

"The apartment's not what I expected," Alan said, as we glanced about again at the crystal chandelier, the fuzzy yellow rug, and the many gilt-framed mirrors and pictures of Jazz with various people, including some celebrities.

"I wasn't sure what to expect," I said. "It is all Jazz, certainly."

"She has a lot of, er, *things*," Alan said, his mouth gaping at a pair of gilt Cupids on the mantel.

"Yes, she does. Expensive, but a tad gaudy, in my opinion."

"As they say, Heath, *Sic transit gloria mundi*."

"Which means?"

"It's a Latin phrase: 'Thus passes the glory of the world.' It has been interpreted as 'Worldly things are fleeting.'"

"True words, Alan. True words."

In due time, Jazz Monroe appeared alone, wearing a blue cotton dress with a yellow ribbon tied round her substantial waist. Her raven black hair was up, and a gold pendant hung from her neck. She wore sensible yellow fuzzy house slippers that matched the rug.

"Gentlemen, what a nice surprise."

"How do you do, Miss Monroe. Detective Barrington, as you may recall, and of course you know Officer Keyes, here."

"Of course, the tall, cute one. To what do I owe the pleasure?"

Even in her own home, her voice boomed. I thought I heard the crystals in the chandelier above tinkle dangerously close to my head.

"I want to ask you a few questions about Mr. Berkett, if you don't mind," I said.

"Shelby? Why should I mind?"

"No reason I know of, Miss Monroe."

"Please, call me Jazz."

"All right, Jazz."

"I was just getting some things ready for the cleaners. Dick made a mess of his pants. Boys will be boys, I suppose, but he's always getting into something."

"And he's not really a boy anymore, is he?"

Jazz shook her head. "No, I guess he's not. Twenty-two this fall. Where does the time go?"

"An eternal question."

"Indeed. May I offer you some tea? Coffee? A cocktail? I believe I have some macaroons, too. I apologize, but I wasn't expecting company. Sunday is my maid's day off."

"Nothing for me," I said, "And we should apologize for not calling first."

She smiled that big, broad smile again, "Not at all. I'm always happy to entertain handsome men. What about you, you fine, young man? Tea, coffee, cocktail?"

"No, thank you."

"Well, then at least have a seat. We might as well all be comfortable."

I took the overstuffed chair, which I immediately sank into. Using the arms, I half-propped myself up, perching above the cushion. Alan took the sofa, and Jazz sat upon the antique Queen Anne, which creaked and groaned under her weight, but she didn't seem to notice.

"Sorry about that chair, Mr. Barrington. I never sit in it because I can't get out of it. Last time I did it took two men to hoist me up. It's filled with goose down, you know."

"It's fine, really."

Her chair creaked louder as she shifted about, until she finally settled into one position.

"By the way, had you been in touch with Mr. Berkett before he came back to Milwaukee?"

Her smile was eerily similar to the one in the portrait above her. "The last time I spoke to Shelby before he turned up here was 1926. As you may be aware, we were not on speaking terms off the stage after what happened back then."

"Did you know he had been cast in Mr. Crane's play before he showed up?"

"Mr. Crane told me, but only after the contracts had all been signed and I couldn't get out of it. But I'm a professional, and we all must do what's best for the good of the show, so I agreed to go on."

"Sounds like you didn't have a choice," I said. "Had you any communication with him at all since he left Milwaukee in 1926?"

She seemed to be deciding before she said, "Well, I did send him a few letters over the years in care of his agent, if you call that communication."

"I do," I said. "What were the letters about?"

"Frankly, I asked him for financial help in raising Dick. It wasn't easy for me, and he was doing quite well back then, according to the newspapers. I wasn't making much money in the early years, and I was hoping he would send a check or two my way. I even enclosed a photograph of little Dick once or twice, thinking that might spur his paternal instincts."

"And what was his response?" Alan asked.

"He wrote basically the same thing each time, when he bothered to respond at all. He said he had no money to spare, and he doubted Dick was his child."

"Did you ever think about consulting a lawyer?" I said.

She laughed bitterly. "A lawyer? And say what, Detective? That I'm an unwed mother who wants to sue the father for support? The reporters would have had a field day with that, and my career would have been ruined."

"You could have kept it quiet," I said.

"No one keeps those things quiet for long."

"I suppose you're right. Did you keep the letters he sent you?"

"I did, though I'm not sure why. They're in a shoebox in my closet, top shelf."

"Is Dick aware of the letters?" Alan said.

She shook her head. "I hadn't thought so, though I wondered. A few months ago, I noticed the box had been moved. I asked him about it, but he denied it. I suppose it may have been my maid. I've caught her going through my things before. Good help is hard to find these days."

"Nothing's the same as it was before the war," I said. "So, when did you first see Shelby when he got back to town?"

"At the theater, of course. First read-through."

"It must have been awkward."

"It was. I admit I was sick about it at first. I didn't want to see him. But suddenly I did, I don't know why. I discovered he hadn't changed much, except he'd lost his hair. God, that awful toupee. But even with that, he was still arrogant, rude, and cocky. It all came back to me, and I was glad, because it made the years gone by easier, if that makes any sense."

"I think so," I said, nodding slowly.

"He acted like we were old friends at first, like nothing had happened. I think he wanted to let bygones be bygones, but I wasn't willing and neither was Jasper."

"That would have been difficult to do after what had transpired," Alan said. "When did he meet Dick?"

"Dick came around after the read-through. I introduced them as I would any two strangers. Shelby stared at Dick for quite a while, assessing him, and I could tell it made Dick uncomfortable. They shook hands, and it was all so polite, but Shelby was cold and distant. I think Shelby was disappointed in Dick's appearance, and the fact that he is a janitor and not a successful businessman or at least an actor. For Dick's part, he had heard the story of 1926 from Jasper and from me, I must admit, so I think Dick was predisposed to dislike Shelby."

"How sad," Alan said.

"Yes, I agree, but it is what is, and it was what it was. We started rehearsals a couple days later, and things were okay at first. But it didn't take long before the tensions started to mount for everyone, as Shelby got on our nerves and he started throwing his weight around."

"Did you talk with him about the past?"

She scrunched up her face. "The weasel came to see me right here in my apartment shortly after we'd started rehearsing.

Oh, I'm sorry, I shouldn't call him a weasel now that he's dead, should I?"

"I understand, Miss Monroe. You didn't care for Mr. Berkett."

She looked at me sharply. "No, I didn't. Most people didn't care for him, and with good reason."

"Of course. But that wasn't always the case with you, was it?"

"No, that's true. As I said, I knew Shelby well back in the old days, naturally."

"Quite well, from what I've heard," I said.

She scowled. "Is that a crack?"

"No, of course not, my apologies."

She glared at me. "All right. Anyway, we dated, thought we were in love even. We were kids. He was still arrogant and rude back then, but he had a softer side, too. That little boy side he mostly kept hidden."

"Interesting."

"Stupid kids do stupid things, Detective. It happened one night, after some drinking and dancing. It just happened. And it happens more than you think. I was a good girl, caught up in circumstance."

"I'm not judging you, Miss Monroe."

"Yes, you are. Everyone judges me, Mr. Barrington. They judge everything I do and have done. It's the price one pays for being a celebrity."

"I suppose so."

"Take my word, but I've gotten used to it. So anyway, after that one night—and it was just one night—I told Shelby about my being with child. His child."

"I can imagine his response."

She laughed harshly, and the crystals in the chandelier tinkled again. "I bet you can. It wasn't long after that the accident happened, *if* it was an accident."

"The Alexander Lippencott and Jasper Crockett accident."

"That's right. Alex died immediately, and Jasper never did walk right again. All because of Berkett," she said. "Jasper carries a lot of guilt around with him to this day, because he survived and Alex didn't. Alex broke his fall."

"You think Shelby flipped the trap door switch?"

"I always have. But I don't think he intended any permanent harm. I think he thought they'd just get banged up a little, bruised, maybe a broken arm. And I don't think it was premeditated. He was near the switch and saw an opportunity to eliminate his competition, so he took it, though he's always denied it. A couple weeks later, the producer came to town, Shelby told him I was expecting, the producer offered Shelby a contract, and he was off to New York, never to return until now."

"You must have been angry back then," I said.

"Oh, I was. I still am. I was also hurt, afraid, and alone. But I got by, no thanks to him."

"How has Dick been since all this? How has he taken the news?"

"It's been a rough time, of course. Hurt feelings, all that nonsense, but he seems better now."

"Finding out about you and Mr. Berkett must have been quite a shock to him."

"I knew I should have told him myself, but I just never figured out a good time to do it. I never would have dreamed they'd meet up. It was easier to keep living the lie, you know?"

"Did Dick come home Friday night after the party?"

"Finally. About two in the morning. I was in bed but couldn't sleep as I was worried about him. It's not like him to run off like that."

"So, what happened?"

"I heard him come in. He had been drinking. I got up, in spite of the fact I had a splitting headache. He asked me point-blank if it was true."

"You mean that you are his mother and Shelby is his father?" Alan asked for clarification.

"That's right. You have to understand women just didn't have babies out of wedlock back in the Twenties, or at least they didn't talk about it. They still don't, but it was even worse back then. I didn't know what to do. I was all alone. I didn't want to give up my career, be blacklisted, shamed. So, I planned to go away to Minneapolis where my friend Donna lives, on the pretense of doing a show there. I'd have the baby, then come back home."

"With the baby?"

"I originally planned to put it up for adoption. But then I saw his sweet little face, and I got attached, which is something I regret. It was a big mistake."

"Why was it a big mistake?"

"Because I had to come back home with a baby in tow and try to get people to believe it belonged to my friend who died in the Minnesota flood. And I had to raise that baby, all while trying to take care of myself and my career."

"I'd say you did okay for yourself."

Jazz glanced about her living room and then settled her big eyes back on me. "Yes, I'd say so, too. But it wasn't easy. Because of Dick, I couldn't travel as much, couldn't do touring companies. I had to survive on my wits and talent here in Milwaukee and keep a big secret all to myself."

"Challenging, I'm sure," Alan said.

Jazz raised her painted-on eyebrows. "And how. And I must admit, I see Shelby every time I look at Dick. He's a constant reminder of the past."

"That's unfortunate."

She shrugged. "It is, in many ways. I try not to let it show, but it's difficult. I admit I'm not always kind to him."

"Maybe now that the truth is known, you can make up some lost time in the mother department."

"Maybe. I hope so, Detective. I'll certainly try."

"So what happened after you and Dick talked?" I said.

"Not much. The next day when it was time to leave for the

theater, I talked him into going with me by telling him I'd buy him dinner on the way. Believe me, I didn't want to go after that awful, humiliating night at Oliver's party, but I'm a professional. The show must go on."

"I can imagine that must have been difficult."

"It was, but I've been through worse."

"You said Mr. Berkett came to see you here a few days after he got in town. Why?"

"Shelby. What a cad. He brought me flowers, can you believe it? I must say I was quite surprised to see him standing there at my door with a cheap bouquet of daisies and chrysanthemums. I put them in water and set them on the table. Then he took off his hat, looked about, and made some crack about the décor. He said something like, 'I see your taste in decorating is like a fruitcake.'"

"What's that supposed to mean?"

"He said, 'colorful but tasteless.'"

"Ouch," I said, suppressing a laugh. Alan was trying not to smile.

"I nearly slugged him."

"I can imagine."

"Then he apologized, insincerely, of course."

"Hmmm. Did Shelby say why he came back to Milwaukee?"

"He made it seem like he was coming back home to see me. He said he wanted us to be friends again, can you imagine? He bragged about how well he was doing, about his beautiful New York apartment, a new show he was thinking about doing. He went on ad nauseam. Of course we now know that was all a big fake. He was flat broke."

"How did you find that out?" Alan said.

"Jasper did some checking with a friend of his in New York who made inquiries."

"Jasper?" I said.

She laughed again. "Don't cross those quiet types. Jasper has a way of getting even with people, slowly, over time, and he wanted to burst Shelby's balloon."

"Sounds like he did just that."

"And how. Good for him. One big prick."

"Excuse me?"

"Jasper gave Shelby's balloon one big prick, and it burst into pieces, metaphorically. Jasper was just as upset as I was about Oliver hiring Shelby for the play. They had quite an argument over it one day at the theater. Jasper even threatened to quit. I thought it was going to ruin their friendship. We all heard it."

"It's certainly understandable that Jasper would be angry," Alan said.

"Yes. Of course, Oliver wasn't around back in 1926 when it happened. He may not have realized the depth of Jasper's and my emotions regarding Shelby."

"I'm surprised Mr. Berkett came back, knowing he'd be seeing you and Jasper," Alan said.

Jazz looked over at Alan. "I think he had a guilty conscience, and he needed the money. Oliver was prepared to pay him far more than he was worth. More than I was getting, even, and I'm the star!"

"I see. And that's the only reason for his return to Milwaukee?"

"Oh, I think he was curious about Dick, too. He had never met him in person, never saw him. I told him Dick was innocent and didn't know who his father and mother really are. I wanted to keep it that way."

"What was his reaction?"

"He said that was fine by him. In fact, he told me he still didn't even believe Dick was really his."

"Why did he think that?"

"Because Shelby Berkett is an ass. Sorry, *was* an ass. I think he didn't want a son. And if he did have a son, he didn't want it to be someone like Dick. Some say Dick's size is my fault, because of my drinking and smoking while I was expecting, but I don't put much stock in that."

"How strange and sad," Alan said.

"You got it, mister. But then, Shelby was a strange fella."

"Did you talk about anything else?"

"Oh sure. He asked if I knew who sent the mysterious telegram."

"Do you know?"

She shook her head once more. "Nope, no idea. Certainly interesting, though. Getting that telegram really shook him up, which is exactly what whoever sent it wanted. And it got him back here pronto."

"What else did you two discuss?" I said.

"Oh, he also wanted to know all about the beautiful Eve Holloway. Those two hit it off right away at first. He wanted to know how her marriage was, what Peter is like, and on and on. They spent a lot of time together at first, but then something happened and it ended just like that. Like I said before, you know, in case you weren't listening."

"I was listening, Miss Monroe. Believe me. It's hard not to when you talk," I said.

"Is that another crack?"

"I'm just saying you command attention."

I could tell she didn't quite believe me. "I see. Anyway, I told him Eve Holloway seemed to be pretty unhappily married, and that Peter is a drunk and abuses pills. All facts, of course. I don't gossip, no sir. It was pretty obvious he was interested in her and was pumping me for information."

"She said she was one of the only ones who was nice to him," Alan said.

"And with good reason. But then Eve found out what he was really like, and that was that. Personally, I think she was hoping for a part in the movie he was up for, but as I said, it ended just like that." She snapped her fingers.

"Apparently so," Alan said. "So, how did the meeting between you two end that day?"

"I told Shelby I'd do the play with him, but I didn't want anything to do with him outside of the theater, and neither did Jasper."

"How did he react?" Alan said.

"He got mad, and I think he was disappointed, hurt. He claimed he was innocent, that he was a victim of rumor and circumstance. I told him Jasper and I didn't believe he was innocent for one second, and that he was lucky he wasn't in prison for Alex's death. Then he said if that's the way we felt about it, there was nothing more to say."

"Then what?" I said.

"He got up, took his cheap bouquet out of the vase, and left, dripping water all the way. Say, what actually did happen to Shelby last night, anyway? There are lots of rumors going around."

Alan looked at me, I looked at him, and then I glanced back at Jazz.

"He was poisoned."

"That is rumor number one. So, just like in the show?"

"Yes, that's right. Cyanide."

"Well, if that don't beat all. Life imitating art, or something like that." She shifted her bosom. "Huh. But how did it happen? How could it have happened? There was nothing but tea in the vial and in the teapot."

"It seems someone substituted poison for the tea, Miss Monroe, or at least, added poison to the tea. Did you happen to notice anything funny about it when you poured it into his cup?"

"No, not particularly, but I didn't pay much attention to it." She stared at us for some time, then her eyes widened. "Say, wait a minute. You don't think I killed him, do you? I mean, I've thought about it, believe me, and I certainly had reason to, but that doesn't mean I killed him."

"No, no, it doesn't. But it doesn't mean you didn't, either," I said.

She crossed her arms below her bosom and scowled. "Well,

this friendly little visit certainly went sour fast. I think the two of you should go. And I think I had better call my lawyer."

"Seeking legal counsel is always good advice, Miss Monroe, but please understand we're not accusing you of anything, we are only trying to gather facts."

Her painted-on eyebrows shot up once more, almost to her forehead. "If you want facts or suspects, Mr. Barrington, I suggest you talk to Jasper Crockett or Mr. Crane."

Now it was my turn to raise my eyebrows. "We plan on talking to Jasper, but you think Mr. Crane is a suspect in Shelby Berkett's death?"

"Of course. He hated Shelby, just like everyone else."

"That may be true, but he didn't really have anything to gain and a lot to lose with the death of the star of the show."

"Excuse me, but *I'm* the star of that show. And Mr. Crane actually did have something to gain. Ticket sales were way down from what he had projected. Shelby wasn't the draw he thought he'd be."

"Maybe so, but what would he gain by killing Shelby? Wouldn't that just make ticket sales even worse?"

"Hardly. You can't buy publicity like this, Mr. Barrington. I'm willing to bet when the show reopens, it will be a sellout."

"Perhaps, *if* the show reopens, but killing someone just to increase ticket sales hardly seems justified."

"People have killed for less. Besides, there's one other thing you may not be aware of. Oliver Crane takes out life insurance policies on all the principal players before every show."

"What?"

"I see by the look on your face you weren't aware of that. It's standard procedure, actually. If a major player in a show has an accident or dies, it puts the show in jeopardy. So, having a hefty life insurance policy allows the producer of the show to pay off its backers and its bills in the event the show closes or folds because a principal player dies or has an accident."

"Are you sure of this?" I said, glancing at Alan, who looked just as surprised as I was.

"Of course. Like I said, it's standard procedure. And in my book, that makes him suspect number one. It's no secret Oliver Crane is in hock up to his snowy-white hair. Ask him yourself if you don't believe me. And I do believe it's time you were going."

I struggled to get out of the overstuffed chair, finally hoisting myself up with both arms. Alan stood as well, putting away his notebook and pencil and dusting off his pants. "Fine. We won't keep you any longer, Miss Monroe," I said.

"I'd say it was a pleasure, but it really wasn't," she said, getting to her feet as well.

"I'm sorry about that. Police work, you know," I said.

"Sure, I know. Just like in the theater. Life imitating art."

"Something like that. One last question, if you don't mind."

She looked up at me suspiciously. "What?"

"Do you love Dick?"

She looked at me hard, her mouth tight, before she finally spoke. "What kind of a question is that?"

"A simple one. Do you?"

"He's my son. Mothers love their sons."

"Most of them."

"I'm not used to being a mother, Detective. It's going to take some time."

"Indeed. We'll be in touch," I said.

"I'm sure you will."

We walked to the entryway and retrieved our hats from the console.

"Good day, gentlemen," she said in an icy tone.

We stepped out into the hall before turning. "Good day," I said as she closed the door abruptly in our faces.

Chapter Twelve

Early Sunday evening, July 13, 1947

"She certainly is something," Alan said, looking at me as we reached the sidewalk out front.

"She certainly is. And she's a good actress, one of the best."

"You think that was all an act?"

"Perhaps," I said. "At least some of it. Let's have another word with Oliver. I believe he said he was picking up Jasper Crockett, so they may both be at Oliver's place by now." I checked my pocket watch. "His apartment is a short walk from here, so we'll leave my car and go by foot."

We got to his apartment in the Blackstone in just a few minutes, deciding on the element of surprise and hoping he would be at home. We followed a woman in through the lobby security door and rode up the elevator to the seventh floor.

"Heath! Alan! What are you two doing here?" Oliver said, opening his door shortly after we knocked.

"We have a few more questions. Mind if we come in?"

"Hmm? Oh, sure, come on in. Sorry the place isn't picked up yet."

We stepped inside, and I noticed the smell of cigar and cigarette smoke still lingered, though the party was two days past by this point.

"Put your hats on the sideboard. Jasper's here with his pup. We were just having a drink. Can I get you one?"

"No, thanks. Hello, Mr. Crockett," I said, nodding to him.

He got to his feet and Pompom followed suit, wagging his tail.

"Hello, Mr. Barrington, Alan. Ollie and I were just talking about the show and what's going to happen. We would have met in his office at the theater, but you've still got us locked out," Jasper said. He was eating gumdrops from a small bag, washing them down with a bottle of beer on the table next to his chair.

"Yes, sorry about that. Hopefully, it won't be too much longer before you two can get back inside. We just came from Jazz Monroe's," I said.

"Really? I was about to call her," Oliver said.

"Were you? Why?"

"I was going to ask her to stop over tonight around six, along with the rest of the cast. Well, the remaining cast, that is. That includes you, Alan."

"What's it about?" Alan said.

"I just want to run some ideas past everyone, some changes, you know, to keep the show going."

"Shelby's not even buried yet, Oliver," I said.

He sighed heavily and looked uneasy. "I know, I know. I suppose it's much too soon, but I get antsy just sitting around with nothing to do, you know? Anyway, I was thinking Henry could take over Shelby's role, and Peter could take over Henry's role if we can keep him sober. Alan here could take over Peter's role as the butler. How does that sound?"

"Gee, Mr. Crane, that would be great," Alan said, beaming in spite of himself.

"Let's not get ahead of ourselves," I said. "We don't even know yet if the show is going to continue."

"What do you mean? I can make it work," Oliver said. "It just needs some fine-tuning, is all."

I glanced at Jasper and Pompom, who had taken their seats

again and were watching the three of us. "Is there someplace we can talk in private, Oliver?"

"What about? Jasper and I go back a long way. If you got something to say, you can say it in front of him, right, Jasper?"

"That's right." He took a handful of gumdrops again and started popping them one by one into his mouth.

I sighed. "All right. Are you sure you *want* to make the show work, Oliver?"

"Huh? Why wouldn't I?"

"The bigger question is, why would you kill Shelby Berkett?" I said point-blank.

Oliver laughed nervously, then stared at me and Alan as if we were crazy. "You're joking, right? Why, Heath? Why would I want to kill the star of my own show?"

"It seems to me that was my question."

"That's nuts. We've been over this before. Remember, I'm not only the director but the producer, too. I have a lot of money tied up in *Death Comes to Lochwood*, a *lot* of money."

"I know that, Oliver. And things aren't going well, are they? Shelby Berkett was turning out to be difficult. He and Jazz were at each other's throats. Rehearsals had gone poorly, and ticket sales were less than stellar. And you just purchased that expensive television set, probably on credit," I said, pointing toward the cabinet on the far wall.

"Yes, so what?"

"You took out a life insurance policy on Shelby Berkett, did you not?"

Oliver shifted uncomfortably on his feet. "You know about that, eh? I suppose Jazz told you. Well, yes, of course I did. I have policies on all the major players, including Jazz."

"I noticed you didn't want me to see his folder earlier. You copied down the contact information and then put the file away. Did you not want me to know about the policy?"

"It's not a secret. It's standard procedure for every production."

"But you failed to mention it. And with Shelby dead, you stand to collect on that policy and make some money whether or not the show goes on, isn't that true?"

He started sweating. "I suppose so, yeah, but I didn't kill Berkett, Heath."

I paced to the balcony doors next to where Jasper was seated, taking it all in, his light brown eyes huge. I stared down at the street through the smoke-streaked glass and saw a Schuster's truck parked next door, making a Sunday delivery, and a rags wagon coming slowly up the alley across the street, pulled by a tired-looking mule wearing a straw hat. Life goes on. I turned back to Oliver and Alan. "I'm not sure what to believe yet. But if it turns out you didn't kill him, someone else in the theater surely did."

Oliver looked incredulous. "I can't believe anyone in the cast could do such a thing."

I looked at Jasper again, now feeding a gumdrop to Pompom. "Maybe it wasn't someone in the cast."

"What do you mean?"

"It might have been someone in the crew, someone who hated Shelby Berkett," I said.

Jasper dropped the gumdrop he was holding and looked up at me, his eyes still large.

"I'm in the crew, Mr. Barrington," Jasper said as Pompom scarfed up the dropped candy.

"I know that, and you certainly had motive and opportunity, didn't you? You alone probably hated Shelby more than anyone. Maybe you even sent that telegram. A passive revenge move, knowing it would get him all stirred up and bothered. As someone once told me, you have a way of getting even with people slowly, over time, and you wanted to burst Shelby's balloon."

"His balloon needed bursting," Jasper said.

"Jasper would never harm anyone," Oliver said, moving closer to him.

"Are you sure, Oliver?"

Jasper set the bag of gumdrops down on the table next to his beer bottle and scratched his little dog behind the ears. "Berkett had a lot of nerve coming back here after all this time. He got what he deserved." Pompom had started licking his fingers.

"Pompom likes the sugar from the gumdrops," I said.

"Yeah, he's got a sweet tooth. He goes crazy for anything with sugar in it," Oliver said.

"Just don't give him too much," I said.

"Oh, I would never do that. As for Berkett, justice has finally been served, but it won't bring Alex back or fix my leg," Jasper said, staring up at me.

"Any thoughts on who might have killed him?" I said.

He picked up his beer bottle and took a swig before answering. "No sir. And if I did, I wouldn't say."

"Why is that?"

"Because. Just because. That's reason enough, I figure."

"All right, fair enough." I turned back to Oliver. "You mentioned the cast is coming by here tonight. Make certain everyone is here."

He nodded as he wiped the sweat from his brow with his handkerchief. "Okay, but what for?"

"Because I want to talk to them and see if we can't get to the bottom of this."

Oliver looked pale, even for him. "Sure, I'll call them right now."

"Good, good, that's fine." I took out my pocket watch once more. "We have a little time yet. Alan and I are going to swing by the police station, but we'll be back before six. Be sure you two stay right here."

"Okay, I understand. See you then."

We got our hats and left, opting to take the stairs down to the lobby instead of waiting for the elevator. Once back outside, we walked briskly back to my car, Alan keeping pace with me.

"What gives, Heath?"

"I want the lab to analyze the key I borrowed from Dick."

"Analyze it for what?"

"The clay stuck in the ridges."

"I don't follow."

"There are several possibilities. Remember Peter Holloway borrowed Dick's key ring to move his car Friday night at the party."

"Right."

"He might have made a clay impression of that key using the missing makeup putty, and then had a duplicate made."

"Yes, I remember you saying that before. I saw that in a movie once. Fiendishly clever."

"Indeed."

"But you said there were other possibilities."

"Yes. Shelby himself might have had a duplicate key made."

"But why would he do that?"

"Maybe the thought of suicide was already on his mind. Maybe he'd already thought it all through and figured on framing Peter or Eve for his suicide by slipping poison into the teapot."

"Gee, maybe, but that doesn't seem likely to me. No offense."

I smiled. "None taken. It doesn't seem likely to me, either. Just seeing if you were thinking."

"Hey, I'm always thinking."

"I know." I reached over and nudged his shoulder.

"So, what's the other possibility?"

"Well, Jazz wouldn't have had to make a clay imprint. She could have made a copy of the actual key since she had access to it. And Dick, Oliver, and Jasper had keys of their own. That leaves Eve, Peter, or Henry who would have needed to use the clay. Any one of them could have slipped into the bedroom at the party and taken the imprint. Remember, Dick had left his key ring on top of the dresser."

"Oh, right."

"You sound disappointed."

"No, I'm not. Not really. It's just that Mrs. Holloway is such a nice lady, despite what Miss Monroe says, and Hank, well…"

"Right. He's something."

"Yeah, he is. But I can't imagine he's a murderer, I just can't."

"I see." I stopped on the sidewalk and faced him.

"What?"

"You tell me," I said, irritated.

"I don't know what you mean, Heath. I said he could be a suspect, didn't I?"

"I don't think you really believe it, though. Do you?"

"I think you want him to be the killer. Your jealousy has clouded your reasoning, and I think that can and will get you into trouble if you're not careful," Alan said.

I scowled. "Why would I be jealous? Just because Henry's smart, charming, intelligent, talented, and stunningly attractive."

"All right, fine. Yes, sure he is. He's all those things."

My heart sank to my knees.

"But so are you," Alan said.

"Thanks."

"I mean it, Heath. You're really swell. I must admit Hank kind of swept me off my feet, though. I mean, we were sharing the theater experience together, sharing a dressing room, and yeah, sure, I'm attracted to him, but nothing happened, honestly!"

"Did you want something to happen?"

"No." He glanced abruptly down at his feet. "Maybe. I don't know. I don't think so, but I'm not sure. I'm sorry."

My heart rose again. I lifted his chin up so our eyes met. "Hey, it's okay. I just want you to be honest."

"I'm trying to be. With you and with myself. Hank's pretty exciting, but you're just you."

I felt my heart sink once more. "I see."

"No! No you don't, Heath. You're you in every wonderful way. You're the one I want to go to bed with, just to sleep with.

My head on your arm, or my back to your chest, the window open."

"You know I don't like sleeping with the window open," I said.

"Just to make it chillier so we have to snuggle closer," Alan said. I felt tears in my eyes. The blush in his cheeks was the color of a fresh pink rosebud.

"You make me feel safe, Heath. Wanted, desired. You make me feel important and attractive, and smart. All Hank ever did was make me feel excited. That was nice, but excitement can't be sustained, do you know what I mean?"

My heart rose up again and started beating so loudly I thought I could hear it. "I-I think so."

"You make me laugh, and you make me think, and sometimes you make me really, really mad, but that's okay. You're smart and witty, and once in a while annoying. You're not perfect, but I think you're perfect for me."

I looked at him tenderly, forgetting the outside world for a moment, forgetting we were standing on a public sidewalk in a busy, residential neighborhood. "I feel the same way about you," I said quietly.

"You do?"

"You know I do."

"You've never said."

"I guess I'm not good at expressing my feelings, but that doesn't mean I don't feel them."

We stood there staring at each other for several minutes until two kids in cowboy outfits and cap pistols came running up the sidewalk and split us apart, ending the moment. We both laughed.

"We'd better get going, I guess," I said at last.

"Yes, we still have a murder to solve."

"And Henry's a suspect, once and for all?"

"Yes, Henry's a suspect, once and for all. As long as you don't think about him any differently because…well, because."

"Deal. And thanks for reining me in, partner." We smiled and nudged each other's shoulders before continuing down the sidewalk.

When we reached my car, I turned it around, aiming it in the direction of the theater.

"Where are you going?" Alan said, puzzled.

"Just a brief stop at the Davidson before we go to the station. I want to pick something up. Fingers crossed I remember how to disarm the alarm. I watched pretty carefully when Oliver did it before."

Luckily, I did remember. I retrieved the can of putty from the makeup room, and we were soon on our way back downtown. I parked in front of the station in a loading zone.

"Wait here, in case a cop shows up," I said to Alan. "I'll leave the keys in it in case you have to move it."

"It's Sunday. Loading zones aren't enforced on Sundays, Detective. You should know that."

I grinned. "Fine, Officer, but wait here anyway. I won't be but a minute." I ran up to the second floor, hoping Fletch would still be there. Fortunately, he was. I was on a lucky streak.

"You're putting in the hours this weekend, Heath," he said as I entered his office.

"I could say the same for you, Fletch."

He shrugged his small, bony shoulders and pushed his glasses up his nose. "I was just about to head home. The wife's got dinner waiting."

I cocked my head. "Can you spare a few more minutes?"

"How did I know you were going to ask me that? It's pot roast tonight, Heath. I don't want to be late for that."

I smiled. "I don't think it will take all that long. I just need you to compare the dried-up bits of clay in the ridges of this key with this bit of makeup putty."

Fletch sighed. "Apparently you've already forgotten everything I said before. Just once I'd like to have you work a day in the lab. There are procedures to follow, tests to run, things to analyze, steps that must be taken in the proper order. Besides, the rest of the crew has gone home..."

"You're right, I know. I'm sorry, Fletch. It's just that time is of the essence."

Fletch sighed again. "Time is *always* of the essence with you. You can be really annoying sometimes."

I laughed. "That's what Alan told me earlier, too."

"Smart man. All right, let me see what I can do."

"Thanks, buddy. I owe you one."

"At last count you owe me twelve. By the way, we got the results back on that broom handle and mirror."

"Do tell."

"Dick Cooper's fingerprints were on the broom handle, but no prints on the mirror except yours and Eve Holloway's."

"It's only natural Dick's fingerprints would be on the broom, but you didn't find anyone else's?"

"Nope. The residue on the broom handle and the mirror were left by some type of tape."

"I thought that might be the case. And the pencil and the ledger? Anything unusual?"

"Since you're so smart, you tell me," Fletch said.

"The pencil showed signs of cyanide on its surface, the ledger was clean."

"Damn it, Heath, how do you do that?"

"It was just a hypothesis, now confirmed."

"So, what does it mean?" Fletch said.

"It means I think I'm on the right track."

"To where?"

"I'll fill you in later. By the way, did you check for fingerprints on the pencil and ledger?"

Fletch sighed and looked annoyed. "No, because you didn't ask me to, and that's not really my job."

"Right. My mistake. Would you do that for me, please? And I really need the putty analysis."

"I'll see what I can do," he said resignedly. "Give me a few."

I grinned again. "Thanks!" I left him to it and went back downstairs, where Alan was still waiting in the car, the window rolled down. I asked him to go inside and call the local radio station, WBSM, and verify some information, followed by a long-distance call to Hamilton Marshall Brach in Hollywood. While he was doing that, I went to my desk in the detective's room and called the woman who shared my mother's party line to see if her son was home. After thirty minutes or so, I headed back to Fletch's office.

"Did I give you enough time?"

Fletch looked up at me, pushing his glasses back up his nose once more. "Honestly, Heath, why do I like you?"

"Because I'm humble and charming, of course!"

"No, that can't be it. But the putty does seem to match the material in the ridges of the key. Same consistency and color."

"Excellent. I suspected it would."

"Of course you did. I also managed to lift some fingerprints off the pencil and ledger, but I haven't had time to compare them to the ones on file from the cast yet. But you probably already know what I'll find, so why bother?"

"Funny, Fletch. I have my suspicions, but I do need them confirmed," I said.

"Now you're the funny one, Heath. Is the fingerprint analysis something you definitely need right now? Because it's pot roast night, as I mentioned, and there will be hell to pay if it's cold when I get home."

"The fingerprint analysis can wait until morning. I can't think of anything else right now, but if I do…"

"*If* you do, it can wait until morning, too."

"Understood. Tell the wife hello for me."

"Will do. She wants you to come to supper again soon, by the way. She really does make a mean pot roast, and she likes you. God knows why. She thinks you're too thin."

I laughed. "I'll take you two up on that, then. By the way, may I borrow one of your clipboards?"

Fletch sighed and heaved his little shoulders. "I'm not even going to ask. Be my guest."

"Thanks, Fletch, I really appreciate it. Thanks for everything. I'll be in touch about dinner."

I headed back downstairs, collected Alan once more, and together we headed out to my car, comparing notes on what each of us had found out.

CHAPTER THIRTEEN

Sunday evening, July 13, 1947

Fifteen minutes later we were back at Oliver's apartment, where everyone had assembled. Oliver had gathered them in the living room and had distributed scripts to Peter and Henry, their new parts underlined. Peter, to his credit, appeared completely sober and was seated next to Eve. Apparently, a truce had been called between the two of them for the time being. Jasper was in the kitchen getting a beer, Pompom at his feet. Dick was seated on the other side of Eve, and Jazz was next to him, with Henry on the other side of her. Henry got to his feet with a grin when he spotted Alan. "Hey, Alan, looks like you will be getting a speaking part after all. Grab a script and come sit next to me. I saved you a seat." He completely ignored me.

Alan glanced at me, and I cleared my throat. "I have a few things to go over before that, Mr. Hawthorne, so you'll have to wait."

"Wait for what?" Henry said. "What things do you have to go over?"

"That remains to be seen."

"What does?"

"We'll see," I said as he scowled at me.

Jasper returned to the living room and took a seat in the chair

Henry had been saving for Alan. Henry did not look pleased. Pompom curled up contentedly under Jasper's chair.

I cleared my throat. "Fine, now everyone's here. Oliver, you may as well have a seat, too. But before you all proceed with rehearsal, I'd like you each to do me a favor and sign in on this clipboard." I handed it and a pencil to Peter, who was seated nearest to me and Alan. He took it with a puzzled look.

"What for? You apparently know who we all are," Peter said, "though I'm not entirely sure who *you* are."

"My apologies. I'm Heath Barrington, Milwaukee Police Detective, Mr. Holloway. We met at the party Friday night."

"Did we? I'm afraid that night is a bit hazy. Are you going to be in the play?"

"No, I'm investigating the murder of Shelby Berkett."

"Was he murdered?" Peter said. "Nobody tells me anything."

"Are you really that clueless, Mr. Holloway, or are you a better actor than you lead us to believe?" I said.

"What's that supposed to mean?" he said indignantly. "My acting is impeccable."

"Humor the man, Peter, and just sign your name, please," Eve said.

Peter sighed, signed his name, and passed the clipboard to Eve, who did the same and passed it on to Dick. Oliver was the last one. He signed it and gave the clipboard and pencil back to me.

"Now what?" Oliver said. "May I start rehearsal?"

"Not just yet, I'm afraid." I handed the clipboard and pencil to Alan, who set them on the sideboard. "You may be interested to know we have discovered someone put poison in the teapot used in the play. It was apparently added in the prop room before the show."

Everyone exchanged glances and murmurs as I continued.

"And it wasn't just any poison. It was potassium cyanide, an extremely fast-acting poison not easily attainable."

"So, who did it?" Jasper said.

I looked at Jasper. "To answer that, we have to ask who had access to that type of poison. Certainly, someone working in a pharmacy."

Henry's eyes grew large. "You mean me," he said.

"You do work at Lempke's Pharmacy in West Allis, do you not, Mr. Hawthorne?"

"I gave my notice yesterday. Besides, I was only a clerk there. I didn't have access to much except hair tonic and liver pills."

"That may be the case," I said, "but I'm sure you would have found a way to obtain it given the need."

"Well, I didn't obtain it or anything else, Detective," Henry growled through clenched teeth.

I looked directly at him. "I had to ask myself, why potassium cyanide? Why not arsenic or strychnine? They are certainly more common and easier to get. Even your average household rat poison would do the trick. I came up with two answers. The first, that the murderer wanted the death to come quickly, onstage, in front of everyone, and potassium cyanide is one of the fastest acting poisons around. Quite dramatic. My other thought was that it may have been suicide."

"Suicide?" Jazz said. "Shelby would never."

"I'm not so sure, Miss Monroe, but I did have Alan check with the director's office in Hollywood. Shelby was indeed in the running for that movie role, so that lessens the likelihood that he killed himself."

"What was your second answer, Detective?" Henry said, his teeth still clenched.

"It comes back to you either way, Mr. Hawthorne. He was competing with you for that movie role, and the fact that you could get the poison makes you a prime suspect, doesn't it?"

"I think you're out to get me, and I think I know why," Henry said, looking from me to Alan.

"I'm not out to get you, Mr. Hawthorne, believe me. I have no need to. I'm just stating facts." I had to admit to myself I liked to rile him up, though. I turned to Dick. "By the way, Dick, you may be interested to know those fragments of clay in your prop room key did match the makeup putty."

Dick stared at me blankly, as did pretty much everyone else.

"What are you talking about now?" Oliver asked.

"My thoughts exactly," Henry said. "I think you're babbling, talking nonsense to make yourself look good."

I ignored him. "The prop room, as you all may know, is kept locked, and only three people had keys to it," I said. "Oliver, Jasper, and Dick."

"So, you're saying it was one of them?" Jazz said. "I don't believe it!"

"Well, it wasn't me," Dick said. "I wasn't in the prop room at all Saturday. I had no reason to be."

"I've told you before I didn't do it," Oliver said. "I wasn't in there at all on Saturday, either."

Jasper stroked Pompom's head nervously as he glanced around the room. "I know what you're all thinking. You're thinking I didn't like him, and it's true. I hated him. He killed Alex and ruined my stage career. My leg's never been the same. But I didn't put no poison in that pot. The last I saw, it only had sweet tea in it," he said, his light brown eyes large once more.

"Clearly one of the three is lying," Peter said, sitting upright. "My goodness, this evening is turning out to be more entertaining than I expected."

"I'm not sure I'd use the term 'entertaining,' Mr. Holloway. And one of them may be lying, but someone else may have had access to that room."

"Who? How? You just said only those three had keys," Henry said.

"Someone could have made a duplicate key. At Friday night's party, Dick left his key ring on the dresser in the bedroom. Didn't you, Dick?"

"Yes, that's right. On top of the dresser in the guest room."

"That would have been a perfect opportunity for any of you to make a duplicate, specifically to press the key into a wad of stolen makeup putty and then later make another key."

The room fell silent until Dick finally spoke again. "I noticed the traces of clay in my key Saturday afternoon and brought it to Mr. Barrington's attention earlier today."

"Yes, you did. You were clever to do so."

"All right, so who was it?" Jazz said, sounding annoyed.

"It could have been you, Jazz. Or Mrs. Holloway. You went in the guest room after Peter's hat and your purse, didn't you?"

She blinked. "That's right, but that's all I did."

"I believe you. In fact, the most likely suspect would be you, Mr. Holloway," I said.

He looked at me sharply. "Me? Well, how fascinating."

"Yes, you actually had Dick's keys in your possession when you went down to move Jazz's car."

"What do you mean he moved my car?"

I turned to her. "Dick had parked Peter in, Jazz. Remember, you two were the last to arrive. Peter moved your car so he could get his out."

She shot Peter a look. "I'll be checking it over for scratches, believe me."

"I'm afraid I don't remember that evening well, Detective," Peter said, ignoring Jazz and looking slightly confused.

"Don't you? Or are you acting? It's difficult to tell, I'm afraid. By the way, your missing pillbox turned up last night, I understand."

"Yes, it was wedged between the sofa cushions. I like to lie there before the show."

"Or did it fall out of your pocket when Oliver and Dick tried to get you to your feet?"

"My pocket? How interesting. I don't recall it being there. I know Oliver has it now, and I'd like it back. It's valuable, you know."

"Indeed it is, I'm sure. But Oliver no longer has it in his possession. It's in the lab at the police station."

"What's it doing there?"

"Traces of the poison used to kill Shelby were found inside it," I said.

"The hell you say. How peculiar."

"It's true, I'm afraid, Mr. Holloway."

Peter scratched his chin. "God, I could use a drink. Oliver, what do you have around here?" he said, looking at Oliver.

I held up my hand. "I don't think that would be a good idea right now, Mr. Holloway."

"Alcohol is always a good idea, mister whatever your name is. Sorry, but I've forgotten."

"Barrington. Any thoughts as to how the poison got in your pillbox?"

He stared back at me. "No. I must admit I am completely baffled by that, but I did not poison that big rat Berkett, much as I would have enjoyed doing so."

I shook my head slowly. "No, I don't think you did, Mr. Holloway. You're not that good an actor. But someone went to great lengths to make it appear you did."

"Then who made a copy of the key?" Oliver said. "It certainly wasn't me!"

"Actually, I don't think any of you did."

"What are you on about, Detective? You just said someone made a copy of the key by using putty," Jazz said.

"I said *if* a duplicate key was made. I believe someone wanted it to appear that a copy of the key had been made."

"Who and why would someone want to do that?" Eve asked.

"Why don't you answer that question, Dick?" I said, walking over to him.

He glared at me but said nothing as everyone turned their attention to him.

"What do you mean, Mr. Barrington?" Jazz asked indignantly.

"I mean, Dick wanted me to believe someone had made a copy of his key."

"Why would he do that?"

"That's a good question, Jazz. But I don't think you'll like the answer. He did it because he did it."

"What? Did what? You're not making any sense, and you're making all of this up as you go. Mr. Hawthorne was right. You're just trying to make yourself look smart. I think we should leave." She picked up her purse from the floor.

"If you do you'll be leaving with a murderer, Miss Monroe, because Dick murdered Shelby Berkett. Didn't you, Dick?"

Jazz dropped her purse, which landed with a thud on the wood floor, and her mouth fell open.

"I don't know what you're talking about," Dick said, staring at me defiantly, arms crossed over his chest.

"I think you do. You found Shelby's letters to Jazz and figured out he was your father."

"Not much of a father," he said.

"No, I must agree with you on that, but you did realize the truth behind Jazz's secret, didn't you?"

"It wasn't a well-kept secret," Dick said. "I never really believed my parents died in that flood. I'm not stupid."

I shook my head. "No, no, you're not. Far from it. You must have been curious about Shelby Berkett, though. What was he like? Why had he never wanted to meet you, to contact you?"

Dick shrugged but said nothing.

"Why wouldn't he be curious?" Jazz said. "I suppose it's only natural. I should have told him, but that doesn't mean he killed him." She looked from me to Dick, but Dick continued to stare straight at me with those round little eyes.

"Sure, it's natural to be curious," I said, "but how to go about satisfying that curiosity? You certainly didn't have the means to go to New York by yourself, and I'm sure you assumed Jazz would never agree to take you there."

"Maybe I would have, if he'd asked."

"No, you wouldn't have, Jazz. Stop lying to me, once and for all." Dick looked at her now, hard.

"You sent that telegram to him about the play, didn't you?" I said.

"Why would I do that?"

"Because you wanted to meet him, to see what he was really like, of course. Signing the telegram Alexander Lippencott was a nice theatrical touch, by the way. You knew it would grab his attention."

"Who's Alexander Lippencott?" Dick said.

"Everyone in this room knows. Anyone who has ever worked in the Davidson Theater in the last twenty years knows, and you know they know. Mr. Crockett told you, and so did Jazz."

"So what?"

"You sent the telegram, knowing it would draw your father back here to Milwaukee, and also that it would bother him."

"I don't know what you're on about."

"Were you hoping for a happy family reunion? Were you expecting him to make it all up to you? To tell you he didn't pull the lever on that trap door?"

"He *did* tell me he didn't do it," Dick said. "But I knew he was lying. I knew the moment I met him he was a liar and a cheat. The way he boasted about himself, how successful he all was, but it was all lies. He lied to Mrs. Holloway, too, and made her believe he was a big shot."

"Yes, he did," I said, "and that drew the two of them close. And when you found out he assaulted her, you hated him for that, too, didn't you? You hated him so much you decided to murder him."

"You're assuming an awful lot, Detective," Dick said.

"This is absurd," Jazz said. "None of this means he murdered Shelby, Mr. Barrington."

I shook my head. "No, not the telegram in and of itself,

anyway. But you were clever, Dick, as I said before. You stole Peter's pillbox to use to carry the poison. You carried it with you when you went to the supply room just after six that Saturday night. And while you were there, you taped the mirror on the broomstick—something you had done before to spy on Eve Holloway through the transom of her dressing room, didn't you?"

"Wait a minute, are you saying this little weasel was spying on Eve?" Henry said, getting to his feet.

I turned to Henry. "Please sit down, Mr. Hawthorne. Dick stole Eve's mirror from her dressing room and used it to spy on her, storing both items in the supply room when not needed. I couldn't figure out at first why the mirror was in the supply room. It didn't make sense. If someone had stolen it to frame someone else, they would have left it in the prop room. And why was it and the broom handle sticky? Then I thought of someone using them to spy through the transoms, but who? Dick is the logical choice. The supply room is his domain, and he's short. The average person would have been able to hold the mirror in an outstretched hand and accomplish the same thing. How tall are you, Dick?"

He didn't answer but just continued to glare at me.

"Cat got your tongue? If I had to guess I'd say you're five one, maybe five two. Mr. Holloway, how tall are you?"

"Six feet."

"Really?"

"Five eleven, then, but what the hell is going on? I thought we were supposed to be rehearsing."

"All in due time, Mr. Holloway, please. And you, Oliver? You're what, five ten?"

"That's right."

"And Mr. Crockett…"

"I'm five ten. Used to be five eleven, but you know…"

"I do know. That leaves Miss Monroe and Mrs. Holloway."

"I'm five seven," Eve said.

"Miss Monroe?"

"Five eight," Jazz said, "but none of that means Dick was spying on her."

"Oh, I think it does. When Eve got up to go to the door and look out, he saw her coming, dropped the broom down, and moved on a few doors, pretending to be sweeping up. Or he ducked into a nearby door."

"I had a feeling someone was watching me, but somehow I figured it must have been Shelby," Eve said, staring at Dick.

I looked at Eve. "Mrs. Holloway, Mr. Berkett made some inappropriate advances toward you, touched you in a private place, and tried to forcibly kiss you. That's correct, isn't it?"

Her pretty pink face flushed crimson. "Yes, that's correct, but how did you know? I never told anyone except Peter, and he doesn't seem to remember it."

"I do remember you were sleeping together," Peter said.

Eve jerked her head toward him. "No, Peter, I wasn't. He accosted me, and I belted him. End of story."

"It's a story anyway," he said, avoiding her eyes.

"I understand you decked Shelby pretty hard, Mrs. Holloway. Gave him quite a bruise below his left eye. He told us it happened when he walked into the edge of a door."

"He had it coming," she said, looking back at me.

"I agree. And all this happened in the privacy of your dressing room, didn't it? Where Shelby thought he was safe from witnesses," I said.

"That's right. But again, how did you know?"

I turned to Dick again and pointed at him. "Because he told me so. And he knew because he was outside in the hall at the time, watching the two of you through the transom."

Once more all eyes focused on Dick, who was turning a bit red himself.

"Is this true, Dicky?" Jazz said.

"No, of course not. And what does that have to do with Berkett's death?" he said.

"I'm getting to that. You already knew, Dick, that the mirror and broom would work for looking through the transoms. So, you figured with the lights out in the supply room, you could use it to peer out the transom and see exactly when Jasper and Pompom left the prop room across the hall."

"I honestly don't know what you're talking about."

"Once you saw Jasper and Pompom leave, you slipped across the hall into the prop room. You located the teapot, took the lid off, and lifted the teapot up to make sure it was full. While doing that, however, you spilled some of the tea on your shoes."

"How would you possibly know he spilled some on his shoes?" Jazz said.

"Because Pompom was seen shortly after licking Dick's shoes enthusiastically. Shelby always had Jasper make the tea extra sweet, and Pompom has a notorious sweet tooth. I remember him licking the sugar off your fingers from the gumdrops, Mr. Crockett."

Jasper bent down again and scratched the little dog behind the ears, Pompom's tail wagging enthusiastically back and forth. "He certainly does like sweets."

"This is ridiculous," Dick said, his arms crossed even tighter.

"Maybe. But I think if we have your shoes analyzed, we will find traces of the same overly sweet tea still there."

"Proves nothing at all," he said.

"It proves something. Once you put the poison in the teapot, you noticed it didn't immediately dissolve. You grabbed the pencil off the desk, where Jasper had placed it to the right of the ledger, and stirred the poison in. But when you put the pencil back, you put it on the left side of the ledger."

He shrugged but said nothing.

"A right-handed person would have placed the teapot lid on the right instead of the left where the mark was, and the pencil was left of the ledger notebook. You're the only left-handed person in this room besides me, Dick, as verified by the signing of names just now. I realized you were left-handed when I noticed you wear your watch on your right wrist, but I wanted to make sure no other lefties were in the room."

"Maybe someone was trying to frame me," he said, his voice flat.

I shook my head. "I think not. Once the poison was in place, you put Peter's pillbox back in your pocket and used the broom and mirror one more time to make sure the coast was clear, and then you stashed them back in the supply closet. You probably put the mirror in your pocket at first, but since it was so sticky you decided to retrieve it later. I remember Jazz saying you'd made a mess of your pants, and I'm guessing it was the tape residue. That can be checked, too."

"Go ahead and check," Dick said, scowling.

"We will. So, you left the supply room, but as you reached the stairs and started down, Mr. Crockett called out to you from the dock door. Your conversation with him roused Peter, who had fallen asleep on one of the sofas near the dock door, just as Oliver came out of his office, Jazz came out of the bathroom, and Eve came in from the stage behind Alan."

"That's right, that's what happened," Jasper said, nodding.

"Shut up, old man," Dick growled, and Pompom growled back at him, his tail no longer wagging.

"Oliver tried to get Peter up, and that gave you an idea, didn't it?"

"And what idea would that be?" Dick said.

"The perfect opportunity to dispose of Peter's pillbox and suggest he was the murderer, because you knew traces of poison would be found on it. In fact, you drew my attention to the pillbox being locked in Oliver's office right after Shelby died onstage, remember?"

"Not really."

"I do. So, while you helped Peter to his feet, you discreetly took the pillbox out of your pocket and dropped it on the floor, making it look like Peter had had it. Oliver picked it up, noted it was empty, and said he would lock it in his office for safe-keeping."

"I'm afraid I'm confused," Peter said. "Are you saying Dick stole my pillbox and tried to frame me for Berkett's murder?"

"It would appear so, Mr. Holloway. Smoke and mirrors, so to speak. Dick stole the makeup putty and made an impression of his own key so bits of the putty would be lodged in it. He then brought that to my attention, knowing I'd put two and two together and realize you had borrowed his keys to move Jazz's car. I wouldn't doubt he parked you in deliberately just for that reason."

"Everything you said is circumstantial, Detective. Nothing would hold up in court," Dick said, his face now smug.

"True, except for three things."

"What would they be?"

"You're the only one besides Mr. Crockett who could have gone in and out of the prop and supply rooms without arousing suspicion."

"Fair enough, but that means Jasper could have done it, too."

"You're also an amateur photographer, correct?"

"So what?"

"Jasper isn't. I spoke with the son of a woman who shares my mother's party line. He's a photographer, too. He confirmed something I had read in the library—that potassium cyanide is used in wet plate photo developing. Meaning you most likely have that poison in your darkroom at home. I can obtain a search warrant easily enough, and we'll most likely find the missing tin of makeup putty, too."

Dick didn't reply.

"That still doesn't mean he did it, Detective. You said yourself Henry had access to that poison, too," Jazz said.

"That's true, Miss Monroe, but there is one other thing. Dick mentioned hearing the commercial for the play on the radio."

"So what?" Dick asked, his arms crossed. "It was a lousy commercial."

"That commercial only aired on Saturday at 6:13 p.m. according to the radio station logs, meaning you were in the prop room at 6:13 while Jasper was out walking Pompom."

"Maybe I heard the commercial somewhere else."

"Where? The only other radio in the theater is in Oliver's office, and he was alone in there at the time with the door closed. You quoted the commercial verbatim, something you would not be able to do unless you listened to it in the prop room while adding the poison to the teapot."

"You have an active imagination, Detective," Dick said.

"So I'm told. You slipped into the supply room about five after six and waited for Jasper to leave about ten after."

"If you say so."

"I do say so. You waited a couple minutes to give Jasper ample time to get outside the building and make sure he hadn't forgotten anything. Then, at about 6:12 you finally slipped across the hall, just in time to hear the radio ad at 6:13."

"Still proves nothing. I'm the janitor. I went in there to empty the trash."

"You stated in front of all these witnesses that you weren't in the prop room Saturday night."

"I heard it in the hall, then, as I was sweeping up."

"Just give up, Dick. The radio wasn't loud enough to be heard through the door, even with the volume way up. I checked. Besides, there's one more thing. You used gloves for the most part, but you can't pick a pencil up wearing them, can you?"

"Huh?"

"The pencil by the ledger. You had to take your gloves off to pick it up. You left a fingerprint." This last statement was a guess, but I figured once Fletch had time to analyze the prints on the pencil, Dick's would be one of them.

"Oh, Dicky!" Jazz said dramatically, tears in her eyes.

Dick glared at her. "What are you on about, Jazz? You hated Shelby as much as I did."

"But to kill him. To murder him. He-he was your father."

"As if you cared, Jazz. It's always an act with you." He looked around the room. "I figure I did us all a favor."

"You did hate him, didn't you, Dick? You hated Shelby in part because you saw him as a rival for Eve's affections, and because you were angry with him for hurting her. The chance to frame her husband for Berkett's death was the icing on the cake. In your wild imagination, you saw Peter being arrested for the murder and the two of you finally free to get together. Isn't that about right, Dick?"

Eve got up from her seat abruptly and moved away from him. Peter sat there looking thoroughly confused.

"Using Peter's pillbox to hide the poison was clever in another way, too, Dick. If Oliver had given him the pillbox back, Peter would have quickly refilled it and, when he took his next set of pills, would also swallow some of the poison. Peter would be out of the picture, and you would be free to get together with Eve."

"You think you're so smart, Barrington," Dick said, glowering at me.

"Not really. But I'm pretty good at puzzles, I guess. I'm sorry for you Dick, I truly am. I'm afraid you're under arrest for the murder of Shelby Berkett. Alan, call for a black-and-white."

CHAPTER FOURTEEN

Monday morning, July 14, 1947

It was back to business as usual as I returned to my desk in the detectives' room and picked up the file I had put off on the Feltchers. It was a good, solid case, and I felt bad for the Feltchers, victims of counterfeiting that cost their small business a great deal, but I just couldn't wrap my head around it yet. I suppose my mind was still on Dick and all that went with him. I was pleased, therefore, when Alan showed up unannounced.

"What are you doing here? Aren't you still on leave?" I said.

"I came to ask the sergeant to put me back on duty now that the play's over. I start patrol tomorrow."

"Yes, Oliver called this morning to tell me he's officially closing the show. I'm sorry to say, *Death Comes To Lochwood* is finished." The phone rang. "Barrington here. Right, send him up." I replaced the receiver and looked at Alan. "Speaking of, Oliver's here to pick up his and Jasper's keys to the theater."

"So goes show biz," Alan said.

I smiled at him. "I'm sorry, buddy. I know you were looking forward to a speaking part as the butler if the show kept going."

"It's okay. There will be other shows, I hope."

"I'm sure there will be, and you'll be great. So, to what do I owe the pleasure of this visit?"

"I was going to ask you if you wanted to have lunch."

"So ask," I said.

"Wise guy. Want to have lunch?"

"With you, always. Oliver won't take long. In fact, here he is now."

I got up from my chair as Oliver strode forward, and we shook hands. "Morning, Oliver."

"Heath, Alan. I wish I could say it was a good morning."

"It is. It will be."

"It will take some time, I suppose. Do you have my keys?"

"They're at the sergeant's desk, down the hall on the left. Just show him ID and sign for them."

"Right. I'll be back in a bit." Oliver replied. He left us briefly and Alan and I debated on where to have lunch, finally deciding on Schwimmer's with the toss of a coin. I was just putting the nickel back in my pocket when Oliver returned.

"All set?"

"Yes, ready to go."

"You look decidedly less than ready," I said.

"I guess maybe I'm not."

I shrugged. "You said you're closing the show, right? Striking the set?"

Oliver smiled weakly. He seemed to have aged several years in the last few days, his hair even whiter than it was before. "Yeah. I know Jazz won't want to go on, certainly not until after the trial. As for the rest, well, I guess I know what I'd have done if I'd been the director of that show back in 1926 when Lippencott died."

"You're making the right decision, and I think you'll find Jazz is stronger than you think, Oliver. She'll get through this, and so will you."

"Yes, I suppose you're right. I should be heading down to the theater. It's almost noon,"

"We'll walk you out. I could use some fresh air, and Alan and I are going to grab some lunch," I said, as I picked up my hat from the rack.

Oliver looked at me. "Thanks, Heath. This has been a crazy few days. It's all so hard to believe."

I nodded as the three of us headed down the stairs.

"What about Mr. and Mrs. Holloway?" Alan said. "What do you think they'll do, Mr. Crane?"

"I called Eve this morning to tell her I was shutting down the show. She told me she's leaving Peter."

"Divorce?" I said.

"Separating, for now. She said she just can't take care of him anymore. Shelby was right about Peter dragging her down."

"And what will happen to him?" Alan said.

"Maybe her leaving will finally get Peter to realize that he needs help," I said.

"He does need help," Oliver said. "A lot of it. Let's just hope it's not too late."

"Agreed," I said as we reached the ground floor. "And what about you, Oliver?"

He stopped and turned to me as we entered the vestibule. "Me? The insurance money will pay off the backers and most of my expenses. I'll get through until the next show this fall. Maybe the time off will do me good."

"Maybe so. Crockett and Pompom could use a break, too."

Oliver smiled. "I'll keep him on salary. He doesn't have much, and I can afford it—barely. He's my friend. I'm using some of the money for Shelby's burial expenses, too. He didn't have anyone or anything, you know. I figure it's only right."

"You're a good man, Oliver. Thanks for not holding a grudge against me for including you as a suspect."

"It's business. Your business. I understand, Heath. Though you really had me scared when I thought you thought I was the murderer."

"I don't think I ever really believed that. Not deep down."

"I'm glad. I'm still in a bit of shock over Dick, though. I have a hard time believing he could have been so cold, so calculating, and against his own father."

"A father he never knew, Oliver. Shelby Berkett was a stranger to him."

"But still…"

"I know. But Dick was infatuated with Eve Holloway."

"Jeepers. I wonder if Dick would have ended up killing Peter if Shelby hadn't come to Milwaukee," Alan said.

"It's entirely possible."

"What was the clue that finally tipped your hat in Dick's direction?" Oliver said.

"Him being the only left-handed person among the suspects certainly was the clincher. And the way he recited the radio ad. Pompom licking his shoes made me curious, too. With those three things, the other clues just fell into place."

"What will happen to him?" Oliver said.

"He'll go to trial. I'll have to give evidence and testimony, so will you and everyone else, but I think he'll be convicted. He may even plead guilty, who knows? He already admitted it in front of witnesses last night," I said.

Oliver ran his hand through his snow-white hair before putting on his hat and pulling it down to shade his eyes. "It's pretty sad. I mean, Berkett was not a nice man, but still…"

I put my hand on Oliver's shoulder. "I know."

"So that's the lot of them," Oliver said.

"Except for Henry Hawthorne…"

"What about him?"

"Hollywood awaits. Isn't that right, Alan?"

"Yes. He wasn't planning on going out so soon, but he told me he figures there's nothing keeping him here now. He's catching the train west next week, on to bigger and better things."

"Maybe we can go see him off."

"You may be seeing the two of them off," Oliver said.

"What do you mean?" I was suddenly afraid Alan had decided to go with him and hadn't told me yet.

"Henry told me Eve's going with him, at least he's asked her to. He thinks there's a future for her in the movies, and he could use a friend out there."

"Do you think she'll go?"

"I do. She's talented, bright, fierce, and lovely. Without Peter holding her down, she can soar to great heights."

"I think so, too," I said.

"Alan, when I figure out what I'm going to do next, I'll be sure and give you a call. I think you're ready for a speaking role."

Alan beamed. "Gee, thanks, Mr. Crane. I really appreciate that!"

We said our goodbyes, and Oliver walked out the door onto the street, his face turned up to the sunshine.

When we were alone again, I turned to Alan in the entryway. "Ready for lunch?"

"Sure thing. I'm still off duty, but you'd better sign out on the board."

"Eh, just this once let's just sneak off."

"Why, Detective, you surprise me. You, breaking a rule?"

I smiled. "Just bending it a little. We'll make it a working lunch to discuss the case."

"But the case is over. There's nothing to discuss."

"We'll review it, then, to make sure I got my facts straight. Good thing you're such a good note taker. By the way, thanks for your help in solving this one, as always."

"You're welcome, as always. But I think you have to thank Alexander Lippencott for his help in the case, too," Alan said.

"The ghost? How so?"

"If we hadn't heard that strange noise in the theater, you wouldn't have investigated the supply room and probably not the prop room, either."

I shrugged. "Probably not. But it was just a strange noise. Happens all the time in old buildings. It probably was a rat in the walls, like Oliver said."

"Maybe. But it also could have been Lippencott trying to get us to discover the mirror and the broom handle. Remember how the noise stopped as soon as you opened the door? And I thought I saw something on the stage just before that."

"I remember. And who knows, maybe you're right. Well, thanks to both of you, then."

Alan smiled back at me. "I'll pass that along to Mr. Lippencott next time I'm back in the theater."

"You really do have the acting bug, don't you?"

"Maybe, I guess. It was fun, you know? To pretend to be someone you're not."

"I suppose, though in a way we both do that every day. I like the someone you are."

"Thanks and likewise, Heath."

"By the way, I have something for you. I was going to give them to you after opening night, but…"

"What is it?" His eyes lit up like a child's at Christmas.

I took the small box out of my pocket and handed it to him.

He unwrapped and opened it enthusiastically, taking out the star-shaped cufflinks and turning them over in his hands, squinting to read the inscription. "Heath, thank you, they're beautiful. But why?"

I couldn't help but feel happy then, my eyes merry. "Just because. Because there are a million stars in the sky, but you're the only one for me, the only one I see."

"What about Mr. Crane? I never said anything, but I couldn't help but notice the way you looked at him sometimes. And his eyes. Cornflower blue, I believe you once said."

"He does have nice eyes, but yours are blue like a cloudless sky. Limitless, vast, and full of possibilities."

Alan smiled. "Thanks. And you never noticed how handsome Hank was?"

"Oh, I noticed. But more importantly I noticed you noticed. And yeah, I noticed he didn't notice me much. But even if he had noticed me, and I noticed him, I would have noticed you more, even if he had noticed me more than you."

Alan laughed. "That didn't make much sense, especially coming from you."

"That's what you do to me, Alan. Anyway, I'm glad you decided not to notice him back."

"Thanks, Heath. For the cufflinks and for just being you. I don't want to ever notice anyone more than I notice you."

"Well, if you do, you do. But I'll always be here waiting. Always."

"I like the sound of that. Let's go get some lunch."

"Definitely. But maybe I *should* sign out first."

Alan laughed. "I thought you'd say that. It's one of the things I like about you. I'll wait here."

"Good, don't start without me!" I turned and hurried down the hall as fast as I could, and when I returned I saw Alan had put the star cufflinks in.

"Snazzy, mister!" I said, admiring them.

"Thanks. Someone I care an awful lot about gave them to me."

"Good thing I'm not the jealous type." I laughed. "Ready?"

"If you're waiting for me, you're wasting your time!"

And we strode out into the warmth of the day and on to lunch and to life.

MYSTERY HISTORY

- The Davidson Theater was an actual theater in Milwaukee. It was built in 1890 and torn down in 1954. It presented plays, vaudeville, films, and musicals.
- The Blackstone apartments still exist in Milwaukee, on the corner of Juneau and Van Buren, and apartment 702, Oliver Crane's apartment, really is a corner two-bedroom with a balcony.
- The private house party Hank invites Alan to is in reference to gay gatherings in people's homes in the Forties before public gay bars were common. They were often raided by police.
- The green dragon, Shelby Berkett's drink of choice, was a popular cocktail in the Forties, along with champagne cocktails and sidecars. The recipe in the book is accurate.
- Television, though still new and expensive, was growing fast in popularity. By 1947, there were approximately 44,000 sets in use in the United States, and *I Love Lucy* was just four years away.
- The Hitchcock movie Shelby and Hank are both auditioning for is *Under Capricorn* (1949), an actual Alfred Hitchcock film set in Australia.
- The Pfister Hotel—the "P" is silent—mentioned in the book still exists in Milwaukee. It is a grand and beautiful building.

- Gimbels department store existed in Milwaukee from 1887 to 1986. The white terra-cotta building still stands, now housing offices, retail, and a hotel.
- The Boston Store department store was founded in Milwaukee in 1897 and remained in business until 2018.
- The Circle Room in the Hotel LaSalle, North Eleventh Street and Wells, actually did host the Nat King Cole Trio in September of 1946. The show was recorded and can be heard in its entirety on YouTube. The author of this book also owns the CD. The Hotel LaSalle still stands but is now known as Cobeen Hall and is part of Marquette University.
- The Cudahy Tower building, where Aunt Verbina lives, still exists on Prospect Avenue.
- Art's diner mentioned in the book is fictitious. The author's husband's middle name is Arthur.
- Party lines were common in the Forties, especially during the war years when copper for the wires was in short supply. A party line was shared by multiple subscribers, and anyone on the party line could pick up their telephone and listen in to someone else's conversation.
- Lois Moran really was a major silent film star. She made a few talkies, too, and then retired to raise a family.
- As mentioned by the character of Mrs. Murphy, movie theaters did have giveaways quite often, including dishes, where each time you attended you got a new piece of the set.
- The great Mississippi River flood of 1927 was a real disaster. Approximately 246 people lost their lives.

About the Author

David S. Pederson was born in Leadville, Colorado, where his father was a miner. Soon after, the family relocated to Wisconsin, where David grew up, attending high school and university, majoring in business and creative writing. Landing a job in retail, he found himself relocating to New York, Massachusetts, and eventually back to Wisconsin, where he currently lives with his husband.

His third book, *Death Checks In*, is a finalist for the 2019 Lambda Literary Awards.

He has written many short stories and poetry and is passionate about mysteries, old movies, and crime novels. When not reading, writing, or working in the furniture business, David also enjoys working out and studying classic ocean liners, floor plans, and historic homes.

David can be contacted at davidspederson@gmail.com or via his website, www.davidspederson.com.

Books Available From Bold Strokes Books

Death Takes a Bow by David S. Pederson. Alan Keys takes part in a local stage production, but when the leading man is murdered, his partner Detective Heath Barrington is thrust into the limelight to find the killer. (978-1-63555-472-4)

Accidental Prophet by Bud Gundy. Days after his grandmother dies, Drew Morten learns his true identity and finds himself racing against time to save civilization from the apocalypse. (978-1-63555-452-6)

In Case You Forgot by Fredrick Smith and Chaz Lamar. Zaire and Kenny, two newly single, Black, queer, and socially aware men, start again—in love, career, and life—in the West Hollywood neighborhood of LA. (978-1-63555-493-9)

Counting for Thunder by Phillip Irwin Cooper. A struggling actor returns to the Deep South to manage a family crisis but finds love and ultimately his own voice as his mother is regaining hers for possibly the last time. (978-1-63555-450-2)

Survivor's Guilt and Other Stories by Greg Herren. Award-winning author Greg Herren's short stories are finally pulled together into a single collection, including the Macavity Award–nominated title story and the first-ever Chanse MacLeod short story. (978-1-63555-413-7)

Saints + Sinners Anthology 2019, edited by Tracy Cunningham and Paul Willis. An anthology of short fiction featuring the finalist selections from the 2019 Saints + Sinners Literary Festival. (978-1-63555-447-2)

The Shape of the Earth by Gary Garth McCann. After appearing in *Best Gay Love Stories*, *HarringtonGMFQ*, *Q Review*, and *Off the Rocks*, Lenny and his partner Dave return in a hotbed of manhood and jealousy. (978-1-63555-391-8)

Exit Plans for Teenage Freaks by 'Nathan Burgoine. Cole always has a plan—especially for escaping his small-town reputation as "that kid who was kidnapped when he was four"—but when he teleports to a museum, it's time to face facts: it's possible he's a total freak after all. (978-1-163555-098-6)

Death Checks In by David S. Pederson. Despite Heath's promises to Alan to not get involved, Heath can't resist investigating a shopkeeper's murder in Chicago, which dashes their plans for a romantic weekend getaway. (978-1-163555-329-1)

Of Echoes Born by 'Nathan Burgoine. A collection of queer fantasy short stories set in Canada from Lambda Literary Award finalist 'Nathan Burgoine. (978-1-63555-096-2)

The Lurid Sea by Tom Cardamone. Cursed to spend eternity on his knees, Nerites is having the time of his life. (978-1-62639-911-2)

Sinister Justice by Steve Pickens. When a vigilante targets citizens of Jake Finnigan's hometown, Jake and his partner Sam fall under suspicion themselves as they investigate the murders. (978-1-63555-094-8)

Club Arcana: Operation Janus by Jon Wilson. Wizards, demons, Elder Gods: Who knew the universe was so crowded, and that they'd all be out to get Angus McAslan? (978-1-62639-969-3)

Triad Soul by 'Nathan Burgoine. Luc, Anders, and Curtis—vampire, demon, and wizard—must use their powers of blood, soul, and magic to defeat a murderer determined to turn their city into a battlefield. (978-1-62639-863-4)

Gatecrasher by Stephen Graham King. Aided by a high-tech thief, the Maverick Heart crew race against time to prevent a cadre of savage corporate mercenaries from seizing control of a revolutionary wormhole technology. (978-1-62639-936-5)

Wicked Frat Boy Ways by Todd Gregory. Beta Kappa brothers Brandon Benson and Phil Connor play an increasingly dangerous game of love, seduction, and emotional manipulation. (978-1-62639-671-5)

Death Goes Overboard by David S. Pederson. Heath Barrington and Alan Keyes are two sides of a steamy love triangle as they encounter gangsters, con men, murder, and more aboard an old lake steamer. (978-1-62639-907-5)

A Careful Heart by Ralph Josiah Bardsley. Be careful what you wish for...love changes everything. (978-1-62639-887-0)

Worms of Sin by Lyle Blake Smythers. A haunted mental asylum turned drug treatment facility exposes supernatural detective Finn M'Coul to an outbreak of murderous insanity, a strange parasite, and ghosts that seek sex with the living. (978-1-62639-823-8)

Tartarus by Eric Andrews-Katz. When Echidna, Mother of all Monsters, escapes from Tartarus and into the modern world, only an Olympian has the power to oppose her. (978-1-62639-746-0)

Rank by Richard Compson Sater. Rank means nothing to the heart, but the Air Force isn't as impartial. Every airman learns that rank has its privileges. What about love? (978-1-62639-845-0)

The Grim Reaper's Calling Card by Donald Webb. When Katsuro Tanaka begins investigating the disappearance of a young nurse, he discovers more missing persons, and they all have one thing in common: The Grim Reaper Tarot Card. (978-1-62639-748-4)

Smoldering Desires by C.E. Knipes. Evan McGarrity has found the man of his dreams in Sebastian Tantalos. When an old boyfriend from Sebastian's past enters the picture, Evan must fight for the man he loves. (978-1-62639-714-9)